"It didn't help my concentration any to lie next to you all night, Zoey,"

Cage mused. "Listening to the soft sound of your breathing. Watching your face while you slept."

She stared at him transfixed, as if hypnotized by that low voice.

"All that in-your-face toughness of yours disappears when you're sleeping, did you know that?" His voice was husky, the finger he trailed down her cheek feather light. "I'm not the kind of man to spend a lot of time thinking about any one woman, but damned if I can figure a way to get you off my mind.

"If you want a mystery to solve, Zoey, maybe you can start with that one."

Dear Reader,

Welcome to another month of fabulous reading from Silhouette Intimate Moments, the line that brings you excitement along with your romance every month. As I'm sure you've already noticed, the month begins with a return to CONARD COUNTY, in *Involuntary Daddy,* by bestselling author Rachel Lee. As always, her hero and heroine will live in your heart long after you've turned the last page, along with an irresistible baby boy nicknamed Peanut. You'll wish you could take him home yourself.

Award winner Marie Ferrarella completes her CHILDFINDERS, INC. trilogy with *Hero in the Nick of Time,* about a fake marriage that's destined to become real, and not one, but *two,* safely recovered children. Marilyn Pappano offers the second installment of her HEARTBREAK CANYON miniseries, *The Horseman's Bride.* This Oklahoma native certainly has a way with a Western man! After too long away, Doreen Owens Malek returns with our MEN IN BLUE title, *An Officer and a Gentle Woman,* about a cop falling in love with his prime suspect. Kylie Brant brings us the third of THE SULLIVAN BROTHERS in *Falling Hard and Fast,* a steamy read that will have your heart racing. Finally, welcome RaeAnne Thayne, whose debut book for the line, *The Wrangler and the Runaway Mom,* is also a WAY OUT WEST title. You'll be happy to know that her second book is already scheduled.

Enjoy them all—and then come back again next month, when once again Silhouette Intimate Moments brings you six of the best and most exciting romances around.

Yours,

Leslie J. Wainger

Leslie J. Wainger
Executive Senior Editor

FALLING HARD
AND FAST

KYLIE BRANT

Silhouette®

INTIMATE™MOMENTS®

Published by Silhouette Books

America's Publisher of Contemporary Romance

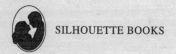

SILHOUETTE BOOKS

ISBN 0-373-07959-1

FALLING HARD AND FAST

Copyright © 1999 by Kimberly Bahnsen

This edition published by arrangement with Harlequin Books S.A.

Visit us at www.romance.net

Printed in U.S.A.

KYLIE BRANT

lives with her husband and five children in Iowa. She works full-time as a teacher for learning disabled students. Much of her free time is spent in her role as professional spectator at her kids' sporting events.

An avid reader, Kylie enjoys stories of love, mystery and suspense—and she insists on happy endings! When her youngest children, a set of twins, turned four, she decided to try her hand at writing. Now most weekends and all summer she can be found at her computer, spinning her own tales of romance and happily-ever-afters.

Kylie invites readers to write to her at P.O. Box 231, Charles City, IA 50616.

For Tom and Leona, my fairy godparents, with love.

Chapter 1

It was an unlikely place for murder.

Spanish moss dripped from huge cypress and oak trees along the winding Atchafalaya River, providing cover for the birds calling to each other in the fading afternoon sunlight. A soft blanket of velvety grass rolled toward the edge of the river, giving way to the reddish-brown soil that lined its banks. There was a quiet splash nearby as a sleek young otter slid into the water in search of dinner. The trio of rabbits grazing several yards away froze at the small sound, ears twitching, before returning their attention to the fragrant clover.

Zoey Prescott lifted the wire-framed Ray·Bans from her face. The tragic death that had taken place here just five days ago had left no scar on this tranquil scene. There was no sinister aura of an unsolved homicide, no lingering sense of evil from the dark soul of a killer. The huge oak straight ahead looked to be a century old. Surely it was the one beneath which Janice Reilly's naked, battered body had been discovered. Her very dead body.

Zoey's writer's imagination could supply the details that were lacking. It wasn't hard to understand why the killer had chosen this spot. The wooded area around it provided seclusion. Its distance from town had ensured that there would be no one close by to come to the woman's aid.

Daylight painted the area with serenity. At night, though, Zoey thought the place would lose its pastoral quality. The draping moss would be menacing against the inky sky, with only a sliver of moon, and the eyes of night creatures reflecting in the darkness. The sounds of predator and prey would seem even more horrifying to a woman trapped by a madman, her fate even more certain.

Despite the hot humid air, Zoey felt a chill prickle over her skin. She couldn't explain why a thirty-second newscast about a murder in rural Louisiana should shatter the writer's block that had begun to seem as insurmountable as a fortress wall. Why hearing of the incredibly sad end to a young woman's life should spark the creation of her next novel. Her agent had once joked that there was something a little bit twisted in all murder-mystery writers. Perhaps he was correct.

She slipped on her sunglasses again. It was time to get back to the small house she'd rented on the outskirts of nearby Charity. Time to return to the unpacking that she'd barely started since arriving that morning. But she tarried for another moment, her gaze fixed upon the giant oak. And before she turned toward her car, she offered up a silent prayer for Janice Reilly.

A more jaded man might have cursed God for creating sultry Louisiana summers, but Cage Gauthier liked to believe they served a purpose. Leaning against the bar in Jonesy's, he contemplated the perfect creature being seated at a table nearby. Her brief denim shorts showed miles of spectacular leg and her white tank top outlined curves that had surely been fashioned by angels.

He tipped a frosty bottle of beer to his lips. It was hard to get worked up about the climate when it was accompanied by such outstanding advantages. Cage liked to think he was a reasonable man. He was willing to overlook the torrid temperatures, the above-average precipitation and the bone-slicking humidity as long as they continued to produce scantily-clad goddesses.

"Oh, my blessed mama," a familiar voice crooned. Tanner Beauchamp fell onto the stool beside him, one hand clutched to his heart. From the direction of his gaze it was apparent that he'd seen the woman. "Who is she, where is she staying and how long must I wait before she jumps my ever-ready bones?"

Cage answered his questions sequentially. "I don't know, I don't know, and I don't even want to *go* there." Setting the half-empty bottle on the bar, he turned to regard his childhood friend. "She's been here long enough to get the word about Jonesy's, at any rate." A couple of miles from town, it wasn't a place most strangers would seek out on their own. The inside was only slightly more inviting than the shabby exterior. Neon beer signs and fly-specked posters of questionable taste adorned the cracked walls. The bar and the tables were scarred, the air-conditioning uncertain. But the tavern boasted the finest grill in the parish. What Jonesy did to rib eye was enough to make a strong man weep.

They watched the woman close her menu decisively and order from Lilah, the part-time bartender, part-time waitress. "Wish me luck, buddy." Tanner straightened and ran his fingers through his dark hair. "That little lady is about to get a megadose of Southern charm and hospitality."

Mildly, Cage raised an eyebrow. "You know, I'm thinking you really don't look her type."

"Oh, I'm her type." Tanner winked. "She just doesn't know it yet." Slipping off the barstool, he walked over to the woman's table, pulled up a free chair and sat down.

With a twinge of disappointment, Cage reached back and snagged the beer bottle with two fingers. Bringing it to his lips, he drained it and signaled Silas behind the bar to bring him another. It wasn't unusual for Tanner to take a running

start on any pretty face in his sights, but it was unusual for
Cage to care one way or another. Since returning to his hometown two years ago, he'd spent more time than he liked to
consider sidestepping genteel marriage-minded ladies of the
parish. He'd be a liar if he denied he got more than his fair
share of attention. Which he enthusiastically returned, but
only within careful boundaries.

Digging a crumpled bill from his pocket, he handed it to
Silas, then turned back to assess Tanner's progress. Things
weren't looking good for his smooth-talking friend. The
woman was gazing at him with an expression that no man
could misconstrue as friendly. Cage wondered what color her
eyes were. From this angle he couldn't see, but he'd bet they
were dark, to match her thick mane of brown hair.

Things happened very quickly then. She leaned forward
and said something to Tanner that had him gaping in response, obviously speechless. Chuckling to himself, Cage
leaned back against the bar and raised his beer bottle to his
lips. It was amazing, he thought as his friend returned, how
a grown man could look so much like a whipped pup slinking
away after a scolding.

"Silas." Cage motioned the bartender over. "A beer for
my disgraced friend here. Something to wash the taste of
humiliation from his mouth."

Tanner shot him a look laden with irritation and grabbed
the beer Silas slid toward him. "Nothing like having an audience watch me get shot down."

"You didn't just get shot down, son, you crashed and
burned." Cage felt remarkably cheerful about the whole
thing. The brunette's list of admirable attributes lengthened
as he mentally added her discriminating taste.

Tanner shrugged and took a long swallow of beer. His ego
was too strong to have been dented by the encounter, though
there might have been a scratch or two from Cage having
witnessed it. "Hard to understand. Most Yankee gals just
plain melt away at this stunning package of Southern drawl
and handsome looks."

"'Yankee'?" Cage looked over his shoulder, appraising the woman again.

"Ice-cold Northerner. Must have some defective genetic trait."

"It's called intelligence." His tone was absent and the insult lacked sting. Craning his neck, he could just make out a dark blue foreign sedan parked out front. No one in the parish drove a car like that. His mouth kicked up in a slow, lazy grin. No one in the parish parked like that. *Illegally.*

Tanner's eyes widened as Cage slipped from his stool. "You're going to try your luck?"

"Nope. Just going to drop her a friendly warning about parking fines. It would be a shame if she were to get on the wrong side of the law while she's here, wouldn't it?" Without waiting for a response, he ambled away.

He stood in front of the brunette for a full minute before she deigned to lift her gaze from the ice cubes doing a slow melt in the glass before her. Not a man to waste an opportunity, he used the time to admire the picture she made. The tank top showed off arms that were toned rather than muscled, and skin the color of rich cream. Her hair was swept back from a finely molded forehead with a slight widow's peak. Then her eyes met his and a fist squeezed his lungs. Instead of the brown he'd expected, they were a deep moss green. And if they could shoot daggers, he'd be lying at her feet, slashed and bleeding.

He grinned and hooked his thumbs in his pockets. "Evening, ma'am."

It took all of three seconds to take his measure. Another small-town Lothario, Zoey concluded, who relied on dimples, charm and boyish good looks to blind the eye and dazzle the senses. She considered herself a gold-plated expert on fast-talking handsome men; experience had taught her just how treacherous they could be.

Her words, and the feeling behind them, were succinct. "Get lost."

"That'd be kinda hard to do." Cage rubbed his chin reflectively. "See, I grew up in this town. I know it like the back of my hand. I don't think there's a spot in the entire parish I'm not familiar with."

"And your point is?"

Patience evident in his voice, he explained, "I couldn't get lost, ma'am. Not even if I wanted to."

Leaning back in her chair, Zoey toyed with her silverware. It really wasn't difficult to remain unmoved by his banter. All she had to do was look at him and see Alan. Slick, smooth Alan, whose gift for numbers was matched only by his expertise in seduction techniques. The liberties he'd taken with her money had no doubt given him far greater pleasure than those he'd taken with her body. She was woman enough to hate him more for that fact than for his crimes.

Her voice cool, she asked, "Do you have a problem understanding rejection?"

Cage cocked his head, as if considering her question. "'Rejection'? No, ma'am, I've been rejected before."

"By a woman holding a knife?"

He glanced at her fingers playing with the steak knife, and his eyes crinkled. "As a matter of fact…" He waited for her gaze to heat and narrow before leaning forward, holding up a bent arm for her to examine. "See this scar?" He tapped a faded white line on the underside of his arm. "That's where Janey Wilson grazed me with a pocketknife when I was nine."

Without thinking, Zoey leaned forward a little to examine the barely discernible wound. "It doesn't look too lethal."

He nearly smiled at the disappointment tinging her words. "No, ma'am, the most lethal wound Janey delivered was here." His fingers went to the buttons on his shirt, and her eyes widened, shocked.

"What are you doing?" Her gaze darted from one side to the other before glaring at him. "Quit that!"

He opened the shirt enough to pull it to the left side, baring the skin molded over a perfectly sculpted pectoral muscle. "See that place right there?"

She couldn't find a safe spot to look. She absolutely did not want to know how many of the locals were watching this exchange, and that expanse of golden skin was the last thing she was going to focus on. "I don't see anything," she said between clenched teeth. "Button your shirt."

"Well, sure, you can't see it," he said reasonably. "But Janey Wilson was the first girl to show me how to kiss, and then she up and dumped me for Robbie James Talbot. He had this space between his front teeth, see, and when the wind was just right he could spit half a city block." He shook his head in remembered admiration. "Now, I ask you, how could I compete with that?"

She blinked, wondering for the first time if she'd been accosted by a crazy man. "What are you talking about?"

Solemnly he answered, "Well, ma'am, Janey near about carved up my heart, dumping me the way she did."

Zoey's grip tightened unconsciously on the knife. She'd been wrong. He wasn't like Alan at all. Alan at least had been sane. Unethical, perhaps. An immoral jerk and a poor excuse for a human being. But sane.

She didn't want to admit to the relief that flickered through her when he buttoned his shirt. "Very amusing. Perhaps Janey should have adjusted her aim a foot and a half lower."

He grinned at that—a brilliant display of perfect white teeth, revealing such good-natured humor that she almost forgot herself and smiled back. Almost. He wasn't as easily dispatched as his friend, and it wouldn't do to encourage him. He'd already proved impervious to the defenses she'd meticulously crafted that kept most men at a distance. Her most valuable weapons—a cool steady stare and a cutting tongue—were noticeably ineffectual with him.

"Ouch. You've got a wicked train of thought. I think I'm glad I didn't know you when I was nine."

"You don't know me now."

"Which brings me to the reason I came over here. Cage Gauthier is my name." She thought, fancifully, that his slow, liquid drawl coated his words like honey. "I'm—"

"In my way, is what you are." Lilah pushed by him with a swing of her generous hips and set a salad in front of Zoey. "Don't even let this one get started, miss," she advised. "He's as pesky as a mosquito. Give him the slightest encouragement and his nonsense will be buzzing in your ear all evening."

"You're a hard woman, Lilah. Unforgiving, too," he added, when she fixed him with a look. "The way you carry a grudge is shameful. I know I promised to marry you when I grew up, but you didn't wait the way you said you would, either."

Lilah arched her brows at him with the familiarity of someone who'd known him all his life. "I'm still waiting, boy. You just haven't grown up yet." She let out a hoot at her own joke and Zoey smiled, picking up her fork. As a hint, it failed miserably. Cage didn't appear to be going anywhere.

"No respect," he muttered mournfully, as Lilah bustled back to the kitchen. He winked at Zoey, inviting her to share the joke, his lazy, disarming gesture loaded with appeal. She felt the effect of it clear to her fingertips, which, along with her palms, had become inexplicably moist. She resisted the impulse to wipe them on her napkin, and deliberately dropped the temperature in her voice a few degrees.

"You won't find any here, either. I'm starving and I'd like to start my dinner. Alone."

Damned if that snooty tone of hers didn't tickle him. She sounded for all the world like she ought to be wearing a jeweled crown and carrying a scepter. He feigned hurt. "And after I came over here to do you a favor."

"If you want to do me a favor, disappear."

"How about a little advice instead?" He leaned forward to cross his arms on the top of the chair before him, and lowered his voice confidingly. "Next time you come to Jonesy's you might want to take a closer look at the curbs. The sheriff is an affable sort, but he can't be expected to overlook flagrant parking violations."

"My car isn't in a no parking area." She was almost sure of it.

His tone was rueful. "Yes, ma'am, I'm afraid it is. Parked smack-dab in the middle of Jonesy's loading zone."

She turned her attention to her salad with an air of dismissal even he couldn't ignore. "I'll take my chances with the sheriff. If I do see him, I'll also ask about his policy on pest control."

The tone was regal, even when she was insulting him. It matched the haughty look on her face, the determined set of her lush lips. He wondered if it was only his imagination that detected a hint of uncertainty softening them.

"You do that, ma'am." Amusement laced his words. "I know for a fact that he never misses an opportunity to discuss parish ordinances with a pretty woman."

She'd made the right decision in coming to Charity. Zoey leaned back in her desk chair and contemplated the willows weeping in the backyard. The churning in her stomach had reappeared only once since her arrival, and a couple of antacids followed by a record-setting eight uninterrupted hours of sleep had alleviated it. The vicious headaches had abated, and she suspected that if she cut her caffeine intake by half, those, too, would disappear. The thought had her reaching for her cup of coffee. It couldn't be healthy to make too many changes in her life at once.

A school of rainbow-hued fish floated across her computer monitor as the screen saver automatically switched on. She didn't notice. She was too busy examining the feeling that had crept up on her unawares—contentment.

She marveled at the emotion; but as foreign as it was, there was no mistaking it. The proof was in the ten pages she'd just finished—the first writing she'd done in nine months that wouldn't have to be trashed. There was more evidence in the normal sleep she'd gotten, and the return of her appetite. Zoey L. Prescott had regained control of her life, and it was sweet, indeed.

She leaned back in her chair and stretched her arms out in front of her, limbering her fingers absently. There were few things, she'd learned, more essential than control. Control was what had gotten her through the grieving when her father had died when she was nine. Her mother had depended on Zoey's strength to cope with raising three children alone. And when her mother had lost her fight with cancer right after Zoey's high-school graduation, it was that same control that had empowered her to set aside her dreams for attending college hundreds of miles away. Carolyn and Patrick had been counting on her to keep the family together.

So she'd changed her plans to include a local college nearby and become mother, father and sister to her younger siblings. At a time when her peers had been pledging to sororities and juggling dates and textbooks, she'd been learning how to be a parent. The fact that her aunt and uncle had been watching closely, expecting her to fail, *wanting* her to, had merely strengthened her resolve.

She'd proved to her relatives and to the courts that she could handle the responsibility of her siblings. She'd proved to the publishing world that the success of her first novel, written when she was twenty, wasn't a fluke, by following it with four others. She'd seen Carolyn through college, Patrick through high school and into the marines. And just when she'd been convinced that she could handle anything life threw at her, Alan had swept in and devastated her world.

Her fingertips drummed lightly on the keyboard. With a sense of wonder she noted that for the first time, thoughts of the man failed to bring that fire to her belly, that sense of helpless rage that had haunted her for so many months. He'd been first her accountant, then her lover. But while she'd been fantasizing about white lace and happily-ever-afters, he'd been draining her investment accounts and preparing to leave the country on a permanent vacation.

It would soothe her ego if she could claim that she'd started looking more closely at her finances because she'd suspected what Alan was up to. But Zoey was brutally honest with everyone, and she'd never spared herself. When it came to trust, she'd been a sap. She'd only begun to examine her assets in order to determine how much to spend on the wedding Alan had started hinting about.

Blowing out a breath, she scowled at the computer screen. It would be a long time before that experience would lose its sting. And even longer before she lowered her defenses again. But there was satisfaction in knowing that she'd made sure Alan Hecox would have plenty of time to contemplate his crimes. Although she'd frequently fantasized about him spending the rest of his life at Attica with an affectionate cell mate, she was content with his sentence of eight years in a country-club prison.

His conviction, however, failed to ease her disgust at the way she'd lowered her guard enough to allow him close to her. She'd begun to depend on him, to—a wince formed at the thought—trust him. Her biggest error had been forgetting for even a short time that she could depend only on herself.

She'd be the first to admit that there had been a hole left in her life by her siblings' leaving home, which a deeper relationship with Alan had seemed to fill. But she would have sneered at the idea that she'd felt lonely, been outraged by the suggestion that she'd been vulnerable. Zoey L. Prescott refused to contemplate vulnerability. She was the strong one, the responsible one. If a return to her customary control meant keeping her emotions tightly wrapped, well, she didn't consider that a disadvantage. Emotions got trampled. Trust got abused. Strength and independence did not.

She watched two squirrels chase each other over the lush back lawn. It occurred to her for the first time that someone would actually need to cut that lawn, probably on a regular basis. She hadn't discussed it with the real-estate agent, hadn't even thought of it. Zoey had been a city dweller all her life, had always lived in a high-rise apartment building. Squirrels and lawns had never been a concern before. The fact that they were now the biggest worries she had brought a smile to her lips.

She pressed the Save command and got up from the desk she'd brought from Chicago. She walked through the compact kitchen and onto the small screened-in porch. She'd been tempted to put her computer out here. With the large trees and hedges bordering the property, there was a sense of isolation about the yard. Unfortunately, there would be nothing there to protect her computer from nature's tantrums. Rather than risk exposing her computer to the elements when the next storm blew in, she'd settled for placing her desk beneath the big window in the kitchen, in the spot most would probably reserve for the table.

There was something almost hypnotizing about that endless spread of grass, she observed idly, leaning against the wall to better contemplate it. She hadn't seen this much uninterrupted lawn outside of city parks for almost a year. She drank in the pleasure of the sight, and savored the first genuinely stress-free afternoon she'd had in months.

The peal of the doorbell was unexpected, but Zoey wasn't startled. The one thing she'd noticed since she'd moved was the friendliness of the citizens of Charity. And though some of them had displayed a curiosity about her that was just short of nosy, they'd been willing to reciprocate with answers to the many questions *she'd* had. She figured it had been an even exchange.

Fully expecting to see one of the ladies she'd spoken with at the grocery store yesterday afternoon, she walked to the front of the house and pulled the door open.

It was the uniform that caught her eye first. With a tiny stab of guilt she wondered if someone had reported to the law that the newest resident in town ignored yellow curbs at will.

Out of the corner of her eye she saw the sleek gold-and-white car with the official seal on its door parked in the driveway. "Good afternoon…Sheriff." This was added after a quick glance at the badge pinned to his shirt. "Can I help you?"

"As a matter of fact, ma'am, I think you can."

She didn't need the man to remove his sunglasses for recognition to overtake disbelief. There was no mistaking the slow liquid drawl, the voice that carried just the barest hint of amusement.

"You!"

Cage raked his fingers through his dark blond hair and nodded, his gray eyes reflecting the smile he managed to keep from his lips. "Yes, ma'am. Cage Gauthier, sheriff of St. Augustine parish. And you're Zoey Prescott, or so the twins told me. And since they manage to know just about everything that goes on around here, I consider them a pretty good source."

The twins. She flipped through her mental files. "You can only mean Lulu and Francine Potter. Something tells me they're the root of a very reliable grapevine in Charity."

She'd met the Potter sisters at Neesom's grocery store. Not only did they share the same physical characteristics, the two octogenarians were blessed with identical talents for eliciting information. They were also, she'd found, local experts on any news that was news in Charity, Louisiana.

"Actually, it was Francine who gave me your name." This time the smile settled on his well-formed mouth. "Lulu just provided corrections, as needed."

The visual image his words summoned was vivid. The sisters seemed to have a system of communication worked out. One did the talking while the other contradicted, inserted and provided additional details. The effect was a bit overwhelming for the listener, but definitely enlightening.

Zoey relaxed against the doorjamb and considered him. She was still having difficulty connecting the smooth-talking charmer from Jonesy's with the chief law enforcement for the parish. He presented two pieces to a puzzle that, try as she might, she couldn't seem to make fit. "You didn't mention your job last night." If he had, she might not have been so eager to get rid of him. Indirectly, the murder of Janice Reilly had lured her to Charity. Cage Gauthier was in a position to know all the details of that murder.

"No, we didn't get around to talking about our jobs." He regarded her with lazy appreciation. An ornately worked gold locket hung from a thin gold chain and nestled in the hollow at the base of her slender throat. Her shorts today were ragged cutoffs, white at the seams. They did just as fine a job showcasing those long legs as the pair she'd worn last night.

With difficulty, he dragged his gaze from that sleek expanse of bare skin. It wouldn't do to get sidetracked right now. "If we had, maybe we could have had this conversation earlier."

She watched him warily. There was a difference about the man that owed to more than the uniform. There was "cop" in his eyes, and in his voice, as it hardened just a fraction. "I understand that you're a writer."

She had no idea why he would make the statement sound like an accusation. "I'm sure the twins make a habit of getting details like that straight."

His smile had vanished. "Yes, ma'am, they do. They also told me that you were asking a lot of questions about the murder victim found near here a while back."

Choosing her words with care, she asked, "Is that a problem?"

His gaze remained steady but shielded. "Actually, Miss Prescott…it is." He slapped his glasses against his palm in a rhythmic motion. "We've had our share of news crews and reporters sniffing around here the last several days." She stiffened slightly at his choice of words, but he didn't seem to notice. "There's nothing like a tragedy to bring out media searching for sound bites."

"I'm not part of the media."

"I know that." He gave a languid nod. His every action seemed leisurely, as if some internal mechanism was fixed in slow motion. Or maybe the trait was a natural by-product of living in the South. The heat certainly had a draining effect on her own energy.

Belatedly, she realized he was speaking again. "Pardon me?"

"I said, it doesn't matter that you're not part of the media. You're doing the same thing the reporters did—asking questions, stirring people up." The glasses were slid inside his shirt pocket. "I don't want my people stirred up."

Frost coated her words. "People have a right to get *stirred up* over murder, Sheriff."

"Of course they do. Homicide is always shocking, but probably even more so in St. Augustine parish. The last murder we had here happened before I was born. But folks have a right to peace of mind, too, and I've been working overtime to make sure they get it." He watched her bare foot cross to her opposite shin, glide down in an absent movement, and he abruptly lost his train of thought. Her skin reminded him of his mother's favorite gardenias—smooth, soft and fragrant. He drew a breath and cleared his throat.

"Maybe peace of mind isn't what the residents of the parish need right now," she argued. "Maybe you should be spending your time warning them of the very real dangers that exist, regardless of where they live. The fact that murder struck in Charity, Louisiana, a small quiet community with no crime rate to speak of is what made it national news."

He slipped his hands into his pockets and rocked back a little on his heels. "You're wrong about a couple of things, Miss Prescott, and so were the reporters. See, Janice Reilly wasn't murdered *in* Charity." That was a fact he was sure Chief of Police Runnels gave nightly thanks for. "The body was found outside city limits, which is my jurisdiction."

His eyes went flinty and his mouth flattened. "And the way I figure it, the victim wasn't killed anywhere around here. The parish was just used as her final resting place."

Chapter 2

Surprise kept Zoey silent. She'd known that the murder victim had been a stranger to the area, of course. But the talk yesterday in town had all dealt with the rumors surrounding the way Janice Reilly had died and the discovery of her body.

"You hadn't heard." Cage felt a measure of resignation. Although he'd emphasized the fact to the local paper, that piece of news couldn't compete with the sensational details regarding the parish's most shocking happening in the last generation.

"No."

He gave a mental sigh, thinking of the work his office still had ahead of them. Soothing the fears of an edgy citizenry was difficult in the best of circumstances. It was an uphill battle when pitted against the very human fondness for gossip.

He narrowed his gaze at the woman before him, and tried not to notice the way the sultry heat had moistened the velvet line of her jaw. "Janice Reilly lived and worked in

Baton Rouge, some fifty miles from here. We know she went to work that day, bought a few groceries, had dinner alone, and then dressed to go out.''

When he didn't continue, Zoey prompted, ''Dressed to go out where? Whom did she meet?''

''It would appear that she met her killer, Miss Prescott.'' There was no mistaking the chill in his voice, and she had a sudden image of the treatment the news crews must have gotten when they approached the sheriff's department. It didn't stop her from asking, ''How do you know she wasn't killed here? Why do you think the murderer would go to the risk of transporting her body elsewhere?''

Since it looked like he wouldn't be leaving anytime soon, Cage took a step backward and propped himself against one of the rounded porch posts. He'd always been a great believer in conserving energy. ''There weren't signs of the crime anywhere in the vicinity.'' Deliberately he added, ''The savage treatment she received would have left a great deal of evidence. Her killer had a sadistic bent.''

He watched her blink, then swallow hard. But there was none of the horrified fascination that he'd seen on the faces of some of the townspeople, none of the zealous greed displayed by the reporters. Instead there was shock, tempered by compassion. Her reaction moved him more than it should have.

''So the killer traveled back roads until he found a secluded place far away from the actual scene of the crime.'' She tilted her head, her eyes alight with interest and intelligence. ''But he didn't just dump the body there, did he? I understand she was tied to that old oak tree by the river.''

He didn't respond to that; didn't intend to. The information he'd given her so far was nothing that hadn't been made public already. It couldn't compete with the grisly facts about the arrangement of the body—facts he was sure the town was still buzzing about. The victim's hand had been nailed to the bark in a macabre greeting for the unfortunate soul who would discover her—in this instance, a teenage boy who'd decided to play hooky and go fishing.

Instead he appeared to change subjects seamlessly. "St. Augustine parish dates back to before the war." With a sudden flash of amusement she realized he was talking about pre-Civil War days. He reached absently into his shirt pocket and withdrew a slim cigar. Running it through his fingers appreciatively, he made no move to light it. "Most of its residents can trace their ancestry to the settlers of the parish and beyond."

Something inside her made her ask, "Including you?"

His fingers hesitated an infinitesimal moment. "My family took great pride in being directly descended from some of the founding fathers. Most of the residents make their living farming, trapping or fishing, unless they work in the paper mill outside of town."

With the earlier steel absent from his words, he sounded like an old-timer in a rocking chair, preparing to render a lengthy lesson on local history for the benefit of ignorant youngsters. Zoey tucked away the recognition of how easily he seemed to switch from laid-back charmer to grave Southern sheriff. It was a curiosity to be pondered at a later date. "What does all that have to do with the murder of Janice Reilly?"

His smile was as slow and easy as the lazy waters of the Atchafalaya. "Are all Chicagoans as impatient as you?"

"Are all Southerners as reluctant to get to the point?" she countered. In the next instant it occurred to her that she'd never told the ladies in the grocery store that Chicago was her home.

He watched her gaze narrow at the realization that he'd done some checking of his own, and admired the way temper darkened her eyes. With more than a hint of regret, he replaced the cigar in his pocket. "My point, Miss Prescott, is that this is an old parish, and a settled one. Most of the families have been living here for years. People don't move around much and they aren't used to big-city problems.

They leave their doors unlocked and the keys in their cars.'' That unthinking level of trust had been shaken, and Cage felt a fresh burn of anger. When he'd been a detective for the New Orleans Police Department he'd encountered murder and death all too often. But murder and death didn't belong in Charity.

She slipped the tips of her fingers into the pockets of her cutoffs, pulling them tighter across her hips. ''So you're saying that life is simple in St. Augustine parish, and that's the way you want to keep it. Your goal is to return everything to normal and let folks get back to their safe worlds.''

He nodded approvingly. ''That's about it.''

''I think you're doing them a disservice. It's not unreasonable for people to be on their guard.'' She waited a beat before adding deliberately, ''Unless you can guarantee the residents that the killer won't strike again.''

''There aren't any guarantees in this life.'' He was in a position to know that all too well. ''But this isn't a Z. L. Prescott novel.''

The note in his voice might have been derision. Her gaze streaked to his. She could see nothing but humor glinting in his eyes. She decided in the next instant that it was as insulting as the emotion she'd expected to see there.

''Unlike some of your plots, there isn't a conspiracy involved here, a sinister family secret or a mad relative with a sharp ax living in a crawl space. Janice Reilly's death was tragic and senseless. But it doesn't mean our citizens are at risk.'' He raised a hand to halt the questions poised on her lips. ''I'm not at liberty to give you details. But what we've learned so far leads us to believe that she was probably killed far away from Charity.''

He let the post take more of his weight and slipped his hands into his pockets, surveying her expression. The lady was a tough sell. She was too smart, too…distrustful, to take anybody's word at face value. He wondered what had happened to her to make her so unwilling to believe in another. And he wondered if she realized that her no-nonsense words were robbed of their effect when uttered in that smoky voice of hers.

"I guess the real reason I'm here is to ask you a favor, Miss Prescott." He indulged himself by watching interest and wariness war in her eyes, and betting on which would win.

"What kind of favor?" It was caution threading through the words, and he gave himself a mental pat on the back for his accurate prediction.

"Just that you help my department do a little damage control. If you hear talk about the murder in town, change the subject. Or better yet, you could bring up the information about the murder occurring somewhere else. Yeah," he mused aloud. "That would be real helpful to the department."

The man was as transparent as glass. "Would I need to be deputized for these duties?" The flash of those masculine dimples sent her pulse into a fast skitter, proving that Alan had only dulled her response to men, not killed it. Under the circumstances, it wasn't a realization that gave her any pleasure.

"No, ma'am."

She watched with more interest than she would admit as he raked a careless hand through the thick blond hair at his nape, which had a tendency to curl in the humidity.

Then that trademark smile bumped up in wattage. "But it sure would be helpful to the department, Miss Prescott. And you'd have my appreciation."

"Your appreciation notwithstanding," she answered wryly, "I think I'll pass."

He nodded, as if her words didn't surprise him. "Okay. It's not really your job, after all. My men and I will keep spreading the word ourselves." He pushed away from the porch post. "Don't be surprised if people are less willing to talk to you in a few days. About the murder, that is. It won't be anything personal, you understand." Turning, he started down her steps.

She regarded his wide shoulders blankly for a moment before saying, "Wait. What's that supposed to mean?"

He faced her again, propped a foot on the first step. "Just that I was serious about calming fears in the parish. You've refused to help us out, but other folks won't. I've known most of these people all my life. When I ask some of them to refrain from talking about the murder anymore, they'll agree."

It may have been couched in the most genial of terms, but she knew exactly what he was saying. The warning had her angling her chin. "You mean you'll tell people to stop talking to *me*."

The hurt look that settled over his face was too innocent to be entirely genuine. "Now there you go, taking this personal. I just told you—"

She started down the steps and stopped when they were eye to eye, fighting an urge to seat him in the dirt. When she was pushed, even indirectly, it was her nature to push back. "I heard what you told me, *Sheriff*. And more, I heard what you meant. You're going to use the fact that I'm a stranger in town to get the people to close ranks. Pretty slick. You'll still get exactly what you want."

Damn. He almost shook his head in admiration. She was as quick as she was pretty, reading him as easily as a dime-store novel. If he didn't have a ironclad aversion to falling too hard, too fast, she'd already have reduced him to a puddle of hormones. His fingers itched for the cigar. Even if he couldn't smoke it, holding it would provide a welcome distraction for his hands.

"Now, don't go thinking folks won't still be neighborly. They'll just be a bit more careful about what they talk to you about." He hesitated a beat before adding, "But since you're not part of the media, that really won't matter much to you, will it?"

He paused just long enough to watch the simmer in her eyes turn into a smolder, before turning toward his car. He could feel her eyes stabbing his back with every step he took. As he drove away he reflected on the damn shame of that.

They really were beautiful eyes.

Zoey sat in the darkness on the front porch and reveled in the slight breeze flirting with her hair. When the heat in Chicago turned beastly, she'd never thought twice about cranking the air conditioner up to glacial and waiting out the high temperatures in the comfort of her apartment. The humidity in Louisiana made Chicago seem balmy by comparison. Yet here she was, sitting in the dark, taking pleasure in the first cool breath of air to move through the area in days. She supposed it had something to do with small-town living. It wouldn't have been safe to sit outside at night in Chicago, at any rate.

The fact that she felt safe doing so now, here, despite a murder victim recently having been found in the vicinity was a bizarre testimony to the change she'd been undergoing since coming to Charity. It certainly had nothing to do with her faith in a certain underhanded backwoods sheriff.

The thought of Cage Gauthier had her spine straightening in the glider she'd bought at the town's only department store. Since he'd come to her house three days ago she'd seen him from a distance, once in his car driving through town, and another time driving by here. On both occasions he'd waved a greeting she'd ignored. She wasn't over being irritated with the man.

It had quickly become apparent that he'd lost no time doing as he'd warned. Each time she went to town, whether it was to shop or to get something to eat at the quaintly named Stew 'N Brew diner, she witnessed the effects of his handiwork. The residents were still friendly, still curious, but it was tempered with a guardedness that was new. Even the loquacious twins were tight-mouthed about any questions she might put to them regarding the murder, and she cursed Cage Gauthier each time it happened. By using her, he'd managed to accomplish exactly what he'd set out to do—quell the gossip that kept the fear fresh, the rumors alive. Although on one level she might have admired his ingenuity, on another she damned him for his tactics.

She stretched her legs out in front of her and enjoyed the way the slight breeze molded the short silk nightgown against her skin. Not that there hadn't been a wealth of information shared during each of her trips to town. A newcomer was just too tempting an audience. She'd heard that Edie Hadley's hair color owed more to her gal at the Beauty Mark than to Mother Nature. Ben Whitley was suspected of fooling around with the widowed teacher at the elementary school. And Josie McCall over at the Gas and Go had been divorced three times and was on the lookout for husband number four. Rumor had it that Josie had inherited her daddy's thick head of hair and restless eyes.

Zoey had listened to the litany of information with something akin to horror. The anonymity of big-city living had a few advantages that she'd never before considered. At least she hadn't had to contend with the entire city knowing all the humiliating details of the disaster with Alan. She valued privacy too much to easily understand the way people here swapped personal tidbits about each other's lives with the casual intimacy of lifelong acquaintants. And although the thought of having that beam of gossip directed at her made her shudder, she couldn't deny an unwilling fascination for each new experience in Charity. That same small-town atmosphere was currently blooming in her novel.

An insect droned near her bare shoulder, and she waved it away languidly. There had been one fact she'd gleaned that had sparked her interest. Actually, it had nearly caused her to reach for the antacids she still carried in her purse. The cozy little house she'd rented had promptly lost some of its charm when she'd heard the news.

Cage Gauthier was her nearest neighbor.

Her lip jutted out in a cross between a sneer and a pout. She really shouldn't have been surprised. She'd long ago accepted that God couldn't resist the opportunity for irony. It would be a long time before Cage's high-handed actions would cease to rankle. Longer still before she let herself be blinded by a super sampling of half-baked charm wrapped up in an attractive package. Not even to herself would she admit just how attractive a package he made.

She heard the car before she saw it. The uneven sound of its engine was punctuated by an occasional backfire. Peering through the darkness, she watched as the vehicle drew closer to her house, and then slowed.

It wasn't a car, after all, she finally observed, but a pickup truck. An old one, from the sounds of it—one that seemed filled to overflowing with men.

Silently she rose and slipped into the house. She shut and locked the door before moving to the front window and pulling aside the curtain. She couldn't see well enough to determine how many men there were, but judging from the hollering going on, all of them had been imbibing freely. Letting the curtain drop back into place, she headed to her bedroom upstairs.

As she slipped between the crisp cotton sheets, she heard a loud whoop and an engine gunned. Grimacing, she directed the fan standing next to the bed toward her and turned it on. Some good ol' boys were going to have pounding heads in the morning, she imagined. She only hoped the pain they suffered was as obnoxious as their behavior tonight.

Somewhere between dozing and slumber, the first sound rang out, rousing her. Blinking groggily, she rolled over, trying to disentangle dream from reality. The second sound had her sitting straight up in bed, confusion fading. Then the noises came in rapid succession.

Gunshots.

Even as she sprang from the bed and pulled on jeans and a shirt, a more rational part of her mind took over. She'd been living in the city for far too long if she was automatically assuming that the sounds were gunfire. They could be fireworks, or, or... Her usually fertile imagination ran dry.

Pounding down the stairs, she ran barefoot to the front door and looked out. The splinter of moon shed little light in the dark sky, but she could see that the street in front of her house was empty. She hadn't expected otherwise. The shots, or whatever the noises would prove to be, hadn't sounded close enough to be coming from her yard.

She went to the telephone and reached for the receiver, then groaned mentally, dropping her hand. Although she'd contacted the phone company the day she'd moved in, her phone had not yet been hooked up. She'd assumed that the service, like so much else in Charity, moved at a slower pace than in the rest of the world. It hadn't been a problem until now.

She scooped up her keys from the hallway table and opened the door. Running down the steps, she headed for her car. There was no way she could return to sleep without alerting the local law enforcement about the sounds she'd heard.

Backing out of her drive, a thought formed in her mind and refused to be banished. Janice Reilly had died brutally, but not from gunshot wounds. Somehow, under the dark cover of the night, that thought failed to comfort her.

It had been a waste of a fine cigar, Cage thought aggrievedly, surveying the damage to his home. He'd been on the front porch, feet propped on the railing, an icy beer in one hand and his nightly smoke in the other. He'd recognized the sound of that sickly engine even before he'd seen the truck. Caution had sent him into the house, flipping off the lights as he went by. Caution may have saved his life. Either that, or damn poor aim.

The first bullet had taken him by surprise, but there had been no mistaking the sound it made, tearing through wood and plaster. Instinct had had him dropping to the faded rug and rolling across the room, in the direction of the holstered gun he'd unstrapped earlier and laid on the table.

The volley of bullets had shattered the front window, raining him with shards of glass. When he'd reached his gun and unleashed some fire of his own, the truck had squealed out of his drive amid more shots and some high-pitched hollering.

He reached an arm behind him awkwardly and pulled out a splinter of glass that protruded partway from his skin. His back felt on fire. No doubt there were countless tiny pieces to be picked out of it. He scowled at the thought. And he hadn't even gotten to enjoy his one cigar of the day.

Crossing to the telephone, he picked up the receiver and punched in some numbers. "Yeah, it's Gauthier," he said when Harriet, the night dispatcher, answered. "I had some trouble out here. Send a couple men." He could feel the faintly sticky traces of blood crawling down his skin. "No, they're gone. And if it's who I think it is, they won't be back."

Hanging up, he skirted the broken glass and headed to the kitchen to get himself a towel—and froze as he noticed the twin spear of headlights coming up his drive at a snail's pace.

Reversing direction, he scooped up the gun he'd laid next to the phone and padded silently into the dark dining room. He unlocked the door and slipped out onto the side porch, jumping nimbly over the railing and landing in the flower bed. He crept around the side of the house and paused. The car had shut off its lights, but no one had gotten out. Training he'd thought long dormant kicked in, and he dropped to his belly, approaching the vehicle at a crawl. If someone had come back to finish the job, he was in for a shock.

He was a yard from the car when the driver's side opened. He lunged to his feet and closed the distance in one smooth motion, clamping his arm around the driver's neck and pressing his gun hard against the temple.

"I never was much for surprises," he murmured matter-of-factly.

The hard body behind her, the pressure of what was surely a gun barrel to her head, had terror sprinting down Zoey's back and pooling nastily at the base of her spine. It took a second for recognition to filter through the panic, another for the dam of relief to break.

"I'll remember to call before dropping in next time," she managed shakily. Even before she'd completed the sentence she heard his muttered curse, then he was releasing her and stepping away.

"What in *hell* are you doing here?"

Temper, she noted, sharpened his words, made the drawl all but disappear. She faced him in the darkness, raised her chin. "I heard something that sounded like shots."

He snorted and half turned away in disbelief, before swinging back to her. "There was a good reason for that, sugar. They *were* shots. Which doesn't explain why you decided to plant yourself right in the middle of the fray."

From the distance he heard a siren approaching and mentally groaned. He should have warned Harriet. That damned DuPrey was like a kid. He'd run a siren for a jaywalker, given the chance.

"I knew they were gone. I saw the truck come out of your drive."

She had his interest now. "You saw the truck?"

As two sheriff's-department cars pulled into the drive, she gave him a rundown of what she'd observed outside her home. "I'm pretty sure it was the same truck that passed me on the road," she concluded. "It's hard to mistake the sound of that engine."

"You're right about that. But next time leave the investigating to the professionals."

"My phone isn't hooked up," she said tartly. "It was either drive into town to report the shots or go back to sleep and ignore the fact that someone could be in danger. If I'd known that the someone was you, my decision might have been different.''

The snooty tone was back. His mouth quirked unwillingly. He'd been the rock his mother and sister had leaned on for long enough to have acquired an appreciation for strong women. Something told him that the woman standing before him was finely forged steel. He didn't know why the thought made him want to see just how deep that steel went.

DuPrey and Fisher climbed out of their units, and Cage turned to face them. He heard her gasp and suddenly remembered what his back must look like. Not that he could forget for long. It felt as though an army of fire ants were marching across each spare inch of flesh.

The headlights of the cars spotlighted the two of them, and the sight of that raw, angry skin sent a tremor through her. ''You've been hurt.'' Her hand lifted, almost reached him, before she snatched it back and tucked it in her jeans pocket.

''Yeah, it was flying glass. Get me a wet towel, would you, honey?''

She watched him saunter away, and just that easily, that casually, she was relegated to nursemaid. She didn't know whether to laugh or snarl.

Minutes later, she was doing neither. He sat on the porch steps giving his deputies instructions while she knelt behind him, wiping away blood. Most of the cuts were shallow, she was relieved to note, but there were a few that still had glass embedded in them. She didn't dare try to remove them. Her nursing experience had been limited to soaking up blood and bandaging Patrick after his various mishaps.

She tended to him silently. But when the two deputies got into their cars, the questions that had been bubbling just below the surface came tumbling out. ''Who are the Rutherfords? Why are you so sure they're behind this tonight? Did you see them?''

He flexed his shoulders gingerly, flinched when he felt a sharp jab. She hadn't gotten all the glass out yet. ''Well, the fact is, sweetheart, I kind of fibbed to you a few days ago.''

Her hands stilled, more from the term of endearment than from the confession. It occurred to her that she'd come a long way from ''Miss Prescott'' in the space of a few days. ''Sugar,'' ''honey,'' ''sweetheart''—some men preferred endearments to going to the bother of remembering a woman's given name. She scrubbed at a trace of blood more vigorously, causing him to release a hiss of breath.

''Take it easy, there, will you? I'd just as soon keep that layer of skin. And it wasn't a flat-out lie, or anything.'' It took her a moment to pick up the thread of conversation. ''When you mentioned there not being any crime to speak of in the parish, I didn't correct you, that's all. Fact is, although this area is quiet by city standards, we have enough going on to keep my department busy. And I'm sure it was the Rutherford boys, because it's just the sort of dumb move they'd make. See, they're plain pissed off at me.'' He turned to look at her over his shoulder, and winked. ''I know you find that hard to believe.''

''Not totally.''

''Yeah, well, I busted up the meth lab they were running in the woods near their place, and hauled their youngest brother, Carver, off to jail. I know dang well the whole clan was in on it, but I only have evidence to charge the one.'' A note of determination entered his voice. ''So far.''

Her hands stilled on his back. ''Meth lab. In Charity?''

''In the parish, at any rate. Running them in rural places is getting more common. I doubt these guys were the brains behind the outfit, since Rutherfords don't run long in that area. Stagnant gene pool,'' he offered by way of explanation. He'd like to turn completely and face her, watch the reactions flit across that expressive face, but was reluctant to pull away from her light touch. He imagined there was a straight route from the tips of her fingers to his veins. He indulged himself for another moment and let himself envi-

sion those hands running over his chest...his stomach...
lower.

"Get the Rutherfords liquored up and they're just stupid
enough to drive their wreck of a truck over and shoot up
my place." His voice sounded slightly strangled, so he
cleared it. "DuPrey and Fisher will most likely find gunpowder on their hands and shotguns that will match the
ballistics from the bullets I'll be digging out of my walls."

"You make it sound so reasonable. Those idiots could
have killed you."

He hid a satisfied smile at the concern in her voice.
Slowly, stiffly, he turned to face her. "Careful there, honey.
You almost sound like you'd miss me."

He was too close, his face only inches from her own. She
swallowed hard when she saw that his eyes had gone to
smoke. "Don't call me honey."

His mouth crooked a little. "Sorry." He reached a hand
toward her, hesitated for an instant when she flinched, then
pushed a strand of hair away from her face. "Zoey." Surely
it was that slow, heated drawl of his that made his voice
sound caressing; that made her name on his lips sound every
bit as intimate as the endearment.

They stared at each other for a moment. She was near
enough to notice the small white scar at the corner of his
eye, to feel the warmth of his breath when he spoke.

"I guess I owe you a thank-you."

Since she couldn't seem to formulate the word, she just
shook her head.

"Yes, ma'am, I believe I do. I usually wait until the third
or fourth date before I ask women to patch me up." A ghost
of a smile played across his mouth. "Hate to scare them
off. But something tells me that you don't scare easily, do
you, Zoey?"

Strange, that the return of his easy charm would have her
lungs easing. His lighthearted banter was infinitely prefer-
able to that moment of tenderness. "Since I hardly qualify
as a date, I don't think you need to worry. And you're not

patched up. At least, not completely. Your next stop is going to be the hospital.''

He took her hand in his and distracted her from the action by arguing. ''Charity doesn't have what I'd call a real hospital. It's more a clinic. Old Doc Barnes gets real ornery when he's woken up, too. He's got the temperament and light touch of a grizzly and uses needles a full foot long.'' He gave a shudder that wasn't totally feigned. ''You could help me more than he could.''

''No,'' she said with certainty, ''I couldn't. Some of those cuts still have glass in them and at least two are going to need stitches. Haul butt, Gauthier. Our next stop is Doc Barnes.''

''Jeez, you're strict.'' But he stood when she did, still not releasing her hand. With her a step above him, their faces were nearly level. Giving in to the impulse that had been riding him since the first time he'd seen her, he coaxed her forward with a slight tug on her hand, and covered her mouth with his own.

He knew better than to rush her, so he eased into the kiss, taking pleasure in each hitch and shudder of breath. Because his senses seemed suddenly, gloriously heightened, he felt the shiver that ran through her, concentrated on the gradual softening that had her body yielding ever so slightly against his.

When her lips parted under his gentle persuasion, he slowly increased the pressure, degree by torturous degree. And finally, he gave in to temptation and swept his tongue into taste.

The step rocked a little beneath his feet, and his free hand went to her back, gathered her closer. He sipped at her mouth, letting the flavors swirl and collide around him, too varied to be easily identified.

He wasn't sure what he had expected. Strength, certainly. Passion. She had both in her. He was unsurprised to taste caution, but found sweetness, too, and a response that was innocent, yet heated. The heat grew with each taste and velvet glide, until her hand rose, fisted in his hair and he obeyed the pressure to deepen the kiss, to drive them both a little crazy.

The soft lazy romance of it smothered Zoey's initial flare of resistance. Resolve melted, priorities shifted. She'd never had difficulty evading smooth words and quick advances. But like everything else about the man, his touch was slow, persuasive, and infinitely devastating. If thinking had been possible, she would have wondered how the clash of tongues and teeth could seem so intimate, so personal. Surely a mere kiss shouldn't make her gasp and shiver, and want, with a vicious craving that sliced clear to the bone.

His mouth drank from hers and with each taste drew a little more of her into his system—a system that was starting to pound and ache for something only she could give him. He had the experience to know that a kiss shouldn't be enough to fire his blood, to bring a shake to his knees and send a dizzying arc through his senses. But nothing he'd known before had prepared him for the intoxicating pleasure of tasting this woman.

His mouth left hers and cruised a warm, moist path down her throat. Her hand left his hair and moved to his shoulders, clutching at him with an urgency that she'd never known before. And when she felt his slight wince, felt the stickiness beneath her fingertips, she froze, then reached for her scattered logic. Even as she pulled away, something feminine inside her that had never before been breached, mourned.

"What in heaven's name are you doing?"

The panic in her voice had his head lifting, his blood cooling. And seeing the panic reflected on her face, he made a conscious effort to soothe. "Just a friendly little kiss. I owed you a thank-you, remember?"

Her gaze flashed to his in surprise. Her question had been directed more at herself than at him. She'd never been one to dive into any experience so recklessly, guided only by heat and emotion. Had never been one to fall, let alone leap, into unfamiliar, uncharted waters.

She took a step back, and then another. She wasn't about to begin now.

"I told you before, no thanks are necessary. If we waste any more time on this porch, I'm going to think that all it takes to cow the mighty sheriff of St. Augustine parish is an irritable M.D. with a wicked-looking needle."

He heard the thin layer of desperation beneath her words, so he smiled easily and backed down the steps. "Sounds like you're beginning to know me too well."

She followed him to the car, already mentally estimating the time before she could drop him back off at home, and return to her house, alone. Away from Cage Gauthier and his troubles. Away from his persuasive lips and coaxing hands. The breath that had been stopped up in her lungs shuddered out of her.

Alone. There was promise in the word, in the thought. She'd cling to that promise in the minutes or hours ahead. Her hand was poised on the door handle when she heard his voice.

"Zoey."

She looked across the top of the car to see him leaning on his folded arms, regarding her steadily.

"It was just a kiss. Nothing too dangerous."

Their gazes meshed for a heartbeat, two, three. Then he opened the door and slid into the car. She didn't immediately follow suit. His words were echoing in her head.

"Nothing too dangerous."

She released a quick, shaky breath. Yeah, right. That's probably the last thing the snake said to Eve before she took a bite of that Granny Smith.

Chapter 3

"Well, it looks like we got us a full house, Tommy Lee." With his hands in his pockets, Cage surveyed the occupants of the three cells like a genial host.

"I reckon these boys come down to see us cuz they heard you was in the mood for company, sir." Tommy Lee Hatcher watched the sheriff with something akin to hero worship in his eyes. Cage Gauthier was the biggest man in the parish, or at least it seemed so to Tommy Lee. And he didn't owe it to who his mama and daddy were, either, nor to the fact that the Gauthiers had always had more money than anyone else in these parts. No, sirree, Cage Gauthier could have stayed in Charity and lived off that money, and no one would have thought the less of him. Instead, he'd gone to some special academy and worked as a detective for the New Orleans Police Department. And come home a hero, no less.

Some might have wondered what had caused Cage to resign his job and come back to Charity to run for sheriff. But it was the best thing that had ever happened to Tommy

Lee. Here he was, twenty years old, and already a part-time jailer for the sheriff's department. He squinted at the cells full of Rutherfords and hitched up his pants in an absent gesture of pride. The only thing that would have made him prouder was if he were allowed to carry a gun. But one of these days he was fixin' to make deputy, and then he'd get a gun for sure. And wouldn't that make Becky Hawkins at the Stew 'N Brew sit up and take notice?

"We got our rights, Gauthier." Lonny Rutherford, the oldest, was spokesman for the clan. "We ain't no dumb homeboys like you used to roust in New Orleans. We each get us a phone call and a lawyer."

"Seems to me, when it comes to brains, you don't have a thimbleful between the lot of you." Cage strolled to the far cell and surveyed Lonny, who, like his four brothers, regarded him sullenly. "Otherwise you'd never have been stupid enough to think I was going to let you get away with shooting up my house. The property damage alone is enough to buy you some jail time, and when we add the attempted murder charge, well…" He shook his head.

"You can't make that stick, Gauthier!" shouted Carver. He wrapped his hands around the cell bars, and didn't seem to notice that his older brothers were shooting him warning looks. "How was they to know you'd be home? Hell, it was Friday night. On the weekends you're usually puttin' it to whatever pookie you're seein' and—" His words ended on a yelp and a curse as one of his brothers obeyed Lonny's unspoken command and cuffed Carver smartly across the head.

Cage's voice remained friendly, but his eyes were hard. "Did you hear that, Tommy Lee? These boys were betting I'd be gone Friday night. I guess that'd just make them cowards, and not would-be killers."

"I reckon they can use that line in their defense, Sheriff." Tommy Lee preened a bit at the exchange.

"Now that's an idea." Cage took the cigar out of his pocket and held it. "I've contacted a public defender to represent the lot of you. Carver's got his own P.D. already. I figured the drug charge would be enough to keep his lawyer busy.''

''We don't need us no damn public defender,'' Luther snarled. ''We got plenty of money. I want my phone call so I can get me a fancy lawyer out of Baton Rouge. You gotta give me the phone call, Gauthier. I know that.''

''And everyone said book learning was wasted on you.'' Lonny had been a few years older than Cage, but after he'd been held back a time or two, they'd ended up in the same class—at least, until Lonny had been sent to a juvenile center for theft. ''And you're right about one thing. You do get a phone call. If you want to use it to hire yourself a different lawyer, go ahead. But be sure and tell him that there's no hurry getting up here. Bail can't be set until Judge Ranier gets back from fishing on Monday.''

He tucked the cigar back in his pocket and looked at Tommy Lee. ''You can take care of the phone calls, can't you?'' When Tommy nodded, he turned and headed to his office. By the time he shut the door behind him the Rutherfords were already fading from his mind.

Dropping into his desk chair he started to lean back, then hissed out a breath when he came into contact with the chair. Straightening, he cursed imaginatively. After Zoey had delivered him home from Doc Barnes's with the advice to get some sleep, he'd spent the better part of three hours trying to do just that. He figured he hadn't had to sleep on his stomach since he'd been in diapers. It appeared he'd lost the knack. By the time exhaustion had kicked in, it had seemed as if the alarm was already going off.

Refusing the pain medication Doc had tried pressing on him hadn't been an act of machismo, as Zoey had accused. He couldn't let anything fog his thinking right now. There were just too damn many unanswered questions. His eyes lifted to the bulletin board above his desk that had been cleared of everything but photos of Janice Reilly. He surveyed a picture they'd obtained, taken a year or two before her death, as if the image wasn't already branded on his mind. She'd been robbed of life in the most savage, brutal way imaginable. He figured the least he owed her was a clear head during the course of her murder investigation.

He picked up the report of last night's ruckus at his place and flipped through it. With his usual methodical precision, Chief Deputy Fisher, head of the criminal investigation division, had typed Cage's statement and the events surrounding the Rutherfords' arrest. According to Charity's gossips, Fisher's personal life had been a shambles since his wife had left him three months ago, yet that hadn't tainted his professionalism on the job. Cage couldn't help admiring the man for that.

Tossing the report aside, Cage reached for the files containing the information they'd gleaned so far on Janice Reilly's murder. Unthinkingly, his hand crept to his pocket, before he caught himself and halted. It was a damn shame, he thought, when a man let nicotine get such a vicious grip on him that the body cried for it without the brain's permission.

Of course, he reasoned, he hadn't gotten a chance for his cigar last night. That meant he owed himself one, didn't it? The Rutherfords had already cost him some new windows, a carpet and a hell of a carpentry bill. There was no use adding to that list by denying himself the pleasure of the smoke he'd missed.

Body and mind in agreement, he took out the cigar and lit it. The first puff was a sweet haze filtering through his lungs. The second was a luxury to be savored, and by the third he was ready to work. He spread the reports before him and proceeded to read every bit of information they had over again. He'd read through them a dozen times before. He'd read them a dozen more before the case was solved.

It was a well-known fact in police work that the twenty-four hours preceding a homicide were as critical as the twenty-four hours following it. Information gleaned from the antemortem was valuable because what Janice Reilly had done, where she'd gone and whom she'd seen all might have a bearing on her death.

The postmortem twenty-four hours were important because the chances of solving the case diminished significantly the more time elapsed after the murder. As the trail grew colder, the killer got more and more of an edge. Cage had been a cop long enough to know that if a case went longer than a week without a solid lead, chances were it would never be solved at all.

It had now been—he did a quick mental estimation—nine days, two hours, and thirty-three minutes since the body had been discovered. And it would take a stretch of the imagination to consider any of their leads "solid."

He pored over the information they'd put together, regardless. Fisher's team had constructed a solid picture of the day immediately before, and the day of the victim's death. But through the endless contacts made with Janice Reilly's family, friends and acquaintances, no real clue had emerged. In a homicide investigation, a law-enforcement officer first looked to those people closest to the victim. Jealousy and greed were the lowest common human denominators. But the victim's ex-husband had been halfway across the country, in a hospital delivery room with his new wife and baby daughter. They had been unable to establish a motive for the man's involvement in his ex-wife's murder, at any rate. By all accounts, their divorce had been amicable.

Cage picked up a five-by-seven picture that was included in the file. That brought them to Jeremy Klatt, the victim's ex-lover who had been, he'd asserted, home alone watching TV the night of the murder. He'd claimed he hadn't seen the victim in over two months, but the deputies hadn't been certain of his truthfulness. The man had also asserted that he'd been the one to initiate the breakup with Janice Reilly, a statement her closest friends disputed. Was his lie merely ego—an effort to save face? Or was it a deliberate attempt to cover up far more? Setting the photo aside, Cage reread the man's statement, before turning to the stack of others the deputies had taken.

When a sharp rapping sounded at his door, Cage looked up, faintly amazed to discover that more than two hours had gone by. A broad torso topped by a fresh-scrubbed Howdy Doody face stuck just inside the door. Deputy Roland DuPrey.

"Sorry to bother you, Sheriff, but we just got an express delivery of the coroner's final report. As long as we've been waiting for it, figured you'd want to see it right away."

"You figured right." He held out his hand to take the envelope from DuPrey, and opened it quickly. Doc Barnes held the official title of coroner for the parish, but the man would be the first to admit that his experience with dead bodies began and ended with the occasional victim of a automobile accident and the final passing of St. Augustine's oldest residents. When the murder victim had been discovered, Cage hadn't hesitated to call Baton Rouge for assistance. Dr. Margaret Wu, the coroner who had worked the case, had seemed capable and intelligent. Normally the final report would be delivered within forty-eight hours of the examination of the body. It was just their bad luck that the crime had occurred within days of a bombing that had wiped out an apartment complex on the city's east side. Both the coroner's office and the labs were backed up with work relating to that case.

Since he was already studying the report in his hand, it was a moment before he realized the deputy was still standing in the doorway.

"Uh…" Roland's throat bobbed nervously at Cage's quizzical gaze. "Would you mind if I went over it with you, Sheriff? Fisher's not in today, and I'm kinda interested, this being my first murder and all. I mean…" Dull flags of color rose in his freckled cheeks. "The first murder in the parish, that is. What I meant was, in recent times…"

Cage took pity on the man. "No, I don't mind." DuPrey was one of his more inexperienced deputies, but he'd been riding with Fisher when the call had come in about the body. From the eagerness Roland showed pulling up a chair next to his, one would never guess that he'd lost the contents of his stomach in the nearby weeds when he'd seen the victim. Cage didn't hold the reaction of the man against him. Death like that *should* shock and disgust people. When it ceased to do so, one would have to wonder just how fine a line separated the savage soul who'd commit such an atrocity from those who hunted him.

Cage began to flip through the pages. "Let's hit the highlights, shall we? Cause of death—ligature strangulation. We knew that." He paused to reread another sentence on the page. When Roland looked up at him, he said slowly, "The marks on her neck indicate that she was choked unconscious several times, then resuscitated."

"Why would he do that?" Roland blurted out, then hunched his shoulders when Cage looked at him.

"Power. He got off on having total control over her, prolonging his pleasure." He'd seen those telltale marks, guessed their significance. It had been the cuts and abrasions on the victim's knees and shins, however, that continued to puzzle him. His gaze returned to the report in his hand. "Ligature marks found on her wrists and ankles...garden-variety clothesline used. Again, nothing new." He flipped a page, read silently, then said, "There was evidence of rape but no samples left by the offender. Damn!"

Disappointment laced DuPrey's words. "Looks like he was lucky."

Luck like that was rare, Cage knew. He felt his stomach clench and grind. Flipping through the pages, he skimmed rapidly. Other than the lack of physical evidence revealed, the report didn't appear to have much more information than the preliminary one the coroner had given them. And some lab work, according to an attached note, still wasn't completed.

"By the time the witness had discovered the body, the victim had been dead four-to-six hours." Out of the corner of his eye Cage saw Roland gape and swing his head toward him, but his gaze remained trained on the report. Janice Reilly had been discovered about 8:00 a.m. That would put her approximate time of death somewhere between 2:00 and 4:00 a.m.

"That's exactly what you said that morning. I thought the coroner would be able to pinpoint it closer than that."

Cage shook his head. "Time of death is tougher to figure than most people think. I was just making an educated guess from the body's temperature, the stage of rigor mortis and…" He shot a look at DuPrey, unwilling to chance a replay of the man's reaction to his earlier explanation of forensic entomology.

But the deputy had already made the connection. "It was the insects, right?"

Cage considered him closely, but, although his face was pale beneath the freckles, he looked steady enough. "Like I told you, they can act as a clock when it comes to time of death. And from the lack of bleeding from the wound in the victim's hand, it was easy to determine she was dead when it was inflicted."

From the look on DuPrey's face it was obvious he failed to see the significance of the fact. Cage began to wish he'd saved that cigar. He was back full circle to the million-dollar questions: Had the site outside of Charity been selected at random? Or did it hold some special significance for the killer?

Becky Jane Hawkins set a bowl of Saturday's special on the table in front of Zoey. The Stew 'N Brew didn't run to the healthier menu choices. Most of their selections featured deep-fat-fried entrées dripping with gravy. But their gumbo, Zoey had quickly learned, was out of this world.

"How's it goin', Miss Prescott?" Becky Jane tarried a moment beside Zoey's booth.

"Just fine, Becky, thanks." She picked up her spoon, but the waitress still lingered.

"Uh...I was wondering..."

Zoey's spoon made a quiet clink against the stoneware as she set it down and looked up at the girl quizzically. With a self-conscious gesture, the waitress smoothed her blond hair, which owed its styling to big bangs and a heavy layer of lacquer. Then she blurted out, "What's Chicago like?"

Her lips curved, Zoey replied, "It's big, noisy. And very crowded."

Becky wiped her hands down the apron covering her pink uniform, hemmed up a good four inches shorter than those of the other waitresses in order to show off her slender legs. She threw a quick peek over her shoulder, but Ethel, the owner, was nowhere in sight. Returning her attention to Zoey, she asked, "Why would you leave it to come to Charity?" Genuine puzzlement shone in her eyes.

Zoey couldn't have offered the girl an explanation had she wanted to. Certainly she'd never before experienced this compulsion to change locales to write one of her novels. But when she'd heard of a murder shocking a sleepy Louisiana town, the inspiration for her next book had struck suddenly. She'd hoped to maintain that intensity by moving to Charity for a time, and her idea seemed sound. Although her novels of murder and mayhem were fiction, this current one owed its flavour to Charity itself.

Her smiled turned wry. No, she couldn't explain that to Becky Jane. She barely understood it herself. "I needed a change," she said simply.

It was plain her answer hadn't satisfied the girl. "That's the same thing Cage—I mean, Sheriff Gauthier—said when he came back from New Orleans. I guess I'll never understand people."

Her words captured Zoey's interest. "Sheriff Gauthier used to live in New Orleans?"

"Oh, yes, ma'am." The fervor in the girl's voice alerted Zoey to the fact that the young woman had more than a slight crush on Cage. "He was on the police force there. And not just as an officer, but as a detective. Isn't that just the most romantic thing?"

"Terribly."

Apparently Becky missed the wryness of the other woman's tone. "He returned when his mama got sick, but after she died he stayed on. I still can't figure why. When I get a little money saved I'm heading out of here on the next bus, and I'll only come back for visits. I'm going to New York, or Hollywood or maybe even Vegas."

Zoey eyed her with amusement. "I'm sure that will make the young man in the uniform who comes in here for lunch most days very unhappy."

"Who? Oh, shoot, you mean Tommy Lee?" Becky tossed her head. Not a strand of her heavily sprayed hair moved. "He's kinda cute, I guess. But I'm not about to get serious about anyone when I'm fixin' to leave and all. It just wouldn't be right."

"I need some coffee over here, Becky Jane," a farmer in overalls and a cap called across the diner.

"Keep your shirt on," she retorted. With a shrug and a cheeky smile she said, "Well, I best get back to work. I'd like to talk to you sometime, if that's okay. About your life in Chicago."

"Sure. Anytime."

Watching the girl move away, Zoey wondered if she'd ever been that young, that impatient to experience life. For her, adulthood had arrived early. She had no thrilling tales to share with Becky Jane about a glamorous life in a big city. Duty, responsibility—those were things she understood. They'd pushed her to grow up faster than most. When she took the time to consider it, she felt no regret. Given the opportunity, she'd make the same choices for her siblings. But glamour and excitement... Her lips curved ruefully and she returned her attention to her lunch. Excitement was something she'd never looked for in her life. And had never once missed.

She didn't bother looking up when the door opened to admit a new customer, but the instant murmur of voices, which gradually rose to crescendo level, had her raising her head. She stifled a groan of dismay. To the delight of nearly every female in the place, the sheriff of St. Augustine parish had just made an appearance.

"Heard you had some trouble out at your place, Sheriff." This from the farmer at the counter.

Cage walked over and gave the man a friendly thump on the shoulder. "Oh, nothing too serious, Cy. Just some boys with more sand than sense. Got the lot of them cooling their heels in jail cells."

Ethel came bustling out of the kitchen and regarded him, her fists propped on her bony hips. "I heard tell Doc Barnes had to sew you up, boy. What in the Sam blazes are you doin' back on the job today?"

The chorus of concerned questions that rose from all the females in the diner would be enough to embarrass most men half to death. Jessamine Walter, the owner and operator of the Beauty Mark, reached Cage first, sliding off her stool and rushing over to run her hand up and down his arm. "Are you hurt bad? Is there anything I can do for you?"

Normally, he would have milked the sympathy for all it was worth, but he'd seen the dark-colored car parked out front. It hadn't taken any of the deductive skills that had once earned him the rank of detective to make the presumption that Zoey was inside.

A quick scan of the diner showed her sitting in the corner booth, rolling her eyes at the crowd of women cooing over him. He smiled at Jessamine—bravely, he thought. "I'm fine. There wasn't even much left for Doc Barnes to do last night after Miss Prescott finished fixing me up." As if on cue, the women swiveled to stare at Zoey, who'd gone completely and utterly still. Inclining his head, he said, "If you'll excuse me, ladies."

It seemed to Zoey that all eyes in the diner were fixed in their direction as Cage walked over to her booth and slid in across from her. Beaming that easygoing, megawatt grin, he said, "Hey. How's the gumbo today?"

All her defenses clicked into place. *Restraint. Command. Control.* The words repeated in her head like a mantra. Those were the qualities she'd possessed in abundance before the debacle with Alan. She'd since methodically reassembled that Zoey Prescott, brick by brick. And damned if she was going to crumble in the face of—unbidden, her memory supplied her with a mental replay—slow hands, a clever mouth and exquisite sensation.

Abruptly, she dropped her spoon with a clatter. "Hard to say. I just lost my appetite."

He reached over and snitched one of the packages of crackers Becky had served with the soup. "Now that's a darn shame. Ethel makes the best gumbo in these parts. She's going to be right put out if you don't manage to eat more than that."

"I know how she feels. I'm feeling a little put out myself."

Pure wicked fire gleamed in his gray eyes, ruining the effect of the angelic expression he wore. "With me? What have I done?"

"I've no interest in becoming the next item of gossip in Charity by having you link our names." Nodding in the direction of the women still openly staring at them, she added, "I have a feeling that any woman seen with you is open to speculation." She added deliberately, "I don't like being the object of speculation."

He'd just bet she didn't. Zoey Prescott was too serious and much too private to allow someone close enough to discover just exactly what made her tick. Carefully, he shifted his weight in the booth, avoiding contact with the back of the seat. The problem was, he was finding himself just about fascinated with the idea of exploring what was inside the woman; and that was cause for concern. Although he'd never begrudged a woman who wanted to be persuaded, he wasn't one to waste his time where Not Interested signs were so clearly posted.

At least, he never had been before.

A corner of his mouth kicked up, slow and engaging. "You didn't expect me to ignore what you did for me, now did you? I couldn't do that, not even last night, when I was near delirious with pain."

Because her lips threatened to twitch, she firmed them. "Well, 'delirious,' at any rate."

He propped his elbows on the table and leaned closer. "My back feels some better today, but it probably wouldn't hurt any to have someone take a look at it. Make sure it's healing okay."

Her eyebrows rose at his blatant flirtation. "Maybe you should get a volunteer from your fan club over there. I believe they're already signing donor cards for you."

Letting loose a laugh that had all eyes zeroing in on the two of them once again, he picked up her hand and sent his thumb skimming across her knuckles. "You're mean, Zoey. I don't know when I started finding that quality attractive in a woman."

She snatched her hand away. "Believe me, I can get a lot meaner."

His dimples deepened. "Since you're only armed with a spoon this time, I figure I'll take my chances."

Zoey gazed at him, allowing herself to wonder for a moment what, if anything, lay beneath that Southern-baked charm and lazy sense of humor. It was pathetically easy to dismiss a small-town Romeo whose ego was reflected in every mirror he passed. It might be harder to rebuff such a man whose mettle ran deeper, stronger. She had no reason to believe that Cage Gauthier was such a man. But still…

She pushed her bowl away. She wasn't in the market for a man—any man—at this point in her life. Given her incredible lack of success with the opposite sex, she wasn't sure she ever would be.

"Listen, Mr.—Sheriff…." She moistened her lips and

tried not to notice the way his attention immediately honed in on the action. "I'm sure you're used to dazzling the female population of the parish, but—"

"Are you going to eat that?"

She blinked. "What?"

He motioned to the soup she'd pushed away. "The gumbo. Are you finished with it? Because it sure does seem a shame to let it go to waste."

"No. I mean, yes. I'm done with it." She watched, bemused, as he took her answer as an invitation to pull the bowl over and begin to finish it off. Using her spoon.

Momentarily sidetracked, she noted the workings of his strong throat as he swallowed, the look of almost-beatific appreciation that crossed his face at the taste. It occurred to her then that the man was a sensualist, taking more than ordinary pleasure in taste, touch. For an instant the memory of the few moments they'd shared last night, when he'd tasted *her,* flitted across her mind, and her mouth went abruptly dry.

"You were saying?"

Her gaze bounced to his. "Pardon?"

He took another swallow of soup. "Before I confiscated your lunch, you were saying something." Because she still looked blank, he said helpfully, "I believe you were telling me I was dazzling."

His words yanked her back to reality with a jolt. "Not exactly. But I'm sure you're used to women finding you so."

"But not you."

She shook her head. "Not me. Sorry." She met his gaze squarely. "I won't be here long, and I'm not the type to indulge in casual relationships."

Her message was coming in loud and clear, as much from the look in those pretty green eyes as from her words. There was a healthy dose of caution there and a glimmer of desperation. Recognizing both, he kept his voice light. "You are careful. I've noticed that about you."

"Too much so to give in to a momentary attraction."

He pointed the spoon at her. "You might call that being careful, I guess. If you were the type to skirt all new experiences to avoid risking one that might just knock you on that pretty butt of yours. Other folks might call that cowardice, but I guess it all depends on the point of view you take."

He tucked the spoon back into the bowl before him and scooped up another taste, pretending not to notice the way her eyes had gone molten.

"'Cowardice'?" The word was a lethal purr.

"That's not my perspective, you understand." He continued eating, talking between swallows. "I'm of the mind that a person does what he or she has to do to get by. The path they take is their own choosing."

"Hey, son, where have you been hiding out?"

Zoey was too busy glaring at Cage to bother looking up at the man who had stopped at the table. He was calling her a coward? He was deliberately mistaking fastidiousness for fear. She gave an audible sniff as he slid out of the booth and clapped the other man on the shoulder. No doubt he was unused to having women restrain themselves from throwing themselves at his feet. She refused to respond to his provocative remarks. Once again she'd underestimated him. He was clever enough to see more than most looked for, and low enough to exploit it.

"Why don't you join us? I was just finishing off Zoey's lunch for her." Cage sat down beside her, and with a friendly nudge, urged her to slide across the seat. She did so, to avoid having him on her lap. "I don't believe you two have been formally introduced. Zoey Prescott, Tanner Beauchamp." He finished off the remainder of the soup and then dropped the spoon into the bowl. To his friend, he added, "Zoey was just explaining why she finds me resistible."

A pained expression crossed Tanner's face. "I know from personal experience that she's very talented in that area."

"Cage is a little more difficult to convince than you were," she said dryly.

"He is persistent."

"Determined," Cage corrected, stretching his arms nonchalantly, then letting one hand drop around Zoey's shoulders. "Tanner and I have been friends since grade school, but he still doesn't know me half as well as he thinks he does."

"Really?" Her elbow caught his ribs with a sharp jab, bringing a satisfying wince to his face. He withdrew his arm hurriedly. "I've only been here days and already I feel I know you far too well."

Tanner chortled, and beckoned for a waitress. "Admit it, pal," he said to Cage. "She's too quick for us." Looking at Zoey he asked, "I'll bet your mama sleeps well at night, assured you're more than a match for any man you happen to meet."

She looked at him silently for a moment, an unexpected spasm seizing her chest. Despite the years that had passed since her mother's death, the sense of loss was never far away. It could sneak up sometimes—an emotional ambush. Aware that the two men were watching her closely, she deliberately smoothed her expression. "My mother died years ago. But I'm certain she'd be relieved to know that I can take care of myself."

Her recovery didn't fool the two men. Tanner reached over awkwardly and patted her hand. "Aw, damn. We're sure sorry about your loss. Cage here lost his mama less than a year ago, and his daddy the year before that. My own father dropped dead of a heart attack at his desk last January. We know what it is to grieve. I sure didn't mean to bring up sad memories."

Because the look he threw in Cage's direction was slightly panicked, Zoey loosened up enough to smile faintly. "The memories aren't sad, it's just the living without our loved ones that's tough."

"That's a fact," Cage responded. There was a trace of sorrow in his eyes and his voice was quiet.

Becky Jane strolled up to their booth, putting an extra sway in her hips for the benefit of the two men. "What can I get for you?"

"Nothing for me," Zoey replied. "Just the check."

Becky obligingly pulled the pad from her pocket and scribbled the price. When she ripped off the page and handed it to Zoey, Cage grabbed it.

"I'll take care of this." He winked at Zoey. "I ate more of it than you did, anyway."

The tinge of sympathy she'd felt for him just a moment ago vanished. She shrugged, unwilling to get into a tussle over the bill. "That's right, you did. Let me out, will you?" He obligingly slid from the booth.

Tanner smiled charmingly. "Miss Prescott. It's always a pleasure."

"It is, indeed," Cage murmured.

With one last long look, she left the two men and walked out of the diner.

The sun was shining brightly overhead. It was hot enough to wilt her a little, even walking the short distance to her car. Surely no one around here ever got used to this brutal heat. She felt as though she was dashing from one air-conditioned place to another.

"You're that writer gal, ain't ya?"

Her attention focused on getting into her car as quickly as possible, she'd missed the figure lingering on the steps of the diner. A woman, she determined, although she was dressed in a man's work shirt, heavy boots and jeans. Her hair was close-cropped and it was a sure guess that she didn't frequent the Beauty Mark for occasional stylings. She looked as weathered and capable as the burly farmer in the diner. She came down the steps and crossed to Zoey with a quickness that was belied by her girth.

"Yes, I'm Zoey Prescott."

"Fern Sykes." Zoey's hand was grabbed in a callused

palm and shaken firmly. "I seen ya around the town. Heard you was interested in that murder we had."

"I had questions, yes."

The woman's blue eyes, made brighter by the dark tan of her skin, fixed her with a direct look. "As you should have. So should everyone in this parish. Everyone with any sense, that is."

Her interest piqued, Zoey said, "The sheriff doesn't seem to think there's any reason for the people to get overly panicked."

The woman snorted. "He would if he knew what I know."

Intrigued, Zoey took a step closer. "And just what is that?"

Tossing a quick look over her shoulder, Fern lowered her voice. "I know who killed that poor girl a few days ago. And I've got me a pretty good idea why it happened."

Chapter 4

Zoey looked around the cabin with interest. She'd never seen such a rustic setting. The walls were split logs, still rough, despite their age. The floor beneath her was unvarnished pine, the furnishings as simple as the rest of the dwelling. Set well back from the road, with trees surrounding it, the cabin blended with nature.

Fern set a mug in front of her and sat down at the table across from her. "Drink it," she ordered brusquely. "It's tea I brew myself. Good for just about anything that ails you."

As she took a tentative sip, Zoey's eyes widened in surprise. It was surprisingly good. "What's in it?"

"Natural ingredients, all homegrown." The woman drank from her own mug, drained the contents, and poured some more from the pitcher she'd put on the table. "Had someone interested in buying the recipe once. That'd be back in the seventies. A man was gonna brew it up by the barrel, put it in fancy bottles and have it on store shelves all over the state."

Zoey lifted the mug to her lips, took a healthy swallow. "What happened?"

Fern lifted a hand. "Oh, my husband was in poor health by then. We just didn't have time to think about it. We lived here together from the time of our marriage till his death. Built the place ourselves."

When she fell silent, Zoey prompted, "You said you had an idea about the murder."

"I know what I said," the older woman replied testily. "I'm not senile yet." She aimed a fierce stare at Zoey. "You in a hurry or something?"

Zoey leaned back in her chair and shook her head. "Not really."

"Good." Fern reached over and poured more tea into Zoey's mug. "Never could abide folks rushing around like their house was on fire. And what I have to tell you takes some leading up to, and I don't like being pushed."

Hiding a smile, Zoey drank from the mug and prepared for a lengthy afternoon. Whether or not Fern Sykes could, in fact, shed any real light on the murder, she was convinced that the next few hours would be entertaining.

"This is an old parish," the woman began. "Families here can date their ancestors back to the settlers in the region. The Beauchamps, DuPreys and Gauthiers were the first to settle around these parts. Gives those families today something to be proud of, seeing as how their folks were the founding fathers and all. Not that the DuPreys have anything to show for it these days. But Jean-Paul Beauchamp, the old scoundrel, he owned the bank in town, passed down to him from his daddy, and his granddaddy before him. That's how Tanner ended up with it. As for the Gauthiers, well, they own just about everything else that's worth owning in St. Augustine parish."

The news should have come as no surprise. The home Cage lived in was pure Old South, needing only women in antebellum skirts and men in frock coats to complete its historic image. He didn't act like a man used to money and

the power it wielded. But she'd learned only too painfully
that she was no judge of what was in a man's heart.

Fern's voice went on, wrapping Zoey in a cocoon of times
past. Zoey drank silently from her mug, refilling it as the
older woman spun tales of times more than a century ago,
of history being made in Charity, Louisiana. And, as ordered, she listened silently—until a familiar name startled
an exclamation from her lips.

"'Rutherford'?"

Fern merely nodded, paused to drink from her own mug.
"Oh, sure, the Rutherfords go almost as far back in this
parish as the Gauthiers. The way I heard it, first man in St.
Augustine parish to be hung as a horse thief was Thaddeus
Rutherford." She squinted, looked at the ceiling. "He'd
have been great-granddaddy of this no-account bunch we
have now, I think. Hard to keep the clan straight, but they're
all related, one way or t'other."

Intrigued, Zoey leaned forward. "Cage…Sheriff Gauthier
seemed to think some people by that name were responsible
for shooting at his house last night."

"No doubt they were. The Rutherfords are noted for not
having a lick of sense between them. That and for being
meaner than cornered rats." She reached for the pitcher and,
finding it empty, went to the refrigerator for another. Ignoring Zoey's protest, she refilled both mugs.

"Tell me about it," Zoey invited. Her tongue felt thick
so she soothed it with another drink of tea.

Satisfied that she had Zoey's full interest, Fern leaned
back in her chair. "Well, we ain't had but one murder in
the history of the parish. Until this last one, that is."

"Cage said this latest murder probably didn't happen
where the body was found."

Fern glared at the interruption, and Zoey sat back meekly.
As the woman had warned, she didn't like to be rushed. The
story would be told, but only in her own time, in her own
way. "It was the summer of '60. Carl Rutherford had a real
nasty way about him, was known to take a hand to his wife

on a pretty regular occasion when he was liquored up, which is to say fairly often. Vella, that was his wife, she learnt real quick to dodge his fists when she could and keep her mouth closed most other times.'' Fern sipped her tea and her eyes took on a faraway look. "Never could figure what made a woman take that kind of treatment from a man. Or what kind of man would dish it out, for that matter.''

She came back to the present and shook her head. "Makes no never mind, at any rate. Some say that Vella had finally had enough, that she was fixing to run off where the old man would never find her again. Others claim she'd taken up with a door-to-door salesman. But there's no disputing the facts. Old man Rutherford came home one night earlier than expected and found her packing. Proceeded to knock her around, as was his custom. No one knows what she said to him, but from all accounts he went a little crazy. Pulled his rifle off the rack and shot her dead, right there in the kitchen.''

Maybe it was a tribute to the woman's storytelling abilities, but Zoey felt the horror of the act wash over her, as if the murder had happened in the present, rather than before her birth. "What happened?''

"Oh, it was a while before what he done came to light. He tried to bury her body in the woods, and act like she was still at home, feeling poorly. She hadn't gone out much anyway—he'd made sure of that. No telling how long his lies would have worked, if her sister hadn't started making a fuss about not being able to see her. The law got involved, and eventually the whole story came out.'' Her blue eyes bright, Fern leaned forward. "You might find it interesting to know that the judge who sentenced Rutherford to life in prison was the sheriff's granddaddy.''

Zoey assimilated that bit of news. History in Charity, it appeared, was a closely woven chain, with past and present intricately linked. She supposed that was common in small towns. She'd yet to see the significance of the woman's fascinating bits of history, but she didn't feel as if the afternoon had been wasted. She was feeling entirely too relaxed for that to be said.

She chose her words carefully. "Well, the story's interesting, but I can't see what it has to do with this last murder."

"It has everything to do with it," Fern snapped. "The way I hear it, the sheriff has a whole bunch of Rutherfords locked up right now, all but the one that most needs to be there. Donny Ray's the meanest of the lot, and that's not the only way he takes after his Great-uncle Carl. He has a habit of using his fists on Stacy, that wife of his. Everyone in town knows it."

Zoey rubbed at a point in the center of her forehead, where a headache was blooming. "Have you taken your concerns to the sheriff?"

Snorting, Fern reached for her mug. "Shoot, folks don't listen to an old woman's ramblings. Didn't do me no good when I told the law what happened to cause my husband's death."

Because it gave her a reason not to respond, Zoey grasped her mug tightly in both hands and drank. She knew, somewhere in the distant corners of her mind, that the connection the older woman was trying to make lacked reason. But somehow, right now it was difficult to summon logic. Her thought processes seemed off-kilter—pleasantly so.

Fern began to speak again, and Zoey focused on her mouth as it formed each word. Her voice seemed farther away, although the woman hadn't moved. She frowned. How curious. Perhaps it was this slight buzzing in her head that made it harder to hear Fern. She propped both elbows on the table and rested her chin on her entwined fingers. The woman's face drifted in and out of focus like a computer-generated three-dimensional image.

"'Course, folks said my Louis had some sickness. But I know what I know. Wasn't nothing wrong with the man before Cain Rutherford fixed him with the evil eye over at the tavern. He started feeling poorly that week, and never was the same after that. Less than a year later, he was dead.''

A vicious blade of sunlight probed beneath Zoey's eyelids and seared her eyes. She groaned, awakening by slow, torturous increments. With each level of awareness came a gradual increase of nauseating sickness, until she lay there, fully awake and praying for a return to unconsciousness—preferably a permanent one.

A raucous chorus of Black & Decker power tools was racketing in her head; her temples thudded painfully in rhythm with the cacophony. Her body felt leaden, immobile. Her first attempt to lift her head an inch from the pillow raised the decibel of pounding to such an excruciating crescendo, she quickly lay still again.

She knew in that moment what it was to pray for death. For several minutes she lay motionless, trying to determine whether the massive headache or her heaving stomach was more likely to result in her immediate demise.

Slowly, carefully, she turned her head, trying and failing to avoid provoking the rising tide of nausea. Upon completion of the single act, she rested against the pillow again. Because it seemed to be a relatively pain-free action, she opened her gritty eyes.

From this position she could observe the reason she was unable to move. A heavy arm slung across her waist held her fixed in place. She slid her eyelids shut, relieved that some weird temporary paralysis wasn't to blame. It was only a man's arm.

Her eyes flew open again.

A man.

With a loud shriek, she sat upright in bed and kicked with all her might at the immobile figure next to her, sending him into an ignominious heap on the floor. For the next few seconds the hammering in her temples and churning sickness in her stomach were secondary. She crouched on the bed, scrabbling to reach the lamp on the nearby table. Yanking its cord free, she held the lamp over her head threateningly.

Cage looked up from his position on the floor, and his eyes widened. As he raised a hand to ward off her action, his voice was low and soothing: "Now, honey, if you throw that, someone's gonna get hurt."

"You're damn right." Her tone was grim as she hefted the lamp for better aim. "And I know who."

If he hadn't been watching so closely, he might not have ducked in time. As it was, the lamp missed his head by only a fraction of an inch and crashed to the floor. Discretion, he'd always believed, should never be mistaken for cowardice. He scrambled awkwardly backward until he was out of throwing range, he hoped. Only then did he rise. His tone reproachful he said, "Now why'd you want to go and do that? There's no reason for both of us to have a headache."

The furious screech she released then seemed hardly human. He would have smiled if he didn't realize just how dangerous a woman in a temper could be. "For future reference, I should tell you that as a wake-up call, I prefer a kiss to a scream most mornings."

Pure evil beamed out of her incredible eyes—eyes that looked more than a little bloodshot this morning. She leaped from the bed and headed toward the dresser. He figured she was after the heavy crystal bowl she had sitting on top of it. It could, he estimated, do a fair amount of damage if hurled with the proper force and trajectory.

Before she got two steps, her gaze dropped to her bare legs and her eyes went wide in horror. Diving back into the bed with a motion that had to have set her head to pounding, she frantically reached for the covers and drew them up. Her hands fisted so tightly, the knuckles showed white. Voice aghast, she accused, "You...undressed me!"

In an effort at accuracy, he felt obliged to point out, "I only slipped off your shorts."

"And slept in my bed!"

"Actually, I was *on* your bed."

Her teeth ground so violently her jaw ached. "Thank you for that illuminating clarification."

Helpfully, he added, "You were in no condition to undress yourself last night, remember?"

She opened her mouth to make a scathing retort, and then paused. Surely it was only due to the harsh clamoring in her head, but she didn't remember. Didn't remember much of anything, as a matter of fact.

"You don't recall?" He shook his head, and pulled his shirttails out of his pants. It was past time for a shower. Sleeping in his clothes never failed to make him feel grungy. "I'm not surprised. You were wasted."

Her eyes went even wider. "I most certainly was not!" Memory, a blessed slice of it, returned. "All I had was tea. Fern Sykes served me tea."

He unfastened his watch and slipped it into his pocket. "Yeah, those tea hangovers are hell, aren't they? Honey, that 'tea' Fern concocts is almost pure alcohol."

She wished she could dispute it. She really did. But her pounding head and rolling stomach were testament to the truth of his words. "Well, how was I to know? She said it was herbs and, and..." She tried to recall just what Fern had said. "She said it was homemade."

He was too wise to smile at that. "I'm sure it is."

Shoving the hair back from her face, she glowered at him. "Well, you're the sheriff around here. Are you saying you let people operate stills in the parish?"

Wounded, he held up his hands. "Is that how you show your gratitude for my help? By attacking me?"

Her voice was strangled. "You expect me to thank you? Your nocturnal assistance was just the latest in the most egregious liberties you have taken with me since we met!"

The smile he didn't dare let settle on his lips crinkled his eyes. "I sure do love it when you talk all fancy and mean like that."

"Stop it!" She jabbed a finger in his direction. "Stop

affecting that demented Barney Fife routine. You're no-where near as harmless as you pretend.''

"But I am." He began unbuttoning his shirt. When it hung open, he headed toward her bedroom door. "I'm always a perfect gentlemen." At the doorway he paused and looked at her. "And last night, I was…perfect."

She stared at his retreating back. His retreating *bare* back, because he'd shrugged out of the shirt and was heading toward her bathroom. "What does that mean?" she yelled, then winced as her voice echoed and reechoed inside her aching head. She heard the bathroom door close, then the sound of the shower turning on.

And she was left to make sense of what little fragments of memory her mind was capable of supplying.

The twenty minutes Zoey spent under the shower's stinging spray had her feeling slightly more human. She dressed and made her way to the kitchen, one hand braced on the wall for support, hating the weakness that still pervaded her limbs. "Feeling any better?" The fact that Cage's tone was solicitous didn't lessen her urge to slug him.

"I've got a dozen demented dwarfs jackhammering in my head," she said testily. "'Better' is impossible. 'Horrible' would be an improvement." She swallowed hard as her stomach pitched violently, then settled into a riotous churning. She eased gingerly onto a kitchen chair.

"The cure for what ails you is coming right up." He shouldn't have looked so at home, moving capably about her kitchen, mixing ingredients he'd obviously searched through her cupboards for. And he most assuredly shouldn't look sexy, rumpled and domestic.

Rumpled. She narrowed her eyes. Although his shirt was hanging unfastened, it was decidedly wrinkled, as were his uniform pants that she wished, for the sake of propriety, he'd taken the time to button. His clothes looked as though they'd been slept in all night.

If she didn't feel so rotten, the belated realization would

have relieved her. Instead, she wondered grumpily why he couldn't just have said so in the first place, instead of leaving her with that suggestive remark. The answer, she suspected, was that he'd taken delight in tormenting her. And as soon as she felt well enough to walk across the room without weaving, she *would* slug him.

"What's that?"

He chuckled at the suspicion threading her voice. "It's an old family remedy. My father had an occasional need for something to settle his stomach on mornings after." He set the glass down in front of her. "In order for it to work, you have to drink it down as fast as you can. It isn't too tasty, but I can promise you'll feel better immediately."

Zoey eyed the sinister-looking liquid. It looked as vile as a witch's brew.

Noting her reaction, he said blandly, "Of course, you can always try the old-fashioned method."

She lifted her gaze to his. "What's that?"

"Waiting for the hangover to pass. Shouldn't take more than, oh—" he cocked his head, pretending to calculate "—twenty-four hours or so."

"Twenty-four hours!" The thought was horrifying. She'd die in that amount of time—slowly, painfully, degree by torturous degree. She looked at the liquid in the glass, then at Cage again. "I'll feel better immediately?"

"Two minutes, tops," he assured her.

Taking a deep breath, she reached for the glass and lifted it to her lips. Gulping it down as quickly as she could, she found that it didn't taste as it looked. It was worse. Far, far worse. Her stomach heaved with each swallow, until she drained the glass and slammed it on the table.

Peering at her closely, he could tell the remedy was doing its work. She was looking more than a little green around the edges.

"That is—without a doubt—the most disgusting, noxious stuff I've ever tasted." She aimed a baleful glare at him. "It isn't working."

He reached into his pocket and removed his watch, slipping it on his wrist again. "You don't feel any better?"

Her face drained of all color. "No, I feel awful. Truly, truly awful." Abruptly she lunged from her chair and raced out of the room.

Cage checked his watch. "Yep. Right on time." Whistling between his teeth, he opened her refrigerator and surveyed the contents. A woman after his own heart, she kept it well stocked. A few more vegetables and a bit less meat than he would suggest, but all in all, he couldn't quibble much with her selections. He took out milk, cheese, butter, eggs and bacon and set them on the counter.

He'd found her pans and had the bacon sizzling and the eggs in the microwave by the time she returned. He threw her a quick glance. She looked depleted, drained, and lethally dangerous.

Dragging herself to a chair, she collapsed into it. "I will kill you." What her voice lacked in strength it made up for in conviction. "So help me, as soon as I can get off this chair, you're a dead man. I'll stake you naked to a hornet's nest and let garden slugs feast on your rotting carcass."

She was obviously feeling better. "The *naked* part sounds promising. I think I'll pass on the rest."

Her eyes narrowed at his cheerful tone. "Kiss your ass goodbye, Gauthier. I'm a Scorpio. We invented the concept of revenge."

"Tell the truth." Expertly, he forked the bacon over. "How do you feel now?"

Horrible. Rotten. She opened her mouth to say the words, then paused as she realized they weren't true. Not quite. And not anymore. Her stomach had settled to a general all-over queasiness and the Black & Decker chorus in her head had softened to a power-drill duet. "I still have a headache," she said sulkily. She fixed him with a malevolent glare. "But don't think you're off the hook. You neglected to mention that in the course of your two-minute cure I would become violently ill."

He opened the door of the microwave and stirred the eggs. "Details. You were better in two minutes, as promised. And we're just about ready for stage two of Dr. Gauthier's Tea-Drinker's Remedy."

"I'm afraid to ask."

Moving competently around her kitchen, he drained the bacon, then began shredding cheese for the eggs. "The next stage is…grease."

"Grease?" She waited for her stomach to roll viciously in response. Instead, it made only a halfhearted rumble that might have been interest. Surely not. Most likely this was yet another step in his torture routine.

"It will coat that acid in your stomach. Then you follow it with eggs, toast dripping in butter, and milk. You still won't feel one hundred percent until tomorrow, but you'll feel human. Believe me."

"You've lost a few points on the credibility scale this morning, Sheriff. And you still haven't explained why you were in my bed this morning."

"*On* your bed."

"Whatever," she said through gritted teeth. He slid a plate in front of her and poured her a glass of milk. "Start talking."

Folding his arms, he leaned against the kitchen counter and surveyed her. "First, you start eating."

Their gazes clashed—hers mutinous, his patient. After several seconds her stomach unsubtly reminded her that she hadn't had anything to eat since the soup he'd finished off for her yesterday afternoon. She picked up her fork, stabbed at the eggs.

He watched, satisfied, as she began to eat—at first testingly, then with real appetite. He turned and filled his own plate and sat down opposite her. "Don't forget the grease."

She picked up a strip of bacon and bit off a piece with barely restrained violence. He knew better than to push his luck. "Fern called me about suppertime last night."

Her hand froze in the act of reaching for a slice of toast. "Called you? Why would she?"

He couldn't resist needling her. "Seems she had Charity's newest resident passed out at her dinner table. I suppose she was fixing to eat and you were in the way." She was making short work of her breakfast, he noted approvingly. It always pleased him to see a woman with an appetite. His mother and sister never used to do more than poke at their food, and complain about the way the pounds went on. He'd bet Zoey didn't have that problem. She usually radiated energy; it fairly crackled from her. It would take ample replenishments of fuel to keep her going at the speed she kept.

"I still don't understand why she would think to call you."

"Maybe she was thinking it was my duty as sheriff to take care of a drunk-and-disorderly call."

Her eyes flashed. "I was not…"

He reached for his glass, his brows skimming upward. "Not…" he prompted, when she didn't go on.

Steamed, she dropped her gaze and shoveled more eggs into her mouth.

"I think we've established the 'drunk' part," he said cheerfully. "As for 'disorderly'—" he tipped his head back and scratched his unshaven jaw "—I reckon that would be pushing things a bit. Actually, you were kind of cute, singing off-key, throwing your arms around my neck when I carried you to the car."

She raised her eyes skyward. God had saved her from death by hangover only to subject her to this? How many times was He going to repay her for putting Mr. Bubble in the church fountain? She'd been eight, for heaven's sake.

"You still haven't explained why you felt it was necessary to spend the night here." She wasn't one to ask for, or accept help readily. However, under the circumstances, she decided there was a period of time last night on which she really didn't feel the need to be updated.

He wasn't in the mood to let her off the hook. "Despite your rather enthusiastic welcome when you saw me…"

She was sure, very sure, that she didn't want to know what he meant by that.

"You were fading fast by the time I got you home." What she'd been was unconscious by the time he'd laid her on the bed, but he was too gentlemanly to remark on it. "You mentioned someone by the name of Patrick several times." His tone, when he imparted the words, was nonchalant. It revealed none of the vicious emotion the name had elicited. Any other man might have identified the emotion as jealousy, but Cage had never been jealous of a woman in his life.

As if the words he'd uttered didn't matter, not wanting them to, he went on. "I know from personal experience that Fern's 'tea' packs a hell of a wallop. When Tanner and I were fourteen we snuck a pitcher of the stuff and drank it at his daddy's hunting cabin. We were sicker than dogs for three days, and had to pretend nothing was wrong, in order to keep our folks from suspecting what we'd done."

He paused, eyeing the toast on her plate. "Are you going to eat that?"

She picked up the piece and bit into it, almost smiling at his look of disappointment. Swallowing, she prompted, "And you stayed because…"

Belly pleasantly full, he leaned back in his chair and stretched his arms. "Well, like I said, I knew from personal experience that you were going to be pretty sick. It was only a matter of time. I figured I'd just stay around to help in any way I could." Because she still didn't look convinced, he added, "You could have had alcohol poisoning. Someone needed to keep an eye on you."

His story sounded almost plausible, so she let it drop for the time being. Fragments of her afternoon with Fern were filtering back. "Fern thinks she knows who killed Janice Reilly."

"Does she?" He picked up his plate and stacked it on

hers with a clatter, reminding her that her headache hadn't completely abated. She watched with more interest than she wanted to admit, to see what he'd do next. A man who could cook a decent breakfast was a rarity. One who would do the dishes afterward was a saint.

She smirked when he piled all the dirty dishes in the sink. It appeared she wouldn't have to worry about having him canonized. She doubted he'd meet those pesky Vatican criteria, anyway. "Aren't you interested in Fern's theory?"

He sauntered back with a wet dishcloth to scrub the table. "Nope."

Astonished, she stared at him. "Why not?"

"Because Fern Sykes is a harmless old woman who rarely bothers a soul. And she believes that Elvis is alive and well and raising mutant kangaroos in Australia. There's not a conspiracy theory that she doesn't subscribe to, not a wacky notion that she doesn't embrace." He walked back to the sink and hung up the wet cloth. "She's called my office six times this year alone to report UFO sightings. In her case, even an eyewitness account of the murder would be suspect."

"She claims that one of the Rutherford family did it." She had to think for a moment to recall the name. "Donny Ray, I think she called him. She seemed to think that he has more in common with his Great-uncle Carl than anyone is willing to believe."

He stiffened very slightly. Then he turned to her, his face expressionless. "Donny Ray Rutherford is a scumbag of the lowest order. There's no denying that. But he'd have no reason to murder Janice Reilly."

Zoey studied him closely. Her words had struck a nerve of some kind, she could tell. "You seem sure."

"As sure as I can be." He heaved a sigh. "Sounds like Fern filled you in on some old history of Charity. Did she also tell you that she holds the Rutherford clan responsible for her husband's death?"

Somewhere that rang familiar in her memory. "I think so."

"Claims one of them gave her husband the evil eye, or some sort of superstitious nonsense." He shook his head. "Fact is, the poor devil was probably eaten with cancer. Neither he nor Fern trusted doctors, the way I hear it. She's hardly a reliable source."

"You're not even going to check it out?"

He walked toward her, propped his palms on the table in front of her and leaned forward. "Zoey." His voice was gentle. "You stick to writing the mysteries, and let me concentrate on solving this one, okay?"

She lifted her chin to a regal angle. "Fine. Who's stopping you?"

"You are." He watched awareness flash into her eyes, followed by wariness. Good. She'd be wise to feel both. "I've got to tell you my concentration hasn't been the same since you came to Charity."

There was a smart retort on the tip of her tongue. Her gaze met his and the words slid back down her throat. Gray eyes should be cold, impersonal. They shouldn't be capable of such warmth, such promise.

"'Course," he mused, his gaze tracing her brows, her lips, "it didn't help my concentration any to lie next to you all night. Listening to the soft sound of your breathing. Watching your face while you slept."

She stared at him, transfixed, as if hypnotized by that low voice.

"All that in-your-face toughness of yours disappears when you're sleeping, did you know that?" His voice was husky; the finger he trailed down her cheek was featherlight. "I'm not the kind of man to spend a lot of time thinking about any one woman, but damned if I can figure a way to get you out of my mind.

"If you want a mystery to solve, Zoey, maybe you can start with that one."

Chapter 5

"Chief Runnels to see you, Sheriff." Patsy, the dispatcher going off duty, gave Cage a sympathetic look before opening the door wide enough to allow Charity's chief of police to enter.

He closed the file he'd been studying. "Boyd." It was more difficult than usual to work up an agreeable tone. It would have been easier, he imagined, after a decent night's sleep. But he hadn't gotten one of those since a pair of serious green eyes had started haunting his every moment.

Twirling his chair around to greet the visitor, Cage crossed one foot over his knee. "Sure is a pretty day today, isn't it?"

"Heat index is over one hundred and fifty already," the chief corrected him. Cage mused that one would never know it to look at Boyd Runnels. The man never seemed to sweat. Nothing so human would be allowed to mar the uniform he wore with rigid pride. A couple of decades older than Cage, he'd come home from Vietnam a decorated war hero, and had exchanged his army uniform for his current one. Two years ago he'd tried to trade in his badge for that of sheriff.

Cage always wondered which fact ate at Runnels more—that he'd lost the election or that he'd lost it to him. He'd never made any secret of what he thought of the hometown boy who had quit the NOPD with a folderful of commendations and a citation for bravery in the line of duty. A record like that might impress some, but not Runnels—not when, to his mind, he had a record to match it.

Cage didn't hold Boyd's feelings against the man. Only those closest to Cage knew how he felt about that shiny medal they'd hung around his neck over two years ago. He'd spent a fair amount of time trying to forget just how he'd earned it.

He focused on the man before him. There wasn't a spare inch of flesh on Runnels's tall, lean frame. His uniform was crisply fresh, his boots polished to a glossy sheen. He wore his gray hair cut short and combed severely back from his narrow face. Whenever Cage spent any time at all with the man, he invariably envisioned him at home with the missus and his troop of kids, all wearing starched uniforms and saluting each other before meals.

Boyd roamed the office, ignoring Cage's offer of a seat, studying the pictures hanging on his bulletin board and the mass of files opened across the desk. "You got yourself a real mess here, don't you, Sheriff?"

Deliberately misunderstanding, Cage said, "Don't you worry about it, Boyd. The janitor will clear away these coffee cups and such after hours."

Runnels shot him a humorless look. "I mean in the parish. First a drug lab, then a murder, and now random shootings." He failed to conceal the satisfaction in his voice. "Yep, I'd say the parish is in a fine mess with this shocking increase in criminal activity."

Cage reached for the slim cigar in his pocket and ran his fingers over it consideringly. "Well, I guess that all depends on your perspective. Some folks might consider the fact that a meth operation was busted up as evidence that our office is tough on crime. Helps that we have charges pending against one of the operators. And there was nothing random about those shootings. The suspects were just released on bail this morning.''

"That still leaves one unsolved murder."

Though his thoughts had darkened, his tone remained even. "Give me time, Boyd. Give me time."

"Well, son, I hope you have time. I surely do." Runnels kept his spine too straight to actually do a good job of leaning, so when he propped one shoulder against the wall he looked like a department-store mannequin, tipped off-kilter. "I'd hate to see you get in over your head on this thing."

Cage contemplated the cigar and gave some hard thought to lighting it. "This isn't the first homicide investigation I've run, Boyd." He let the words hang in the air between them, noting the way the other man stiffened at the reference to his experience.

"You've got a suspect, then?"

His voice noncommittal, Cage replied, "We're following up on some leads."

"My office is at your disposal. Anything you need help with, just let me know."

The offer was perfunctory, and both men realized it. " appreciate it. Maybe I'll take you up on that."

Civilities over, Runnels added, "Of course, with only two officers, I don't have the manpower to offer you much assistance in the actual investigation."

"I think my men can handle the job. Thanks for the offer." Cage stood, in an effort to hasten the man on his way. Runnels peered over his shoulder at the open file on his desk.

"Pretty grisly stuff." His gaze met Cage's. "I expect the man who found the killer would be something of a hero in these parts."

With great care, Cage replaced the cigar in his pocket and wished unwelcome memories could be tucked away as easily. *Hero.* It was a term society used too freely, applied too generously. It seemed ironic to herald as a hero a man who did nothing more than react to a crime. And when that reaction came a split second too late, the word could ring with its own resounding mockery.

"It's been my experience, Boyd, that when these things are over, the only heroes are the survivors."

Two hours later Cage's car was crawling down the road to his house. Despite the long days and sleepless nights he'd had recently, the peace of his home failed to beckon. Usually he looked forward to his evening routine of warming up the meal Ila—the housekeeper for as long as he could remember—had prepared and relaxing after dinner for a much-deserved nap in the hammock. He'd always done his best thinking sprawled out in that hammock strung between two giant cypress trees. A little relaxation with an icy beer in his hand and a hat tipped over his eyes did wonders for a man's ability to reflect. That the image failed to tempt him now was serious indeed.

He laid the blame for that firmly on Zoey's creamy white shoulders. Never before had he allowed the pesky thought of a woman to worm its way into his mind and make it churn in a way that was downright exhausting. Sexual attraction was pleasant and uncomplicated. It didn't cause the brain to fog and the senses to slow. At least, he thought with a hint of a scowl, it never had before.

On impulse, he eased the car off the road and up a badly rutted lane lined with overgrown grass and brush. The house that sat in the clearing had probably known paint once. There was still evidence of the original white coat clinging to cracks and hollows in its siding. But Cage didn't remember a time when the McIntire house had looked other than it did right now—like a structure doing a gradual slide into complete deterioration.

The porch still listed badly to one side. But the corner post that had been missing for decades had been replaced recently, and judging by the neat pile of lumber on the ground, it looked as though the steps were the next to be repaired. Cage took the improvements as a positive sign. Billy must be going through a good spell.

As he was getting out of the car, the front door opened. Billy McIntire stared silently at him for several moments. Cage crossed his arms on top of the open car door and greeted him.

"Hey, Billy." He nodded at the porch. "Looks like you've been keeping busy lately. Hot work in this weather."

"Sheriff." The big man lumbered down the sagging steps and stopped just shy of the car. Billy had to be close to Boyd Runnels's age. They'd gone off to fight in the same southeast Asian jungles within five years of each other, but it was the way they'd come home that had differed. There had been no medals pinned to Billy's chest, no tales of glory surrounding his return; just a quiet discharge for a young man deemed unfit for duty, a man whose mind had been unable to adjust to the killing and carnage he'd been immersed in.

Cage couldn't be sure what kind of changes Billy's experience had wrought in the man. But he knew for certain that no one could look upon what one human being did to another and remain unaltered. When the flashbacks that still lingered became too intolerable, Billy took to the woods, retreating farther from civilization until the ghosts that haunted were under control. Cage didn't fault him for his methods. He knew for a fact that if a man didn't find a way to conquer his personal demons, they would swallow him whole.

"Place is going to look some different when you're done," Cage remarked. He let his gaze shift to the house once again. "You're a good hand with a hammer and nail. Always have been."

Billy reached up a crooked finger to push back the straw hat he wore over his fading red hair. "It ain't so much." He hitched up the strap of his denim overalls with a shrug and scratched at a heavily muscled bare shoulder. He wasn't comfortable with company and small talk, but he could tolerate Cage Gauthier more than he could most folks. Cage was at ease with words and manners in a way that Billy could barely remember ever being; but he didn't use them to judge and condemn a man whose ways weren't his own. There was a look in his eyes sometimes that made Billy wonder if Cage didn't have his own ghosts that brought him screaming out of sleep.

"Well, I can see you have your hands full out here." Cage leaned against the car door and admired the job that had been done on the porch. "I was just on my way home and started thinking about the work you did for me last summer. The yard sure did look fine when you got done with it. Don't think it's looked better since my daddy died. I can't seem to find the energy or will to mow these days. Ila's been chewing my ear off about it. I suppose you're too busy to consider taking the yard work over for me again this summer."

Billy swatted at an insect that had settled on his forearm and mulled over the offer. "That riding mower of yours still working?" His voice was rusty, as if from disuse.

"Should be. Had it up to Carson's garage for a tune-up and I don't know what all else. Got those pruning shears sharpened, too. I'd sure appreciate you taking the yard off my hands for me again this year, if you're feeling up to it."

It was a roundabout way of asking Billy if he had a good grip on the ghosts that still rose to haunt at times—the ones wearing dying Asian faces. But Cage would never say so in words, and Billy appreciated the courtesy.

"I reckon I can take that yard work off your hands."

"I'd be obliged. Be willing to pay you a dollar more an hour than last year, if that sounds fair to you."

"Sounds okay to me." Billy's hunting dog came around the corner of the house then, ambling toward the men with a long-suffering maternal air. Around the dog's feet three puppies gamboled, tripping and tumbling over each other in youthful frolic.

Cage's face creased in a delighted grin. "Well, looks like you've got pups on your hands again, Billy. Nice-looking litter, too."

"I'm thinking to keep a couple this time. Ol' Lucy is getting up in years. She's been slowing down some."

One of the pups made a beeline for Cage, its tail wagging so hard it set its whole hind end swaying. He bent to scratch behind one long floppy ear, and soulful puppy-dog eyes turned up to meet his. A part of his heart that remembered the twelve-year-old boy he'd been turned to mush.

"Well, shoot. He's a cute little thing, isn't he? Reminds me of the dog I had when I was a kid."

"He's yours, if you want him." Billy removed his hat and wiped the sweat from his forehead. "The pups are weaned already. You can take him with you."

Cage eyed the dog, which was busily chewing at his bootlace. It was stupid to even consider it. He was gone most of the day, and having a rambunctious pup around the house would just be another headache for Ila. The animal picked that moment to flip on its back, growling in imaginary combat as it wrestled with the lace, and succeeding in tangling two of its paws in it. The puppy gave a startled yelp, and emotion abruptly triumphed over logic.

Cage bent to scoop up the animal. "I'm much obliged, Billy. I guess I'll take this little guy home with me after all."

Driving with the mutt in the car proved to be a distraction. The dog paced the width of the front seat and decided that Cage's lap was the best place to ride. No amount of coaxing or demanding could convince him otherwise.

"Don't get used to it, pooch. You won't be calling the shots when I get you home." The pup yawned, clearly unimpressed by the warning. After another few miles it was fast asleep.

"Yeah, you're going to be in for a real eye-opener,"

Cage continued, stroking the dog with a gentle hand while he drove. "You're not going to find me one of those permissive masters. As for Ila... If you're brighter than you look, you'll steer clear of her. She's not the type to be taken in by big brown eyes and long droopy ears."

When he got close to Zoey's house, the car slowed without his conscious permission. He told himself that it was just difficult to keep a steady pressure on the accelerator with the mutt using him as a cushion. Lord knew, the smartest thing to do would be to keep his distance from her until he got these unfamiliar emotions leashed again. The car pulled off the road and into her driveway.

He'd always had the damnedest time doing the smartest thing.

The car idled in the drive as he tried to talk himself into reversing and heading home where he was less likely to get himself into trouble.

The decision was made for him when Zoey strolled around the corner of the house, her fingertips tucked in the front pockets of her white shorts and wearing a skimpy blue top the color of Caribbean waters. Before she looked up and saw his car he had a moment to observe her, to note the solitary air she always seemed surrounded by. She looked like a woman used to being alone. If he made the mistake of asking, he was sure she'd say she liked it that way. But he wasn't sure he'd believe her.

Turning off the ignition, he hoisted up the pup in one arm and opened the car door, calling out, "Why, if it isn't Z. L. Prescott. All through plotting murder and mayhem for the day, ma'am?"

"I was. Until now." Instincts more basic than logical urged her to retreat. She held her ground. Ever since he'd left after cooking her breakfast yesterday morning, his parting words had been ringing in her head. She refused to reveal the confusion they'd caused. No doubt he was a man well practiced in the art of polished phrases contrived to keep a woman off-balance. Pride demanded that he never know how well he'd succeeded.

She sent him a cool look, which lost most of its starch when he got out of the car and she caught sight of the puppy.

"Oh, how sweet."

He looked modest. "Well, gee, thanks, Zoey. But I thought we'd already agreed that I was dazzling."

She crossed the yard toward him with that long stride of hers. "Not you, idiot. The puppy."

The dog wriggled in Cage's arms, so he set him down and watched him bound over to charm Zoey. She bent down to pet the pup's thick brown fur and then let out a soft laugh when he propped his front paws on her knees and attempted to lick her face.

The sound of that husky laugh sent a burning arrow of lust straight to Cage's loins. The sensation was almost a relief. Desire was familiar—a natural, pleasurable part of being a man. For the first time since he'd kissed her, he felt a return to steadier ground. He was comfortable with wanting, without the tangle of stickier emotions.

She beamed a smile, one that lit her face and danced in her eyes. "He's adorable. Is he yours?"

His earlier sense of satisfaction splintered abruptly. The effect of her genuine smile kicked him in the chest and left his lungs straining for oxygen. It was a moment before he could gather his thoughts, another before he managed an answer. "As of about ten minutes ago."

"What's his name?"

Cage hauled in a huge gulp of air and jammed his hands into his pockets. "I haven't thought of one yet." The dog spotted a butterfly near the porch and dashed off. The adults followed at a more sedate pace.

"Where'd you get him?"

It occurred to Cage that Zoey had spoken more freely in the last few minutes than she ever had in the time he'd known her. There was nothing like baby animals to lower defenses. He wasn't above using that knowledge to his advantage.

"I stopped in to talk to a fellow I know down the road." He climbed the steps, dropped to the top one and cast a lazy eye on the frolicking pup. "He wanted to get rid of one, and this mutt seemed to take a liking to me." He shrugged uncomfortably under her amused look. "I've been thinking of getting a watchdog, anyway."

"A 'watchdog'?" She watched the puppy shake himself violently, one long ear landing inside out across his eyes. "The term seems something of an oxymoron in his case."

"Well, there you go. That name would fit as well as any." At her blank look he explained, "'Oxymoron.' Look at the size of his feet. When he's full-size, 'Ox' will be a fitting name for him." The dog picked that instant to start chasing his tail. "And at times like now, 'Moron' seems rather apt."

Zoey scooped up the puppy and cuddled him close, sending Cage a chastising look. "You can't call him by a disparaging name. You'll damage his self-esteem."

Damned if the mutt wasn't looking at him with reproach in his big, doggy eyes. "Well, I'm open to suggestions."

She cocked her head thoughtfully for a moment, before saying, "I'll have to think about it. Right now he looks thirsty. I'm going to get him some water." Setting the puppy down beside Cage, she turned toward the house.

"I'm thirsty, too," he called after her. "A beer sure would taste mighty fine after a long day of keeping the parish safe from dangerous criminals." The screen door banged behind her. There was no indication she'd heard his words. He reached down and ruffled the dog's fur. "I suppose you think you're some kind of babe magnet. Don't let it go to your head. One accident on the rug and you'd be pooch history."

The pup cocked his head, then decided that Cage was really asking for a thorough licking. When Zoey came out again, he was pushing the mutt away before it could drown him. She put a bowl of water on the porch and coaxed the dog over to it.

"Here, Oxy. There's a good boy."

Cage raised an eyebrow. "I thought you wanted to think of a different name." With only mild surprise he took the beer she handed him.

She lifted a shoulder and sat down next to the dog. "I don't have a lot of experience thinking up names for animals."

They both watched as the pooch quenched his thirst, then circled three times before deciding that Zoey's lap was as good a place for a nap as any. Cage couldn't fault the dog's instincts. And he was beginning to credit his own. Something more fundamental than reason must have led him here. Certainly it was demanding that he stay.

Zoey was normally so closemouthed that he couldn't pass up the opportunity to learn more about her. "What do you mean, you didn't have any experience? Didn't you have pets as a child?"

She shook her head. "We always lived in apartments."

"Not even goldfish?"

Her fingers speared through her hair, pushing it carelessly back from that fine forehead. His gaze followed the gesture, and lingered. "No dogs, no fish. By the shock in your voice, I imagine you had a menagerie."

Turning to face her more fully, he settled as comfortably against the railing as his healing back would allow. "I had an assortment of animals over the years. The house was off-limits, though. My mother wasn't the type to overlook pet hair and puddles on the floor." He tipped his beer up, drank with enjoyment. Despite his initial reservations, he couldn't imagine a better way to end the day than sitting on Zoey's porch and gorging himself on the sight of her.

"Only had one dog," he continued. "His name was Tooner. We were inseparable." The memory made him smile. "Nice thing about a dog is it's always willing to accompany a boy on adventures, and it doesn't tell tales afterward.''

Zoey tried, and failed, to suppress a smile. "I'm guessing you had lots of adventures that you didn't want tales told about."

"I can't deny it."

Unbidden, a visual image unfolded in her head, of endless summer days and a young Cage Gauthier, with a large loping dog at his side, wheeling along Charity's country roads. He'd have been blonder then, the merciless sun having bleached his hair to nearly white. The boy's face would have been a younger version of the man's, but she guessed the charm and glints of wicked fire would have been present even then. Try as she might, she couldn't shake the mental picture from her mind. It suited her to blame that on her writer's imagination.

"Whatever happened to your dog? Did he die of old age or did you run him ragged keeping up with your mischief?"

"Tooner? He went off one day and never came back." Cage's voice was silent for a moment, as if the memory still pained him. "I always figured that he chased something into the woods and tangled with a creature far fiercer than he was." He reached to stroke a hand over the pup's warm fur. "My daddy offered to get me another dog. Even brought one home once. But I never felt right getting one to replace Tooner. We'd had him ever since we moved to Louisiana, when I was four. He seemed to go with the house, somehow."

He'd managed to surprise her. "You haven't always lived in Charity?"

Stretching his legs out, he took another swallow of beer. "I guess there have been Gauthiers here since the time the parish was settled, or thereabouts. My great-great-granddaddy built the house I still live in. Tradition always played a big part in my family, but my daddy had a mind to see what he could accomplish on his own. Shortly after he married my mama, they moved to Florida and he started his first business there. That's where I was adopted.''

Her gaze flew to his, but his eyes were as steady as his tone. "How old were you then?''

"Two. My birth mother was charged with neglect. She gave up her rights.'' That much his adoptive parents had told him. Because it had seemed to bother them when he asked, he'd tried not to question them overmuch about it. His life, his memories, began after he'd become a Gauthier. That had been enough for his parents, and had been enough for him for a long time. Since his adoption had taken place in Florida, he doubted there were many in the parish who even knew the truth of his birth. It wasn't until he'd become an adult that his own questions had become more persistent.

As if she were able to read his thoughts, Zoey asked, "Do you wonder about your birth family?''

He finished the beer and set the bottle on the porch beside him. Somehow, without even trying, he'd snagged her interest. Her curiosity was strong enough to pierce the guard she usually wore. And it had landed unerringly on a subject he was still wrestling with.

He drew the cigar from his pocket and took his time lighting it. "Do you mind?'' he asked belatedly. She shook her head with barely restrained impatience. He drew in deeply and then exhaled with pure enjoyment.

"Do you?'' she prodded. "Wonder about it?''

"There sure are a barrel of puzzles in this world.'' He squinted into the distance, observing the thin stream of smoke rising over the top of a cluster of trees. Cleve Hawkins must be burning his ditches again, despite Cage's warnings about the dry spell they were having. Almost absently, he went on. "I wonder about a lot of them.''

"Like?''

He blew a smoke ring and contemplated it as it hung in the air. "Like why the Howells took all those clothes for what was only a three-hour cruise. It was almost like they were figuring on getting shipwrecked. And how come Darrin never let Samantha use her witchcraft?'' That one was a real enigma, and he cocked his head in bafflement. ''You'd think he'd have at least let her use it to help with the housework.''

She released a breath she hadn't been aware of holding and barely restrained the urge to punch him. ''Yeah, those old sitcoms are mysteries, all right. Aren't you ever serious?''

His lips twitched at her reaction. ''Something tells me that you're serious enough for both of us.''

He was right, of course, though she wouldn't give him the satisfaction of telling him so. Life, she'd found, was a serious business. ''I'm sorry for prying.'' It pained her to make the apology, and her words were stiff. ''I don't especially enjoy having people poke around in my life, either.''

Somehow, without trying, he'd offended her. The topic may have been one he'd been avoiding dealing with, but he didn't resent her interest. ''Zoey.'' He waited for her gaze to meet his. ''I was teasing. Just joking around, all right?'' When she didn't respond, he let out a breath. ''Boy, you're tough. Okay, yes, I have thought about my birth mother. It didn't take much to figure that she probably wasn't a real loss. But the fact that there might be other family—I did wonder about it. Enough to write to the state of Florida and have my adoption records opened.''

He succeeded in throwing her one curve after another, one minute clowning and the next serious. She wished she could manage indifference. But glimpses of the man beneath the charm and affability were too fascinating to ignore. She refused to consider what that meant.

Her fingers stroked the dog's soft fur unconsciously. ''What did you find out?''

Narrowing his gaze against the haze of smoke trailing from his cigar, he took his time answering. ''I don't know.''

Sharply, she looked at him. He raised the slim cigar to his lips and inhaled. ''I waited until after my parents—my adoptive parents—had died before looking into it. Seemed only right, somehow. When I told my sister—did I mention I have a sister?'' He waited for the shake of her head to go on. ''Nadine is three years younger than me. She was adopted as an infant shortly before my folks decided to move back to Louisiana. Married a lawyer a few years back and they're living in Atlanta. Anyway, when I told her what I'd done, she really lit into me. Accused me of being unfaithful to our mama and daddy's memory.''

His words glossed over the unpleasantness of the scene. Like a true Southern-bred lady, Nadine was adept at maintaining a perfectly civil tone as she cut a man off at the knees. He was no stranger to guilt, and the accusation she'd aimed had hit its mark. His sister had never questioned her roots, had been comfortable with the Gauthier legacy her adoption had entailed. He hadn't considered that his questions about his birth could be construed as betrayal. Beau Gauthier had been a strict disciplinarian, but intelligent and fair-minded. His wife, Althea, had been genteel, good-humored and loving. Neither of them had ever once made him feel that he was less than their natural son. He wondered if the questions still circling inside him could manage to do so.

Zoey sensed a thread of melancholy tracing through his words, and felt an unwilling tug of empathy. ''There never seems to be any shortage of people in our lives who think they know what's best for us.''

He glanced at her, wondering at her rueful tone. ''Spoken like someone with firsthand experience.''

''Yes.'' She surprised him, and herself by explaining. ''When my mother died, I went to court to fight for custody of my brother and sister. My aunt and uncle were convinced they would be better guardians. It was…tense for a while.'' The process had, for better or worse, molded Zoey into who she was today. Self-assured, slightly arrogant and supremely competent. As she'd been described by her aunt and uncle on occasion, not always flatteringly. She'd accepted those descriptions of herself, embraced them. Even at times when her knees had knocked with self-doubt—*especially* at such times—she'd cultivated a veneer of confidence. Her relatives would have pounced at the first sign of weakness from her. She had already lost too much to risk letting that happen.

While he pondered her words, Cage offered a bent knuckle to Oxy, who chewed it obligingly. She couldn't have been very old when she'd assumed responsibility for her siblings. There was no denying the sheer guts it had taken for her to do so. He wanted to probe further, but he'd felt a part of her shift away almost as soon as she'd finished speaking, as if she regretted sharing the little she had.

The dog lost interest in them, and started down the steps to investigate the bushes. Mildly Cage said, "Family loyalty is an admirable thing. Trouble is, seems like everyone's got a different opinion on just what it entails. You did what you thought was right for your family. I still have to figure out what's right for mine. I've never blamed Nadine for her opinion, you understand. She has her views, and I have my own. Doesn't make either of us wrong."

It wasn't the first time he'd espoused such a sentiment. Zoey wondered if he could possibly be as tolerant as he let on. Many people, she'd learned, saw the world in black-and-white. And while that might be a comfortable view, it seemed to be the shades of gray in between that she was most familiar with.

"At any rate—" he took a last puff of the cigar with real regret, before dropping it to the step and grinding it out "—she made me stop and think. When I got a packet of information from Florida's Department of Human Services a few months ago, I stuck it away in my desk at home. It's been there ever since. Unopened."

Her jaw dropped. "How can you stand that?" His utter placidity about the matter was incomprehensible. "Doesn't it drive you crazy to think that you might have the very information you've been wondering about, and not even look at it?''

He could have told her that he was no stranger to regrets. He knew how guilt could weigh on a man. But it was imperative to him that he not unseal something else that could prove difficult to live with. A man wasn't always given a choice about those matters. ''Something Nadine said made sense to me. Warned me not to ask the questions until I was sure I could live with the answers.'' His face, his voice were sober. ''That seemed like good advice. So I'll wait until I'm sure.''

She shook her head, genuinely baffled. ''I'll bet you were the kind of kid who didn't sneak peeks at your Christmas presents, either. Never once went on a search to see if you could find them before they were wrapped, did you?''

The words were almost an accusation. He felt his seriousness slip away. ''What fun would Christmas morning be if there were no surprises?''

''What good are surprises if you have to wait forever to find out what they are?''

His lips curved. He could almost see her as the impatient kid she must have been. When he bought her a present, he'd have to hide it well. He could already imagine the fun he'd have before holidays, torturing her by dropping hints and driving her slowly insane.

It occurred to him then that the scene he was imagining entailed some sort of long-term relationship with Zoey— something he'd carefully managed to avoid with other women. The impulse should have been cause for panic. Instead, it beckoned with a sweet warmth that layered over the need he was accustomed to feeling. The emotion was unfamiliar, but too tantalizing to be feared.

The puppy bounded up the steps then, and made itself at home on Zoey's lap. Seeing the picture they made, Cage suddenly became thoughtful. Her isolated air seemed muted somehow as she held the animal, and an idea formed, began to gel.

Scooting over to pet the dog, he braced his hand on the porch behind Zoey, close to the curve of her hip and that sweet, shapely behind.

She looked at him sharply, suspicion evident on her features. "Isn't that a little pathetic, Gauthier? Using a poor dumb animal to facilitate a seduction scene?"

Her choice of words never failed to tickle him. "Is that what I'm doing?"

At the genuine amusement in his words, her tone grew less certain. "Isn't it?"

"You're skittish, Zoey." With a gentle push he urged the dog off her lap, and pretended not to notice the woman beside him inching away, as well. "Makes me think that there was a man sometime who disappointed you."

Because his guess was too close to the truth, she ignored it. "Just because I happen to have better sense than to be taken in by some small-town Romeo..."

"Was it this Patrick you mentioned?" The name released a burning fist in his gut, but he thought he did a decent job of keeping the emotion from his voice.

"'Patrick'?" Her tone was puzzled. "What's my brother got to do with anything?"

"Your...brother?" Relief flooded, and the world looked a little brighter. "Not Patrick, then. But someone hurt you." He paused expectantly, giving her an opportunity to respond. When she remained silent, he said in an amiable tone, "I reckon you'll tell me about it in your own time. Right now, I've got a proposition for you."

She stiffened at his choice of words and wished, in an instant of cowardice, that the porch post didn't prevent her from putting more distance between the two of them. Pride kept her from rising. Months ago, she'd ceased giving a man—any man—control over her emotions.

He felt her body go rigid and his voice went low and soothing. "Actually, it's more a favor. An exchange of favors, I guess you'd call it."

"What?"

He wanted to grin at the caution underlying that sing
word, but was far too savvy a strategist to do so. "We
the thing is, I really don't have time to spend with the pu
right now. The carpenters aren't done with the repair wor
yet, and my housekeeper, Ila, isn't one to have the patienc
to train a dog. I was wondering if you'd agree to keep hi
for me." When she didn't answer, he added hastily, "Ju
until this murder investigation is over. I'll have more tin
then."

She looked at the puppy, which was trying to avoid tun
bling down the steps. "Seems to me, you should hav
thought of that before you got him."

"I couldn't be sure he'd still be available, could I?" N
waiting for an answer, he went on, "If you can't be bot
ered, I'll understand. Seems a shame to have to tie the litt
guy up most days, but I can if I have to."

She cast another look at the dog. "That doesn't see
quite fair."

As if he sensed she was weakening, he added quickl
"In return, I can arrange to have your lawn taken care c
That'd be one less thing for you to worry about. Yo
haven't lined anyone up, have you?"

As she shook her head, he observed the Potter car slowir
as it drove by her house. Thursdays were always Francine
day at the wheel, although she was doing more gawkir
than driving at the moment. By noon tomorrow it would I
all over Charity that Cage Gauthier and Zoey Prescott ha
been seen sitting close on her front porch. He shot a quic
glance at Zoey. She hadn't seemed to notice. He alread
knew her well enough to predict how she'd react to becom
ing Charity's latest item of gossip.

She eyed the dog doubtfully. "I really don't know mud
about animals."

"It'll be a new experience for you, then."

Though his tone was bland, his words had her turning
look at him sharply. Zoey was suspicious enough by natu
to wonder if his offer was a thinly veiled excuse to continu

to come by here. But she was far too uncertain of her femininity to completely believe it.

Her gaze returned to the dog, which seemed to be watching her hopefully. She pursed her lips, considering his offer. There had been little about Cage's behavior today to set her inner alarms clamoring. The visit had seemed almost neighborly in its innocence.

Her teeth closed over her bottom lip as she pondered. "Well," she said finally, "I guess I really do need my lawn mowed."

He was unprepared for the jagged edge of desire that tore through him as he watched her teeth worry her lip. Her words were slow to register. He wanted, badly, to kiss her. It took far more effort than it should have to resist.

"You know, around here we seal agreements in one of two ways." He waited for her to look at him before going on. "When I was a kid, the two of us would have to draw a line in the dirt and spit on it." Her nose wrinkled. "Over the years, however, I've found the most satisfactory way to seal a bargain—" his voice dropped infinitesimally "—is with a kiss."

Zoey leaned against the post at her side, pressing another inch of space between them, and managed a steady voice. "And if I find both prospects equally revolting?"

Damn. Amusement traced through him. He doubted there was another woman alive who could still make him want her even while she was insulting him. "Then I guess we'll have to settle our bargain in a more traditional way." He stuck his hand out.

Zoey contemplated his not-quite-innocent smile distrustfully and allowed her palm to be engulfed in his. When his fingers closed around hers, she experienced an instant of very feminine panic.

"Great. We have a deal, then."

"Yes," she agreed, and wondered why she felt as if she were making a pact with the devil. "We have a deal."

Chapter 6

The first order of business, Zoey decided the next morning was a trip to town for puppy essentials. Oxy had come close to being an absolute pain during the night. Despite the cozy bed she'd made for him out of an old quilt at the bottom of the stairs, he'd whined so pitifully she'd gotten up to tend to him several times. Finally, in exasperation, she'd given up and taken him to her room. He'd started the night curled up beside her bed, but she'd awakened to find him nestled against her, his small sides moving rhythmically as he slept the beatific sleep of the innocent.

She felt as though she'd failed her first test of dog-sitting. She was fairly certain that dogs shouldn't sleep on beds. They were going to have to get serious about his training before he learned all manner of bad habits.

Oxy gave her a pitiful look when she shut him in the kitchen, but she steeled herself against the plea in his big doggy eyes. It would be a lot cooler for him in the air conditioned house than waiting in the car while she shopped.

As she drove the short distance to town, she reflected on the turn of events that had led to her having a dog, however briefly. When she'd seen Cage's car in her driveway her system had undergone rapid freeze. It was the only way to keep the blasted man at a distance. The fact that it had taken such a serious effort on her part was something that had given her more than a few sleepless hours last night.

Somehow her practiced ice-queen routine failed to have the predictable effect on Cage, and she didn't quite know what to do about that. Most men in her acquaintance were easily turned away by an indifferent manner and a cutting tongue. Those few whom she'd allowed closer had quickly learned that the ice was slow to thaw, much less melt and sizzle into heat.

That was a fact she was determined Cage Gauthier would never find out for himself. Just the thought had little licks of panic flickering in her veins. She'd come to terms with her own lack of passion. Oh, not that she was abnormal in that respect; she had the same needs and desires as the next woman. But when it came time for the ultimate intimacy with a man, there was a part of her that closed off, that wouldn't be breached. Most men never noticed. She had a feeling that the laid-back Don Juan of St. Augustine parish would. And that would be the ultimate humiliation.

The flowers in the yards she was passing made brilliant splashes of color in the bright sunshine, but Zoey didn't notice. When sleep had failed to visit last night, she'd gotten up and written a long letter to Patrick. She missed talking to him, but he was on one of his three-month stays at sea, so letters were the only form of communication they had. A persistent stab of guilt had forced her to write a rather stilted letter to her aunt and uncle, as well. There was nothing to prevent her from phoning them, other than her own reluctance. They'd never forgiven her for winning custody of her siblings. No doubt her biggest sin had been doing a decent job of raising them.

Afterward, she'd called Caroline's answering machine.

She hadn't had to be concerned about waking her. Her sister was still in Paris, taking advantage of a two-week trip Zoey had arranged for her. Her lips curving, Zoey doubted that Caroline had been able to tear herself away from the art museums to bother with sleep for her entire stay. But she was due back in the States in a few days, and Zoey had left a message for her to call when she got home.

Pulling up in front of Charity's lone department store, she got out of the car and felt the slap of solid heat that thickened the air and squeezed the lungs. A few quick steps and she was pushing the store door open, breathing more easily in the cool air pumping through the place. Louisiana summers had made her newly grateful for the miracles of technology.

Cruising the aisles, she found the pet supplies and began to load her cart. A blue-cushioned bed, which would no doubt only fit Oxy for a couple more months, two red bowls, a black collar and leash. She paused for a long time before the dog food, reading the labels. She was fairly certain that the three hamburgers she'd fried for the animal last night would not have qualified as proper puppy nutrition. She was wrestling a twenty-pound bag of dog kibble into her cart when a voice behind her spoke.

"Well, Zoey, it looks like you've acquired a pet."

Turning, she saw the Potter sisters. She was almost certain it was Francine who had spoken.

"I'm just keeping a dog for…a friend for a little while."

"Cage Gauthier's dog, isn't it?" Francine spoke with authority, while Lulu nodded in agreement. "Saw them both at your place yesterday evening."

Gritting her teeth, Zoey nodded. "Yes, it's Cage's dog."

"I guess he'll have a reason to come over frequently, then." There was no mistaking the satisfaction in Francine's tone. "To see that dog of his," Lulu added.

Zoey looked from one sister to the other. Their identical white-coifed heads were nodding in unison. That their remarks so closely resembled the suspicion she'd had yesterday shouldn't have surprised her. Her need to convince them otherwise did. "He said he won't have much free time until this murder is solved."

"If I know Cage Gauthier…"

"And we do…" interjected Lulu.

"He never fails to make time for a pretty woman."

"Unfortunately, I'm not going to be able to make time for him," Zoey said firmly.

"Then you're not as smart as you look." Francine's voice was tart. She lifted a thin, blue-veined hand dismissively. "Oh, don't raise your eyebrows at me, young lady. I may be in my eighties but there's nothing wrong with my eyesight. Cage Gauthier is the kind of man that makes hearts flutter regardless of age. Why, he's as handsome as the devil himself—"

"He has a real kind heart—"

Francine continued as if she hadn't heard her sister's interruption. "He's rich as Midas and best of all, none of it appears to have spoiled him overmuch."

"Leastways, no more than willing women ever spoil an attractive man," observed Lulu.

The forced smile on Zoey's lips felt like a grimace. "No doubt he's a real paragon, but…"

"Now, I didn't say that," corrected Francine. She was the elder of the sisters by eight minutes, and considered it her duty and privilege to be the spokesperson. "The boy's had a streak of wicked in him that those dimples never could disguise. He was forever letting that dog of his get away from him."

It took a few seconds for Zoey to follow their train of thought back twenty-odd years.

"Constantly digging up our garden, too," interjected Lulu.

"Cage, or the dog?"

Francine never missed a beat at Zoey's dry question. "That dog of his, of course. But we never did tell Cage's daddy. We figured between the mischief he and that Beauchamp boy cooked up, he got his share of whippings already.''

"Every time we could catch him, though, we'd put him to work. To make up for the damage his dog did.''

"He was always real sweet-natured, not like that sly Beauchamp boy.''

Zoey felt as though her head was ringing with the two women's litany of Cage's virtues. She refused to let the image they painted unfurl in her mind. There were far too many uninvited thoughts of him crowding there as it was.

"It's amazing, isn't it, that such a prince should still be single?" Zoey inched her cart away from the two sisters, but they followed her relentlessly.

Francine said, "A smart woman, mind you, would have that boy roped and hog-tied in front of a church, singing his I-do's and thanking her for the chance to wear a tux.''

Try as she might, Zoey had no success at keeping that mental image from unfolding in her mind. She shook her head, as much to dislodge the picture as at the words. "As...enticing...as the thought is, I'm really not in the market for marriage. With anyone.''

The sisters looked at each other, their eyebrows climbing upward. "Sometimes," Francine said, "what we want isn't necessarily what we need.''

"Sometimes," Lulu intoned, with an arch smile at her sister, "life has a way of deciding things for us.'' They moved away then, perfectly in step, leaving Zoey to grind her teeth ineffectually.

Pushing the cart with more force than necessary, she wheeled it toward the back of the store. She shouldn't let the two good-natured busybodies bother her. Things were done differently in Charity, it appeared, with every citizen feeling free to offer advice on the most personal of matters. Zoey doubted she'd ever get used to having others focus on her affairs, and she knew for a fact she'd never like it.

She stopped before a selection of dog toys. She supposed a puppy needed something like that rawhide bone to chew on. There were also some balls he'd probably dearly love to catch, and toys that squeaked when squeezed. She added several more items to her cart.

"Oxy's going to think he's died and gone to puppy heaven."

Stiffening slightly, Zoey looked up into Cage's lazy smile. Bumping into the man, almost literally, so soon after she'd been subjected to the sisters' discussion of him made her tone less than welcoming. "I'm just picking up a few things to help him feel at home. He had trouble sleeping last night."

His smile grew wider. He had no trouble imagining where the dog had ended up sleeping. The pooch hadn't looked slow to him. "What you need is a hot water bottle and an old-fashioned alarm clock—one with a real loud ticking. It'll make him feel like he's curled up next to his mama, listening to her heart."

She hated to admit that his idea made sense. "I guess I'm not done shopping then." When she would have pushed her cart past him, he reached out a hand to stop its progress.

"I was wondering if I could ask you to do me a favor first."

"Seems to me that's why I'm here to begin with."

The smile was still there, but his attention was diverted, as his gaze swept the store. "This is a bit different. See that truck out front?"

She stared at him, but he wasn't looking at her. Slowly, she turned and glanced over her shoulder. And then backed up for a better look. It appeared to be the same truck she'd seen in front of her house—the one that had passed her on its way from Cage's home.

Retracing her steps, she asked, "Is it the Rutherfords?"

"One of them, I expect. Here's what I'd like you to do, Zoey. Go up to the front and position yourself beside the big window. Pretend you're looking at magazines, or whatever. Just do your level best to block the view the truck's driver has into the store." His gaze met hers then, with a serious light she rarely saw there. "Will you do that for me, honey?"

"But why..." He slipped around the aisle, and her words tapered off. Muttering to herself, she considered for an instant, just an instant, going about her business and letting Cage play his games with someone else. But then she looked at that pickup again and remembered the damage that had been done to his home that night; the injuries to his back. With a sigh, she guided the cart toward the front of the store and parked it with seeming nonchalance right in front of the store window.

She plucked a few magazines from the rack and pretended to riffle through them, gauging her position carefully. And then she turned to see what Cage was up to.

It shouldn't be a surprise to see him deep in conversation with a woman. But her initial disgust dissipated when she studied the woman more closely. No amount of makeup could disguise the rainbow shades surrounding her puffy eye. And there could be few reasons a woman would choose to wear long sleeves in the Louisiana heat. Apparently Donny Ray and Stacy Rutherford had come to town.

Casting another surreptitious look out the window, she replaced the magazines on the rack and pretended to take her time choosing some others. Donny Ray was fidgeting in the front seat of the truck, craning his neck to get a better view of the store. Zoey remained firmly in place. Turning her head slightly, she checked on Cage's progress.

The woman was looking around furtively, and then accepted something Cage handed her, slipping it into her pocket. Wondering about it, Zoey looked back outside, and then froze. Donny Ray was out of the truck and headed for the front door of the store.

Impulsively, she threw the magazines in her cart and wheeled it around, halting before the door as he began to enter.

"These darn things," she said in a ringing voice. She shrugged apologetically at the man, whose way she was blocking. "Seems like I always choose the cart with a stubborn wheel." Hoping that her ruse had warned Cage, she pretended to right the cart and slowly moved it out of the man's way.

From the corner of her eye, she saw Stacy scurry to the front counter with her purchases. Donny Ray stood watching her, his gaze sweeping the rest of the store. Zoey did the same. But other than the Potter sisters, who were conversing with the store owner's wife, there was no sign of anyone else.

She didn't breathe easily again until Donny Ray had hustled his wife out of the store and the truck had pulled away from the street out front. Wheeling the cart around toward the checkout, Zoey started at the voice behind her.

"Looks like I owe you one."

She whirled around to find that Cage had made a reappearance. The shelf of aspirin he was leaning against was a perfect backdrop for him, she thought unkindly, since he seemed to be an incurable headache.

"Mind telling me what that was all about?"

His smile was slow and engaging, but his eyes remained sober. "Nothing cloak-and-dagger. I just wanted to talk to Stacy Rutherford. Without Donny Ray seeing."

"Did she tell you how she got those bruises?" Even the memory of the black eye the woman had sported was enough to make Zoey's spine go stiff.

"Stacy and I sort of have a deal. She doesn't spin fairy tales about her injuries anymore. At least, not to me." All semblance of affability had vanished. His face was set and hard. "I do my part by not letting that piece-of-scum husband of hers see me near her."

This was a new side of him—one she couldn't help but be intrigued by. "What did you give her?" At his sharp look she added, "I saw you slip her something."

He stared past her shoulder pensively. "Nothing I haven't given her before. Just an address and a phone number of a place that would provide help. If she ever decides to take it.''

She understood his meaning. There were shelters for abused and battered women. But first Stacy Rutherford would have to overcome her fear, or whatever tangle of emotions she felt for her husband, and leave him.

"Women like Stacy," he continued softly, "sometimes feel like they have no other choices, no one to turn to. I just like to remind her when I can that she has both.'' A moment later, his gaze returned to hers, that familiar grin curling one side of his mouth. "You understand why that doesn't make me real popular with Donny Ray.''

What Zoey was beginning to understand, at least about him, was threatening to shred the deliberate defense she'd carefully maintained. It was comfortable to believe in that veneer he affected, the slightly-addled good-old-boy routine that was contrived to disarm. These hints of the man beneath that surface softened something deep inside her—enough to coax an inner door, one she'd thought was tightly closed, to creep open.

She drew a shaky breath. "I'm surprised that he's out of jail. I'm sure that was the truck I saw the night your house was shot up.''

"You're right about that. It is Donny Ray's truck.'' A masculine dimple flashed. "The clan must have drawn straws to see who was going to drive. I'll bet Donny Ray was ready to spit glass when he found out he wasn't going to get to take part. Ended up being the only thing that kept him out of jail. We can't prove he was the driver, of course, and since there was no trace of gunpowder residue on his hands, we had nothing on him.''

"That's too bad,'' she said grimly. "At least if he were in jail his wife would be safe from him for a while.''

"Not for as long as you'd think.'' He watched her closely, wondering at the faint shadows beneath those incredible green eyes. If Oxy had been the cause of a sleepless night, he owed her for more than the cartful of merchandise before her. "His brothers made bail a few days after their arrest. All except for Carver," he added. "I did manage to convince the judge that he was a flight risk on the meth charge."

The outrage on her face was a delight to behold. "They got out? After shooting at you?"

"Darn lawyer is going to make a good case that the boys weren't aiming to hurt me at all, just blowing off steam. He'll go for criminal mischief." Absently, he crossed one foot over the other, slipped his hands in his pockets. "Guess it will be up to the prosecutor to make something more stick."

"That is totally disgraceful!" The anger bubbled up inside Zoey and spilled over. "People can't get away with endangering others' lives, or their property. I'd like to talk to that prosecutor myself."

Something lightened inside him as he watched her work herself into a lather. Her creamy cheeks were flushed with emotion and her eyes were hot. No doubt she'd claim that she was upset about what she considered a miscarriage of justice. It suited him better to believe that her anger stemmed at least in part from concern for him.

"Trial's set for three months from now. You going to be around by then?" Although his tone was casual, his intent wasn't.

The question took her off guard. "I—That depends. Probably." She shook off the indecision that had colored her answer and added more firmly, "I'll be here until I finish the book. That will take a few more months."

"And then what?"

Something about his steady gaze was disconcerting, and made formulating an answer difficult. "And then...I'll go back to Chicago."

"To what?"

Her eyes narrowed. "To my life. My apartment. My friends."

He nodded, as if accepting her answer, but there wasn't

acceptance in his head, in his gut. She spoke of leaving so nonchalantly, as if Charity had been merely a stopping place—one easily left, easily forgotten. The thought of her leaving burned, and he didn't want to consider the reason for that. "Seems to me there must not be much in Chicago to go back to."

Because there was more than an element of truth in his words, she angled her chin and straightened her shoulders. "Why would you say that?"

"Because you came here." His voice was gentle. "You don't leave Chicago to write each of your books, do you?"

She opened her mouth to answer, then closed it again. He was skirting too close to matters she'd rather not remember, much less discuss. She didn't want to be reminded that the emptiness in her apartment these days reflected a larger void in her life; didn't want to admit just how little appeal going back home actually held right now.

Instead, she avoided the question, and his eyes. "Every book is different."

"I'm sure it is." With a slow nod he gave consideration to her words. "And I expect you'd be the one to know if it was only the book that sent you from Chicago, or something more. I do know that there's a damn sight more to be found here than ideas for a new story."

It was probably a rare occurrence for Zoey Prescott to be speechless, and, back at his office, Cage took pleasure in the memory. She'd regained her voice quickly enough when she'd heard him tell old man Kreger to bill her purchases to him, but he'd ducked out the back door again, and had let her argue it out with the store owner.

He'd surprised himself as much as her with his words, but he didn't see much point in denying the feeling behind them. She would probably like to believe that the distance she maintained with him was due to a lack of interest on her part. Hell. His mouth quirked upward. She'd done her best to convince him of that very thing. But she hadn't been successful—not because he thought of himself as irresistible, but because more than once he'd caught a glimpse of an uncertainty in her eyes that was totally at odds with her usual cool manner. She was a woman who liked—no, *demanded*—control in her life. But she wasn't nearly as certain in her dealings with men. He didn't know why he should find that contradiction so endearing.

There was a rap on his door, and then it was opened by Tommy Lee. "Excuse me, Sheriff. Someone to see you." He stepped aside to allow the coroner from Baton Rouge to enter the office.

Before requesting assistance from the Baton Rouge Coroner's office, Cage had known Dr. Margaret Wu only by reputation. It was a reputation, he'd since learned, that was totally deserved. She was sharp, efficient, and thoroughly professional. She marched into his office right now, her diminutive height aided by the heels she wore, and took a seat, waving Cage back into his.

"No formalities, Gauthier, it's too damn hot for them."

"Yes, ma'am." Despite his agreement, he waited until she'd sat before resuming his seat. Manners were too ingrained in him to be relinquished easily. "I guess that means I don't need to offer you some of that strawberry Nehi we started stocking lately."

She let out a bark of laughter. It hadn't taken him long to discover her sweet tooth, or to start pandering to it. "Well, I guess I wouldn't turn one down." While he was sending Tommy to fetch one, she slipped off her shoes and rubbed the arch of one foot. "I'm just on my way home from a conference in Shreveport. There's not another thing in this world that would convince me to put on panty hose and a dress in this miserable heat." She accepted the bottle from Tommy gratefully and tipped it to her lips.

"I'm assuming you have some test results for me."

"You'd be right about that, Sheriff. Don't know what you'll make of them." She put the bottle down with visible reluctance, and opened the briefcase she'd carried into the room. She withdrew a file and handed it to him, then reached for the bottle again.

"That's the analysis of those fragments we took out of the victim's knees and shins. Some splinters were so deeply embedded, I would have had to do surgery to remove them. Didn't see the point. They certainly paled in significance compared to her other wounds."

"Redwood chips," Cage murmured, then lifted his gaze to the doctor.

"That's right," she affirmed. "The same kind used for landscaping around shrubbery. What do you make of it?"

Cage flipped the file closed and leaned back in his chair, hooking one foot over his knee. "There wasn't anything like that around the apartment building she lived in. It was a condo unit right on the street. No trees, no courtyard."

Dr. Wu's dark eyes sparked with interest. "You think this guy did her outside his house?"

"If he did, this evidence isn't going to help us locate where he lives. Half of suburbia probably uses redwood chips in their yards. Damn." He tossed the file onto his desk and raked his hand through his hair. "I was hoping for something that would provide a better lead."

Dr. Wu grunted. "The only clue this gives you is what the victim was kneeling in hours before her death." Swallowing the last of the soda, Dr. Wu set the bottle on Cage's desk. "Sorry we didn't come up with anything more substantial. I did find one more thing that was kind of curious. Not sure if it will be any more helpful, though. There was glue residue on the victim's fingernails." At his uncomprehending look, she explained, "The kind they use to attach false nails."

He stared at her for a long moment. "The victim wasn't wearing false fingernails."

Placidly, Dr. Wu raised her eyebrows. "No, she wasn't, was she?"

His mind racing, Cage rose as the doctor did. Taking one

of her hands in both of his own, he bent over it. "Margaret, it's been a pleasure."

She gave another bray of laughter. "Always the charm, Sheriff. You were born a century and a half too late."

His gaze shifted to the photo of Janice Reilly hanging above his desk. "I hope for her sake that's not true."

Cage followed the doctor from his office to the front door. As she exited, he turned to look at Patsy. "Where's a woman go to get her nails done?"

The older woman looked unfazed by the question. "Well, Norma over at the Beauty Mark always does mine. Charges me an arm and a leg for it, too, and truth to tell, she isn't always as careful as she should be. That polish she uses chips so easily, I swear I'm going to start bringing my own—"

"Patsy."

She blinked at his interruption. "What?"

"Where would a woman go for false nails? The kind they have to glue on."

Wheeling her chair away from her desk a little, she shot him a frown. "Well, Norma would put those on, too. I just don't go in for that kind of thing myself. But she went to a special class to learn how."

"What about in the cities? Say, Baton Rouge. Do they still do that kind of thing in the beauty parlors?"

Cocking her head, Patsy considered the question. "I expect so. I know there are some specialty places in the malls and such, but lots of the hair salons have someone, too. It's more convenient for a woman to just have it done the same place she gets her hair fixed. 'Course, most would shop around a bit, look for the best price...." Her voice trailed off as she realized she was talking to his retreating back. "And you're welcome, too," she grumbled, swinging her chair to face to her desk.

After flipping through the volume of material they'd acquired in the course of the investigation, Cage found the information he was seeking. He reached for the phone and started making calls. When Delbert Fisher knocked and entered the room, Cage waved him to a seat.

Minutes later he replaced the receiver and sat slowly back in his chair, spearing a look at his deputy. Fisher waited stoically for him to speak.

When he did, his voice was mild. "How are you coming along on the meth investigation?"

"I've got Sutton and Baker tracking down all the suppliers of ether in the state." Ether was a main ingredient in the manufacture of meth, and its sale was restricted. "They're working their way down the list, contacting every place on the list that's reported a robbery."

"They're showing pictures of each of the Rutherford boys?"

At the deputy's nod, Cage went on. "If they strike out, have them start contacting the hospitals." The man nodded again, and Cage switched topics. "I just finished talking to Janice Reilly's hairstylist down in Baton Rouge."

Placidly, Fisher said, "I spoke to her myself last week, Sheriff. It's in the report."

Cage nodded. "I saw that, Delbert. What I didn't see in the report was any mention of the fact that the victim also made regular visits to the same establishment to have false nails applied and cared for."

The deputy looked stunned. "I... That is... The lady I talked to didn't offer that information."

Cage studied the man soberly. It wasn't his nature to pry, but this was a murder investigation. The stakes didn't get much higher than these. "It's not like you to miss something this obvious, Delbert. I wouldn't be doing my job if I didn't ask. I know the last few months have been rough on you. Is your personal life affecting this investigation?"

Fisher flushed a deep, dark red, and his hands clenched around the arms of his chair. "I missed something on that statement. I admit it. But don't tie it to Betsy's leaving, Sheriff. That's a damn cheap shot."

Cage inclined his head, studying the man closely. "I suppose it sounded like it. I hope you realize the reason I asked." Silence stretched, seconds ticking by in a vacuum. "You still haven't answered my question."

For a moment he thought the man would explode. Every muscle seemed to tense, as if Fisher was preparing to eject from the chair in a furious burst of energy. Then, just as suddenly, the tension seeped away from the man's body. His wide shoulders hunched, and he seemed to fold in on himself. "It's been three months since Betsy left, Sheriff. That's more than enough time for an intelligent man to figure she ain't coming back." His jaw worked furiously, and he looked away. "Suppose you heard the story. This damn town always seems to have the details. She's living with some guy in New Orleans." He let loose a bitter laugh. "A shoe salesman, for God's sake."

Giving a sympathetic grimace, Cage said, "Well, that's enough to bust up a man's life but good for a while, isn't it? I'm not looking to kick you while you're down, Delbert. You're the best asset I have in the investigation unit. If you need to take some time, just say the word."

Fisher's gaze jerked to his. "The last thing I need is more time alone to think about Betsy. This job is about all I've had to keep me sane lately. I messed up when I questioned the beautician, Sheriff, but don't blame it on my personal life. I'll make sure it doesn't happen again."

Nodding, Cage said, "If you tell me you're fit to do your job, that's good enough for me. Anyone can make a mistake." Pausing a beat, he added, "But if you make another one on this case, I'll have to remove you. It's too damn important for me to take chances with." Their gazes held.

"Fair enough, Sheriff." Fisher nodded at the report lying before Cage. "Why don't you fill me in on what I missed?"

His desk chair gave a protesting squeak as he leaned back in it. "Well, it appears as though the victim had false nails reapplied two days before her death. Coroner found the remnants of the glue on her natural nails." He waited patiently for Fisher to process that information.

"We didn't find any false fingernails on the body, at the crime scene or in the victim's apartment." Fisher looked grim. "You think the killer removed them?"

Cage inclined his head. "That's what I think."

"Well, you guessed the killer was highly organized. He must have thought we'd find traces of his skin beneath her nails."

"Seems to me that he's more than organized." More than lucky. More than smart. Cage scrubbed his hands over his face, acidic snakes churning in his stomach. Whoever killed Janice Reilly had been careful. Murder was a nasty business. It was his experience that killers tended to mess up. They got scared, or remorseful, or sloppy. Janice Reilly's crime scene had yielded no clues to the identity of the killer. Which meant that the murderer had taken precautions to avoid detection.

"What do you mean, Sheriff?"

He heaved a sigh and wished to hell that he weren't so certain he was right. "I mean he didn't just get lucky. And I don't think the lack of clues is merely the result of careful planning. I think our killer has had practice." He looked at his deputy, watched the grim mask settle over his face. "I'm beginning to doubt Janice Reilly was his first victim."

Chapter 7

*U*nder the cover of night, the killer stalked, his movements swift and sure. There was no hesitation in his steps, no hint of caution. Detection was unthinkable, capture impossible. He was invincible.

The anticipation had started building the moment he'd chosen his next victim. He'd learned to savor that anticipation, to stoke it for days, weeks, until the timing was right. It made the final moments razor sharp, the culmination almost unbearably sweet. That first rush of power when he seized his prey, that pure, godlike feeling when he held the decision on her life and death in his hands. But there was really no decision to be made. He chose death, every time. Her death.

She walked by him, unsuspecting, as blind as all the others. He drew in a deep, soundless breath, letting the dizzying rush of his own power roar through him like an out-of-control locomotive. One step. And then his hands reached for her....

Zoey's fingers stilled on the keyboard for a moment, and

she raised her unseeing gaze as she considered what came next. Like a movie playing in slow motion, the next scene unfurled in her head and she automatically translated it into words. Her fingers poised again, then faltered.

It took long moments for reality to break through the self-induced world she was lost in. One instant bled into the next, as she stared through the window at the stranger's face; saw the sun glinting brightly off the lethally sharp blades in his hand.

She stood abruptly, stumbling out of the chair in her haste. A scream rushed to her throat, balled there. In the next instant, even while panic was pounding through her veins, she felt the first thread of comprehension, swiftly followed by a sense of foolishness.

She watched as the stranger crossed her yard a few feet, bent over a bush, and brought up those shiny blades again. Pruning shears. She expected they came in handy when trimming bushes.

The breath streamed out of her and she propped one hip against the desk. There could be few things more humiliating than overreacting to a scene of her own making. The only thing that saved her from complete mortification was that there were no witnesses to her momentary flight from her senses.

There was a slight sound at her feet, and she dropped her gaze to where Oxy watched her hopefully, his new black collar lending him a dapper air.

"Some watchdog you turned out to be," she scolded. "Shouldn't you at least bark or something when someone is outside?"

The pup cocked its head and looked at her quizzically.

"It's just the man Cage arranged to have do the lawn, but that's no excuse. I don't know who looks more stupid over this scene, you or me." Oxy gave a doggy grin, his tongue lolling out one side of his mouth. "Yeah, you're right. I *do* know."

There was a sound of a motor starting up outside, and

she went back to the window for a look. The man had
climbed on a riding lawn mower and was proceeding to cut
her grass, which was long overdue for a trim. She looked
from her computer to the window again, and then gave a
sigh. The mood was definitely broken. She wasn't going to
get any more writing done until her lawn was finished, that
was clear.

She pressed the Save command on the computer and
turned back toward the room, nearly tripping over the dog,
which had tangled itself in her feet. "You're getting close,
real close, to earning the second half of your name. And
wouldn't Cage just get a kick out of this scene," she muttered, stepping around Oxy.

It would be satisfying to blame her stupidity on that in-
furiating man. Although he'd promised to have her lawn
taken care of, he'd never given her a hint of when it would
be done. But she knew she had only herself, and her some-
times-overactive imagination, to blame. Admittedly, it
wasn't the first time it had gotten the best of her. What,
besides pure inventiveness, could ever have blinded her to
Alan's deviousness for so long? Others might make excuses
for poorly formed decisions made in the name of love. Zoey
didn't make allowances readily enough to be any less unforgiving with herself.

The puppy dashed to the front door, then turned back to
her, waiting hopefully.

"Oh, all right," she said, following him down the hallway and opening the closet for his leash. "We'll go for a
short walk. Maybe by the time we return he'll be done."

Oxy seemed to approve of the plan—at least until she
fastened the matching leash to his collar. Then he gave a
very good impression of a doorstop.

After several minutes of undignified tugging, Zoey
dropped the leash and propped her hands on her hips, glaring at the dog. He remained where he was, haunches firmly
planted on the floor. "You have to get used to the leash,

because I'm not about to engage in a tug-of-war with an animal that seems to be losing IQ points as we speak.''

Unimpressed, Oxy gave a huge yawn and lay down. Zoey stared at the puppy from narrowed eyes. If she opened the door right now, he'd be outside in a flash. But he liked to make his visits to nature without the bothersome trappings of civilization, like leashes. And since she'd learned from experience that he had a streak of wanderlust in him, he couldn't be trusted to stay nearby.

The answer, she decided, was in being smarter than the dog. She went back to the kitchen and opened the cupboard, taking out a box of puppy treats. The quiet clicking of toe-nails on linoleum told her that she had an audience. Oxy had already shown that he had disgracefully poor willpower where such treats were involved. While he watched, she took a handful, then slipped them into the pocket of her shorts. This time when she went to the front door, he was at her heels. Pausing for her sunglasses and a baseball cap, she swept all her hair up and pulled the cap over it. When she reached down to pick up the leash this time, Oxy came willingly.

She smiled smugly. She just needed to be smarter than the animal. Locking the door behind her, she led him down the porch steps.

It took a doggy treat every several yards to ensure Oxy's continued cooperation. Fortunately, he didn't seem to discriminate between part and whole treats, so she was able to feed him pieces each time. She knew she would have to conserve the blasted things in order to get him home again. There was no way she was going to carry him back to the house when the time came.

Right now he was expending more enthusiasm than sense, running in and out between her legs, tangling her in the leash and nearly tripping her.

Muttering a few disparaging comments about the dog's parentage, Zoey stopped and unsnarled the leash. A car slowed on the road, and its electric windows lowered.

"Where's that dog taking you, Zoey?"

She looked up, saw Tanner Beauchamp grinning at her from the driver's seat. Giving a mental sigh, she gave one last hard look at Oxy. "He's practicing walking on a leash."

Tanner guided the car over to the side of the road, parked it and got out, leaving it running so the interior wouldn't heat up again. Propping his hands on his hips, he surveyed the two of them. "It does look like he needs a lot of practice."

The sight of the man wearing a lightweight summer suit of a quality she recognized made her grateful for her own casual clothes. The sun hadn't diminished in strength, though it was already past five-thirty. She mentally estimated how long it would take Tanner to melt where he stood.

Oxy made a dash to sniff out the newcomer, and when the leash jerked suddenly in her hand, Zoey barely managed to avoid landing face first on the ground.

"I think his training may be beyond me. He's going to need some classes." She shot the dog a dark look. "A lot of classes."

"Hey, fella." Tanner squatted down and gave Oxy a vigorous ear scratching. "So what I'm hearing is that you're a little on the slow side. Is that right?"

Uninsulted, Oxy closed his eyes and enjoyed the attention.

"He's going to be a big one. Look at the size of those feet." Tanner lifted his gaze to hers. "Are you figuring on taking him back north with you?"

It was the second time in as many days she'd been reminded of her home in Chicago. The second time she'd found that reminder strangely unappealing.

"He's not mine." Surely that wasn't a pang of emotion for the little beast who was even now shaking himself off and investigating Tanner's shoelaces. "I'm just keeping him for Cage for a while." Under the man's sudden scrutiny, she added uncomfortably, "Until he has more time for him."

Tanner rose, still staring at her. "Well, I'll be." His gaze went back to the dog. "You know, I think this is Cage's first dog since Tooner. Has he told you about the dog he had when we were kids?"

For some reason, seeing the thin line of perspiration trickle down the side of Tanner's throat made him seem more human. She nodded. "He told me it accompanied the two of you on your share of misadventures."

Teeth flashing, he agreed, "That's a fact. And in case that's disapproval I detect in your voice, I'll assure you we got our share of wallopings for the mischief we caused."

Brows arching, she asked, "Was it worth it?"

This time his grin was wicked—a sudden, vivid reflection of Cage's. "Every last minute of it." He chuckled richly at the memory, one hand going to his tie to loosen it. "My daddy was a real enthusiastic disciplinarian. But Cage caught heck as often as I did, because he lacked any imagination when confronted with the evidence of our misdeeds."

Involuntarily, a smile pulled at her lips. "Neither of you seems to have suffered overmuch for it."

"You have no idea." His grin was rueful as he spread his suit jacket wide. "I still can't bring myself to wear a belt."

"Obviously cause for years of intensive therapy."

He shook his head in mock sorrow at her unsympathetic tone, but his eyes were gleaming. "You're a hard woman, Zoey. Does Cage realize that?"

The question had her spine stiffening. "Why should Cage's opinion matter to me?"

The chuckle sounded again, and his face was alight with real amusement. She wondered, fleetingly, if it had been that overdose of charm that had first bonded the two men together so many years ago, or their simple need for adventure.

"Why?" He finally addressed her question. "Maybe because you and he have been dancing around each other since the day you stepped into town. If we were still in fourth grade, we'd be saying you two were sitting in a tree, *k-i-s-s-i-n-g.*"

He'd managed to annoy her. "Unlike your ancestors, Beauchamp, I don't do my kissing in trees."

He threw his head back and laughed. "Oh, you're a match for him—no doubt about it. You're…perfect. I wonder if he sees it." He looked at her, his eyes still crinkled. "Chances are, he does. Although I've often chastised the boy about his deplorable sense of honesty, one thing he's never been is slow. You just might be the one to help him forget the reason he came back to this place."

His words reignited her irritation, while at the same time lighting a spark of interest. "And what reason would that be?"

But Tanner was already looking as though he regretted his words, his gaze shifting slightly away. "Oh, just losing his daddy. And his mama was in real poor health by then." His voice was a shade too innocent, his inching movements toward the car too furtive. "I'd ask you to Jonesy's tonight to discuss dog training over rib eye, but I know you're going to be busy."

Although she was intrigued by his words about Cage, she refused to pump him for more information. There was something distasteful in the thought of gossiping about Cage at the side of the road, even if it was with his best friend. "You must be a well-rounded individual, Tanner, to add mind reading to your list of talents."

Opening his car door, he said, "Wish I could claim psychic abilities." He winked at her. "Fact is, before I came upon you walking your dog, I saw Cage heading up to your house with an armful of groceries."

Whirling toward the direction of her home, she heard his parting chuckle, but never saw his car pull away. There was no sign of Cage on her front porch, but a vehicle she'd never

seen before sat in the driveway. She flinched as Oxy remembered which pocket held doggy treats and jumped up
for some, his nails scratching her bare legs.

She paused long enough to break off a treat and toss it
to him, before starting for home. She told herself that the
anticipation she felt certainly wasn't caused by the thought
of seeing Cage Gauthier again. She almost believed it.

Her kitchen was a fog of steam and there were heavenly
smells coming from one of the pots on top of the stove.
Although her traitorous stomach showed instant signs of interest, her mind wasn't so easily mollified.

She leaned against the doorjamb and surveyed the man
moving competently about her kitchen. As a concession to
the heat generated by the boiling water, he'd unbuttoned his
shirt partway down his chest, revealing a wedge of smooth
golden skin. "You know, I could have sworn I locked the
door when I left."

At the sound of her voice, Cage's head jerked around
and he didn't quite manage to wipe the guilty expression
from his face. "You thought you locked the door?"

Thinking of the start she'd gotten when she'd been scared
witless by the stranger's face at the window, she nodded
slowly. "I know I did. So you have two things to explain—
how you got into my house and what you're doing in my
kitchen."

She wasn't demanding that he leave yet, he noted, and
took that as a sign of encouragement. "Actually, your front
door was locked, but the back-porch door wasn't. A woman
living alone really ought to be more careful. I figured it was
my duty as sheriff to watch over things until you got back."

She frowned and tried to remember the last time she'd
used the back door. She was almost certain she'd checked
it before retiring last night. "Does your duty as sheriff include making supper in empty kitchens?"

He stirred the spaghetti sauce with a long-handled wood

en spoon he'd found in one of her drawers. "Only pasta, and only in your kitchen."

"And why is that?"

"Because pasta is good for the soul, and it's impossible for you not to invite me to dinner when I'm making it."

She should have demanded an explanation. She should have been outraged that he'd entered her house without her permission. But when he'd turned around for that brief moment, there had been a look in his eyes that had given her pause. And beneath his bantering words was a tone she hadn't heard from him before, one she couldn't identify. The debate about his high-handed actions could wait while she took time to discover what was bothering Cage.

"I'd think breaking and entering would hinder the digestion."

"Now that's a mighty harsh way to describe an unexpected guest, Zoey." He managed a hurt tone as he opened the oven door and checked on the French bread. "Especially when he's intent on feeding you. How do you feel about dinner?"

She pushed away from the doorway and followed Oxy into the kitchen, bending to unfasten his leash. "Interested enough to consider letting you stay."

He sent her a quick grin. If she hadn't been watching so closely, she might not have noticed that the usual charm of it was slightly off the mark. There was something missing, a part of him that wasn't quite focused on her. Without a thought, she went to the cupboard and took out two wineglasses.

It wasn't her nature to pry; she was a woman who valued her own privacy too much to feel comfortable intruding on another's. But she recognized the air of someone troubled by more than he would say. Her recognition of it, however, didn't explain this unnatural urge she had to soothe.

Taking a wine bottle from the refrigerator, she filled both glasses and handed him one. She pulled a chair out from

the table and sat down, sipping and watching him over th
rim of her glass.

"Do you want to talk about it?"

He stiffened, then turned slowly and leaned against th
counter, taking a reflective drink.

He didn't evade or pretend to misunderstand her. His gaz
met hers across the kitchen. "It's the case. And it's n
something I can talk about. I don't even have it straight i
my own mind yet."

"All right."

And it was just that easy. He marveled at the matter-o
fact way she accepted it. Other women might have whee
dled, some would have pouted. But Zoey better than anyon
would allow a person a little space. He didn't know wh
that trait of hers should feel so welcome right now.

He sat next to her, cradling the wineglass in his hand
"Did I ever tell you my Great-great-uncle Lamar was
celebrated chef?"

She released a breath she hadn't realized she'd been hol
ing and forced back an unconscious sense of disappoin
ment. Not even to herself was she willing to admit just ho
much she'd wanted to hear what was weighing on him. Th
would take a level of trust she didn't even want to conside
Certainly it was one she was never going to return. Shakin
her head, she said, "I don't believe you did."

"Well, he was. He had himself the best possible place
show off his talents, too, in the kitchens of the Blue Ros
the finest brothel in St. Augustine parish."

"Really?" Recognizing the beginning of the story for th
distraction it was, she settled back to enjoy the tale. "
wouldn't think that the…ladies of the evening would hav
had especially hearty appetites."

He gave her a wicked wink. "Oh, their appetites wer
everything you'd expect for women in their positions, b
like I said, this was a real high-class place. Gentlemen cal
ers would come for companionship, as well as for less ho

orable reasons, and there would be singing and dancing before everyone sat down to an elegant dinner.''

''Much like the one you're preparing tonight?''

He waved a hand toward the stove carelessly. ''Heck, spaghetti can't hold a candle to the dinners Lamar could serve. The way I heard the story, he was torn between two loves—one for cooking and the other for Sarah May, the most beautiful and talented of the Blue Rose's occupants.''

She wondered if it was her imagination that made him seem a little less tense, as if the act of storytelling could accomplish what she couldn't. ''Something tells me that his two loves led to his downfall.''

''There are folks who would agree with you. On the night in question, Lamar was aiming to serve his famous roast duck. The governor was passing through, you see, and it was to be a very special night at the Blue Rose. But Sarah May slipped into the kitchen while Lamar was preparing the meal. Seems she was partial to his lemon-cream tart, not to mention a few other specialties best not mentioned in polite company. Well, one thing led to another. Old Uncle Lamar didn't have his mind on watching the duck, and by the time his attention was diverted from Sarah May, most of the kitchen was in flames. Way I heard it, the fire never did get far out into the dining room, but the governor is said to have panicked. Ran out of there, vowing never to return and the owner, Rose herself, saw the reputation of her place go out the door with him. Luckily Lamar figured he wouldn't be too welcome around there much longer, and had already slipped away before Rose charged into his room with a Smith & Wesson in her hand and murder in her eye.'' He paused to enjoy the sight of Zoey looking at him, her lips turned up, eyes alight with interest and humor.

''And what happened to him?''

''Well, being swift of foot, he'd gotten clean away and taken Sarah May with him. They knew they'd best get out of the area, so I'm told they headed for New Orleans, where

Lamar opened a little café and settled down with Sarah to raise a family.''

"Is that a true story?" Zoey demanded.

He loved the way she looked, her mouth twitching between laughter and disbelief. The sight lightened something inside him. "As the saying around here goes, if it's not, it oughta be. I do know my daddy could hold his own in the kitchen when my mama would let him try, and he's the one who taught me a thing or two about cooking."

She watched while he set his glass down and went to the stove, stirring the sauce and poking at the spaghetti with a long-handled fork. There was something restful about watching a man moving about her kitchen, preparing a meal for her. Something definitely odd, but homey too. She tried to imagine Alan showing up at her apartment in Chicago and cooking for her and the thought proved too elusive to contemplate.

Finally, at some good-natured grousing from him, she roused herself enough to set two places at the table, and helped him find some serving dishes for the bread and the sauce. When they settled down again to eat, each with a plate mounded with spaghetti and with Oxy parked hopefully at their feet, the atmosphere took on a cozier feel.

Determined to ignore it, Zoey focused intently on her meal. Surely it was only her imagination that the air seemed to get thicker by the second, wrapping them in a cocoon of intimacy. Cage didn't appear to notice it.

She shot him a glance from beneath her lashes. He was eating with obvious enjoyment, sipping occasionally from his wineglass. To look at the man, one would believe he was dining with a favorite elderly aunt. The thought rankled. She tried to remember that only minutes ago her goal had been to offer him comfort. Now it was taking a masterful effort on her part to resist an equally strong urge to kick him. Hard.

Driven to move, she got up and retrieved the wine bottle from the counter and filled his glass, before tipping more wine into her own. As she slipped back into her chair, he lifted his glass in a half salute.

He watched as she reached for her glass, his eyebrows climbing when she drained half of it. Something had her nerves tightening and he wondered whether she sensed the chemistry sparking and humming between them. It pleased him to think that she did. It gave him even greater pleasure to believe it was the cause of her sudden unease. He found the thought infinitely more enjoyable to focus on than the niggling fear that had been troubling him since his conversation with Fisher.

To distract them both, he reached for her hand and sent his thumb skating across her knuckles. "I've been wondering about something. How come you use your initials on your books?"

"It was my agent's idea." She made a face, giving a discreet tug to free her hand. It was held fast. "He thought my first books would sell better if people didn't know they were written by a woman. Sexism," she added dryly, "is alive and well in the publishing world."

"I've been giving the thought some consideration," he said seriously. "I believe I can guess what your middle initial stands for."

"Somehow I doubt it." She was unable to keep the smirk from her voice.

"I'm thinking something imaginative. Not the usual 'Linda' or 'Lisa' for you." He pretended to mull it over for a moment before guessing, "'Lillabelle.'"

She wrinkled her nose in disgust. "Not even close." She'd never been crazy about her middle name. For the first time she reflected that it quite possibly could have been worse.

"'Lolita.'"

She gave a shake of her head.

"'Louisa.'"

She narrowed her eyes at him. "You cheated."

Amused, he tightened his fingers around hers, holding them as she tried to pull away. "How could I cheat?"

"I know for a fact you did some checking up on me when I first came here." She didn't bother to keep the annoyance from her tone. The idea still irritated. "You probably found out then."

"Nope. That would have violated my impeccable sense of fair play. It fits, you know. It's almost as if your parents knew you'd be a writer."

Since she was having no success in freeing her hand from his, she let it lie limply in his grasp. "Somehow I have difficulty picturing you as a literary type."

"You're surprised I recognize Louisa May Alcott? I'll have you know that when I was fourteen I couldn't wait to get my hands on a copy of *Little Women*."

"Don't tell me. You thought the book would be about an acrobatic troupe of circus midgets."

Her wry comment was close enough to the truth to have him grinning. "Not exactly. I might have imagined a book of memoirs written by pygmy members of the world's oldest profession." Though she made a rude sound, he went on, "But despite my overwhelming disappointment, I finished the book."

She was amused despite herself. "Was that your last foray into literature?"

"Not at all. I've even read a novel or two by Z. L. Prescott." He enjoyed surprising her. "I have to admit to getting a chill or two from your description, although your research on the investigation of murder scenes needs work."

The quick bloom of pleasure caused by his first words was doused by the rest of his statement. She was certain her contact in the Chicago police homicide division would feel as offended as she did. "That's a bit strange, coming from someone who did his damnedest to make sure I did *no* research concerning the murder in his parish."

"I had my reasons," he said equably. "Good ones. And the talk has quieted down, due to the measures my office has taken. It's easier to run an investigation when the phone lines and officers aren't tied up with people jumping at shadows or seeing bogeymen behind every corner. It's also better for the town when folks can sleep at night.''

She refused to see the simple logic of his words. "Is that what brought you here today? An urge to make sure I wasn't wreaking some kind of havoc in your parish by getting it 'stirred up' again?''

He smiled at that, with a rueful curve of his lips, but his eyes were alight with an emotion she was afraid to identify. "Honey, you've been stirring things up since you got here.''

Tearing her gaze away from his, she strove to focus on his words. The expression in his eyes, on his face, was enough to terrify her. "Well, despite your lack of cooperation, my novel is shaping up just fine.'' It was, in fact, developing into what she thought would be her finest work. The murder had ignited some dormant spark in her creativity, but it was Charity itself that was breathing life into the story. The small Southern town she'd created was purely fictional, but there was no denying that it owed its origin to the homespun atmosphere she'd found here. Like the murderer responsible for Janice Reilly's death, her own villain hadn't identified himself to her yet. A chill crept over her arms despite the late-afternoon heat. Just as life imitated art, there were many possibilities.

He reached down to give the pup an absent pat, his gaze never faltering. She could feel it, hot and intense, compelling her to look at him. It was a compulsion she was determined to ignore.

"Well,'' she said with forced brightness, "since you fixed dinner I guess I can do the cleaning up.'' It would give her an excuse to escape that warm grip, that equally warm gaze. It would also give her an opportunity to get her suddenly jittery nerves calmed again.

But her plan was waylaid by Cage's insistence on helping. It was impossible to keep her guard up while the man regaled her with imitations of just about every citizen of

Charity while he dried the dishes. He was a wicked mimi
and had each individual's mannerisms and speech pattern
perfected to a *T.*

His nonsense soothed her earlier edginess, and when h
declared it time to retire outside for the long-honored tra
dition of porch sitting, she could only follow bemusedly.

And so it was that she found herself sitting on the porc
glider next to him with his arm stretched out behind he
The glider's slow, rhythmic movements were a perfect me
ronome for the music of Cage's drawl. His long langui
tales of Charity's history and his own childhood could mak
her smile in appreciation or listen with barely suspende
disbelief—but always, always, with rapt attention.

And as they sat and rocked, laughing a little, talkin
more, darkness was slow to fall and the heat was slower t
lift. His placid voice lent a dreamy sort of magic to the ai
His words didn't so much drawl as meander, strollin
through story after story like a leisurely walk in the wood
The cadence was hypnotic.

Fireflies were dancing and glinting in the twilight befor
the first stirrings of cool air brushed their skin. Both ha
grown quiet, content to watch shadows gather. Mellow fro
the wine and the peaceful drifting of time, Zoey let her hea
rest against the back of the glider, felt the strength of h
arm against her neck. His fingers, as harmless as the ligh
breeze, toyed with the ends of her hair. She tilted her hea
to watch with heavy-eyed fascination as he absently presse
his still-cool beer bottle against the wedge of skin bared b
his half-buttoned shirt.

"This is the very same brand of beer that Tanner and
favored, mostly because it was the kind my daddy filled ou
refrigerator with." Because her attention was still focuse
on the bottle he was smoothing down his chest, she didn
see the smile on his lips, but it sounded in his voice.

Her words, when they came, were huskier than norma
"I saw Tanner earlier this evening while I was walking Ox

I've already concluded that the two of you deserved every beating you got, and then some.''

His chuckle was low and amused. "No sympathy. You know, sugar, somewhere along the line you've gotten the worst possible impression of me.''

She wished his words were true. They certainly had been at first. It would be comfortable if she could go back to believing that there was nothing to the man but surface charm and laziness, but she'd discovered more beneath the surface—much more. The shallow, glib picture wouldn't fit the man who tried, repeatedly, to help a battered woman find the strength to leave her husband. It didn't begin to describe a man who cared so deeply about his adoptive family that he worried about betraying parents already dead.

He tipped the bottle to his mouth and she was close enough to see the moist path it had left on his skin; close enough to wonder if the spot would be cool to her lips, to her tongue. Dimly, a warning bell rang in her mind. Whether the wine or the close-wrapped intimacy was to blame for it, she ignored it.

"It's true that Tanner and I were the curious sort. And any trouble that came along, we got into together.'' His fingers moved against her neck, not quite casually, and a delicious shiver slid down her spine. "His mother left when he was young and his daddy was a hard man. Tanner spent more time at my house than he did at his own. My mama always said it was like raising twins.''

Cage set the bottle on the porch floor and reached for her chin, sliding his fingers along her jawline. His voice was low and as smooth as velvet. "I guess some things haven't changed much. I'm still curious. And I still have the damnedest time avoiding trouble.''

His thumb gently skated across her lips, following their contours. She registered the need to move away—a need born of self-preservation and logic. She didn't move. For once, Zoey Prescott wasn't going to listen to that sneaky little voice that warned of lies, distrust and betrayal. Her lips parted and she tasted the rough pad of his thumb, heard the uneven breath he drew in. She tipped her head up to meet his descending mouth with her own.

For once, just this once, she was going to let herself feel.

Emotion drenched her the moment his lips met hers. She'd forgotten just how quickly his touch could mist her mind with emotion. How sweet that descent was as they drifted into sensation. She raised a hand, speared her fingers into his hair. When he shifted her onto his lap without releasing her mouth, she gave a gentle sigh and sank into the kiss.

Cage drank in the release of her breath and gathered her closer. He lingered over her mouth, taking his time with her to draw out the moment. The smooth glide of tongues mating, teeth scraping, were sensations to be savored. The velvet skin beneath her jaw begged to be investigated, and the soft secret place behind her ear smelled of her perfume. He inhaled deeply, then grazed his teeth over her earlobe, pleased by her quick shudder.

There was something about his mouth, she thought dreamily, that was tormentingly languid, as if time were inconsequential. He could take her by surprise, alternating the soft lazy pleasure with unexpected darts of pure fire that caused her nerve endings to flash and sizzle. She guided his lips back to hers, eager to swamp herself in his taste and texture.

His hand slid under her T-shirt and splayed against her back. She had no choice but to feel. He was nudging her emotions to the surface with each velvet stroke, each leisurely glide. Somehow she'd known from the first that he was a dangerous man; one who could effortlessly summon all kinds of sensations that she normally kept tightly guarded—emotions that, once released, couldn't be so easily contained again.

He released the snap on her bra and then his warm fingers were closing around her bare breast. She arched into his touch in helpless response. Her nipple tautened against his palm and she wanted him—fiercely, with a pure, reckless need that was as exhilarating as it was foreign. She slid her hand to the strong column of his throat, then lower, to the smooth skin bared by his half-buttoned shirt. There was just a hint of moisture there, and she pressed forward blindly, seeking it with her tongue.

His breath sawed out of him, his heartbeat sounding raggedly in her ear. "You told me once you didn't take this casually." His voice was a low rumble in the shadows. "There's nothing casual about this, Zoey." He cupped and shaped her breast with clever, knowing fingers. His kiss held the merest edge of desperation. "I've never been more wrapped up in a woman. I guess I'm asking you to trust me on that."

Trust. The word triggered a response she was helpless to prevent. Ice shot through her veins and her body stiffened against his. Desire and longing battled against defenses long relied upon. She knew there was no hiding her reaction from him. And she knew he'd guess at the cause.

His hand stilled against her skin and for an infinite moment they sat, gazes locked. She would have understood anger, expected frustration. But she wanted to cry out at the glimpse of utter desolation she caught in his eyes.

Then he was smoothing her clothing into place and shifting her away from him. "I rushed you." The words were even.

"No," she denied. She wouldn't take the easy out he offered. Wouldn't let him make it simple for her. "I wanted you." Her hand lifted, touched his jaw. "I still do."

He caught her hand, pressed a soft kiss in the palm and brought it down to her side. The gesture might have seemed loverlike. She wondered achingly why it appeared more as if he couldn't bear her touch.

"A woman has a right to make up her own mind." He stood, looped an easy arm across her shoulders, walked with her toward the steps.

"Are you sure—" her voice quavered and she felt like fool "—you won't come inside?"

He ran his knuckles gently under her chin, pent-up desir churning and frothing in his gut. It joined another emotion— one that came from a bleak and barren place deep insid him, one that could spring forth without warning. "I don' think so." The kiss he pressed against her lips was hard an brief. "Lock your doors. Both of them."

He turned before he could change his mind. The familia despair was coupled with a heavy dose of sexual frustration Something told him he'd better get used to both feelings.

In the deepest part of the night, the darkness was absolute Naked, Cage trod lightly across his porch floor, the age boards murmuring beneath his feet. The front door stoo open behind him, the interior of the house as full of shadow as the secluded yard. One shoulder propped against a sturdy column, he drank from a beer he didn't want, to quench thirst he didn't have.

Sleep refused to beckon. It was just as well. This was the kind of night that summoned unwanted memories, Techni color reruns of nightmares that refused to fade. At least in the balmy night air his clogged lungs eased a bit. But the ghosts had followed him outdoors. He'd brought them with him.

Already drops of condensation were forming on the bottle in his hand. He raised it to his lips, swallowed the coo liquid. He didn't know how long he'd spent sitting in the den staring blindly into the darkness. He hadn't needed light. The display on the wall behind his daddy's antique desk was branded into his mind.

In the distance a night creature wailed a long, mournfu note. He remembered when Nadine and his mama had proudly shown him what they'd done with the commenda tions and letters buried deep in cardboard boxes. Each had been matted and framed, arranged carefully above the desk that now belonged to him.

And in the center of the arrangement hung that polished medal, suspended patriotically from a red, white and blue ribbon. He could still remember its weight as the New Orleans Chief of Police had placed it around his neck, still feel the wash of self-doubt and guilt that had accompanied the award.

He drank, wishing the effects of the beer would summon sleep, knowing it would fail. *A citation for bravery in the line of duty.* Would the phrase never lose its mockery? Certainly the four survivors had agreed he was deserving. They'd even attended the award ceremony with their families.

But he'd known the truth. The truth had been in the woman who was absent. The woman whose crumpled, lifeless body had lain with that of her killer.

Cage squeezed his eyes shut for a moment. Then, in a sudden burst of violence, he hurled the beer bottle as far as he could. The sound it made when it smashed among the shadows in the yard failed to satisfy the savage rage that still lingered. Rage born from a sense of failure that refused to fade. He leaned his head against the forearm he'd braced against the porch pillar.

One instant. Just one split second of indecision could result in ghosts that haunted for a lifetime. He'd never forgive himself for his millisecond's hesitation that had cost Amy Lou Travers her life.

It was the most bitter of ironies that Zoey had frozen the way she had tonight. Lips twisted, he stared blindly into the darkness. He'd had some nerve, asking her to trust him.

It had been over two years since he'd been able to trust himself.

Chapter 8

Ordinarily, Cage was a pretty amiable person in the mornings. But when night melted into day without a minute's worth of sleep, a body was entitled to feel a little irritable. As if in direct reflection of his mood, the weather had turned sultry, with clouds boiling and bumping across the sky. Most likely they were in for a much-needed thunderstorm before the day was over, but not before they'd been treated to several hours of suffocating humidity.

He wasn't in a welcoming mood when he pushed his office door open and saw the visitor sitting in his chair, feet propped on the desk before him.

"What the hell are you doing here?"

Tanner raised his eyebrows, then handed him one of the steaming cups of coffee sitting before them. "Rather testy this morning, aren't you, son?"

Cage grunted, took the cup and sipped. Aiming a telling look at his desktop, he pulled up another chair. Tanner obligingly swung his feet to the floor.

Peering at Cage closely, he noted, "You don't look like

ou slept much. Now that could mean one of two things, ut given your temperament this morning, I think I'm safe n guessing that you struck out with your lady love and spent ours last night cursing your ineptitude in the dalliance de- artment." He shook his head in mock reproach. "You now if you need help in that direction, you've only to ask."

If possible, Cage's foul mood worsened. He suggested hat Tanner perform an anatomically impossible act, and ritted his teeth at the other man's bellow of laughter.

When Tanner finally sobered, he said, "You should have topped in at Jonesy's. You and I haven't been out together or a while. I was there until the wee hours showing Mari- nne Jamison a little sleight of hand." He winked.

"I wasn't in the mood."

"Might have done you good. You could have told ol' Jncle Tanner all about it." He whirled his chair to face Cage expectantly. "C'mon," he wheedled when his friend emained silent. "I tell you everything."

"Yes. And I've asked you to stop."

Chuckling again, Tanner sipped cautiously from the teaming brew. "All right, then. I won't regale you with ales of my exploits with the fair Marianne. No one ever ccused me of insensitivity." He ignored the other man's nort. "I didn't have the best day myself yesterday. Had to o to Baton Rouge and meet with our branch manager there. Seems we had a teller who was tucking away a bit of money or a rainy day. Spent a couple of hours with a Detective Fuller filling out a report to file charges." He drank reflec- ively. "He said to tell you hey."

Cage slouched lower in his chair and tipped the cup to is lips. The coffee was succeeding in making him feel at east half human again. "Lloyd Fuller? Tall fella, thinning dark hair, wire-rimmed glasses?"

After giving careful consideration to his light-colored rousers, Tanner crossed one leg over his knee. "Don't now about the thinning hair. Looked plumb gone to me, ut that sounds like the detective I met."

Cage scratched the chin he hadn't felt like shaving tha morning. "I'll be. I worked with him in New Orleans. didn't know he'd transferred to Baton Rouge."

"Spent the better part of the afternoon trying to get tha mess sorted out. Then on my way home I was nearly run off the road by another old friend of yours." Tanner raised his glass in mock salute. "None other than good ol' Donny Ray."

His attention arrested mid-yawn, Cage went still. "Re ally? Where was he coming from?"

"Looked to be the same direction as me, Baton Rouge Recognized that decrepit old truck when he practically side swiped me. No offense, son, but it's a fact that there isn' an officer of the law around when you need one. Not tha the boy ever could drive worth a damn. Do you recall when you beat him in a race out on the old Bonneyville black top?" He leaned back, clearly lost in old times. "You had that sweet little souped-up Mustang, and he was running tha '72 Chevy pickup."

"I remember." But Cage hadn't followed his friend back some fifteen years. He was too busy wondering what kind of business Donny Ray had had in Baton Rouge. "Was he hauling anything?"

Tanner threw him a surprised look. "Hell, no, don't you remember? Bucky Hanover did the judging and he made sure you emptied out your trunk and Donny Ray cleared ou the bed of the truck. He wouldn't even let me ride with you the little twerp." He gave a frown, as if the memory stil rankled. "Always regretted missing the opportunity."

"I mean yesterday," Cage said with all the patience he could muster, which wasn't much. "Was Donny Ray haul ing anything yesterday?"

Tanner lifted a shoulder. Clearly the events of a day ago couldn't compete with the memory of a childhood victory more than a dozen years previous. "Didn't notice. Hap pened to see him last night at Jonesy's, though, and gave him my opinion of his driving abilities." His teeth flashed. "He accepted it with his usual good grace and humor."

Cage winced. No doubt Stacy Rutherford had taken the brunt of her husband's temper last night. He made a mental note to send one of the deputies out on some pretext to check on her. A familiar powerlessness filled him. Some way, he had to convince the woman to leave her husband and seek safety. He did what he could, but slipping her a card and a few extra dollars now and again dimmed miserably against the realities of the life she led. He wondered how he would deal with it if the day came that Donny Ray used his fists on her once too often. He was afraid he already knew.

Belatedly, he realized Tanner was speaking again. "I said, the obvious aside, how are you coming along in the courting of Zoey Prescott?"

"None of your damn business."

"You sound a bit peevish, Cage, m'boy." Clearly enjoying himself, Tanner rocked back in the chair. He wasn't above needling his friend when the opportunity arose. "If the lady is sick of your pretty mug already, could be she's in the mood for a change. Maybe she's ready to appreciate my more heroic qualities. Don't know how she failed to see them the night we met," he mused aloud. "Usually I'm like glass when it comes to women."

"Give or take a few letters." Driven to move, Cage rose and threw his cup into the trash.

It suited Tanner to ignore Cage's last remark. "Could be I'll just ask Miss Prescott if she'd like to see a little more of the parish. There's nothing like a moonlight drive to allow the most interesting developments."

His smile humorless, Cage said softly, "Don't."

Their gazes met—Tanner's amused, the other man's dangerous. Slowly, slowly, the teasing smile faded from Tanner's face and he gave a long, tuneless whistle. "Well, I'll be. Looks to me like you're smitten, boy."

There was a dull throb beginning in Cage's left temple.

"You know, I've got about one nerve left, Tanner, and you're on it."

His friend's eyes crinkled. "Yep, smitten is what you are. Don't know of anything else that turns a normally easygoing man into the snarling beast I see before me right now." He held up a hand to ward off the obscenity Cage mouthed. "Now don't you go getting riled up. It was bound to happen to one of us sooner or later, and it's just my good luck that it happened to you." Chuckling at his own joke, he glanced down at his watch.

"Shoot." He rose swiftly to his feet. "I've got a meeting with the bank auditor in five minutes."

"By all means," Cage said with mock politeness, rising to throw open the door. "Don't let me keep you."

When he got to the door, Tanner turned. "As much as abhor seeing my best friend go through the pangs of true love, I have to say I do admire your taste." He winked. " couldn't have chosen better if I'd picked her out for you myself. And in a manner of speaking, I did." He had the good sense to duck, and missed the halfhearted swing Cage sent his way.

Hand propped on the doorjamb, Cage watched his friend stride away. He could and did blame his foul mood on the sleepless night he'd just spent, but he'd been shocked at the burst of pure primal possessiveness that had had him warning Tanner off Zoey. It had been immediate, and completely involuntary. Any idiot could have recognized that Tanner was merely baiting him, but the visceral response Cage had felt at his friend's words hadn't stemmed from logic.

He took a deep breath, released it slowly. A damned sorry state of affairs, indeed, to get this heated up over a woman who had told him, in a reaction clearer than words, that she didn't trust him. It shouldn't matter. He wished like hell he could figure out when it had started to matter all too much

He pushed away from the door and headed down the hall in the opposite direction to the one his friend had taken Entering the room labeled Investigative Services, he absently returned the greetings of the deputies seated at their desks and made his way to the bank of computers at the back of the room.

Progress, he thought, as he sat down before the main-frame computer, was a wonderful thing. Given enough local funding, law-enforcement officials around the nation could tap into a huge database of information compiled on un-solved crimes throughout the U.S. Eyes intent on the computer screen, he keyed in his command and waited for access.

Of course, there wouldn't have been sufficient funding available to bring twentieth-century technology to the St. Augustine sheriff's department without philanthropic con-tributions. Cage didn't consider it strange that he'd donated an amount ten times his annual salary to the sheriff's office after he'd been hired to bring its investigative abilities up-to-date. He'd been raised to understand that being born to wealth entailed certain obligations. Although he'd never given it much thought growing up, he'd been aware that his parents had contributed freely to the town and the parish. The new addition to the school, and the two fire trucks the parish volunteers kept polished to a gleaming shine were evidence that the Gauthier tradition of charity was contin-uing. Or at least, that of the most recent Gauthiers. He seemed to recall having heard a thing or two about his granddaddy's ability to keep two sets of books and every penny he ever made.

Cage squinted at the screen and tapped in the information he wanted to access, narrowing the search to Louisiana: *Homicide female unsolved.* As the volumes of data began downloading he prepared the printer and turned to the dep-uty nearest him, Bob Sutton. "Some time this morning I want you to run out to Donny Ray's place. Check up on Stacy." The man nodded. It wasn't the first time the request had been made. As a wave of resignation swept over him, Cage knew better than to hope that it would be the last.

* * *

The day had been a total loss. Zoey shoved away from the computer and rose to pace. She had the self-discipline to keep herself at the screen all day and the determination to type eight new pages. She also had the insight to realize every word she'd written would have to be trashed.

Unfortunately, concentration had been far more elusive to summon than self-discipline had been—unless she was willing to admit that her concentration had been focused solely on Cage, and the events of last night.

In a strange sense, she felt as though she'd failed some test, one she couldn't even put a name to. The thought of putting a stop to their growing intimacy had never entered her mind, not once that slow, persuasive mouth had met hers again. Not after those warm lips had cruised up her jawline and unerringly found the sensitive spot below her ear. Not after he'd cupped her breast in his clever fingers. And especially not after she'd touched him, tasted him.

A shiver ribboned down her spine. No, she'd elected just for once to feel, and feel she had. The explosion of desire had been more raw, more primitive than anything she'd experienced before. She hadn't considered backing away. Logic simply hadn't entered the equation.

Until one little word he'd spoken had shattered the spell.

She turned sharply, and nearly tripped over Oxy, who gave a startled yelp, then looked up at her with reproachful eyes. She knelt down to give him a soothing pat. She'd been a fool to react so violently to something Cage had said half in jest. Even now, she could remember his easy tone and the heat in his eyes as he'd uttered the phrase.

"You'll just have to trust me on that."

Surely he hadn't meant the words to be taken literally. And certainly her response must have surprised him, embarrassed him—almost as much as it had embarrassed her.

As if he understood the emotions churning within her, Oxy reached up and swiped her face with his tongue. She hunched her shoulder, wiped her cheek on her shirt. One little word. So silly, really. Easy to utter, but, oh, so difficult to give. She drew in a shuddering breath and gathered Oxy close. Why, then, did it feel like a personal failure on her part?

She sat there holding the dog, rocking a little, until Oxy began to wriggle and squirm out of her arms. She released him and stood, resolve forming. She'd spent the entire day wondering what Cage was feeling, what he was thinking. Was he still worrying over the investigation the way he'd been when he'd come to her last night?

Turning, she headed toward the stairs. In some odd way Cage had needed her last night, in more than just the physical sense. A compulsion that ran far deeper than simple emotion demanded she find out if he still did.

Zoey took a quick shower and blow-dried her hair. Then she dressed with slightly more care than usual, applied some makeup and went to her dresser for the locket she kept there.

Funny. She frowned, looking into the crystal bowl on top of her dresser. She wore the locket so frequently she rarely put it away, electing instead to drape it over the side of the bowl. But there was no sign of it now, neither in the bowl nor, a quick search determined, in the jewelry box where she sometimes kept it.

Glancing at the clock on her bedside table, she paused for a moment, indecisive, before turning on her heel and heading down the steps. She'd look for it tomorrow, first thing, she promised herself. Right now there was something much more pressing to do.

She went to the kitchen, took out a sack and then opened the refrigerator to examine its contents. Before she could give her better judgment time to talk her out of it, she put some food in the bag, scooped up Oxy, locked the door and headed for the car.

It wasn't until she was standing on the front porch of the stately Gauthier home that her knees began to shake. It took all of ten seconds in the still, suffocating air for dampness to form along her spine. Stalwartly, she stepped forward and rang the bell.

And waited.

She rang it again, clasping Oxy a little tighter. For the first time it occurred to her to wonder what she would do if Cage wasn't home from work yet. Or worse, if he was home, but didn't want to see her. Or even worse, if—

The door swung open and Zoey's gaze fixed on the woman filling the doorway. Surprise, and a healthy dose of awe, kept Zoey silent.

"Well?" The woman crossed her broad arms and began to tap what was surely a size-twelve sneaker. Her brassy gold curls bobbed as she swept Zoey with a look that didn't miss an inch, top to bottom. "If you're selling something, miss, I'm not the lady of the house."

"No." She was unable to say more, unable to do more than stare.

The woman's three strands of brightly colored beads jingled as she tapped more furiously. "No? What do you mean, no? No, you're not selling something, or no, I'm not the lady of the house?"

Fascinated, Zoey watched the woman's heavily rouged cheeks deepen in color. "No, ma'am. I'm—ah—not selling anything."

"Well, good, because I'm about to go home and I just don't have time to watch a demonstration of dirt being sprinkled on the carpet and vacuumed all up again. Lucky for you, too. Last salesman did that to my clean carpet limped for a week."

Zoey didn't doubt it. "Actually, uh, ma'am...I was wondering if Cage was home."

The tapping stopped. The woman peered at her more closely. "Well, of course you are. Don't know a salesperson who brings a dog with her." She shot Oxy a suspicious look. "Fact of the matter is, don't know one of Cage's women who travels with one, either. Is he expecting you?"

If there was a God in the heaven, the earth would open up and swallow her right now. Seconds ticked by. The earth remained solid. Natural disasters were notoriously unreliable.

Zoey cleared her throat. "Yes," she lied baldly.

"Humph. Never said a thing to me about it, and I can't say as I recognize you, either. You're not from around here, that's for sure. I know nearly everybody in the parish...." Her mouth made an O of discovery. "Well, I'll be... You're that writer from up north that moved in, ain'tcha?"

Oxy squirmed in her grasp, and Zoey tightened her hold on him. The woman before her—Cage's housekeeper, if she didn't miss her bet—didn't look the type to be charmed by animals, no matter how adorable. "Yes, ma'am."

The blond curls bobbed emphatically. "Don't know why it took me so long to see it. I've had my ears filled with news about you since the day you drove into this town. So you've come to sniff around my Cage?"

Zoey's brows rose and her chin angled. Cage would have recognized the frigid tone. "Certainly not." It was a moment before Zoey unbent enough to observe the twinkle in the woman's eyes.

"Actually, the way those Potter sisters tell it, the boy's got his sights set on you, but you've been giving him the cold shoulder. Never known him to put forth this much energy before on the chase." As if to discover the reason for the anomaly, she gave Zoey another thorough once-over.

She was a contained one, Ila noted, with the confidence to stare down the devil himself. Intelligence shone from those surprising green eyes and there was stubbornness in the angle of her chin. Cage wouldn't have this one falling at his feet with a little sweet talk and his effortless charm. At the realization, Ila's estimation of the woman rose. Cage wasn't family, but he was the closest thing to it, and Ila wasn't getting any younger. She wouldn't mind a few surrogate grandchildren tearing through the house while she was still around to enjoy the experience.

She swung the door wide. "Cage isn't home from work yet, but since he's expecting you, you'd better come in and wait. Mind you, now, I don't want any messes in the house.''

Zoey was almost certain that remark was directed at Oxy.

The other woman turned away and headed toward what, Zoey remembered from her previous visit, would be the kitchen. "I'm Ila, by the way. Been housekeeper here since Cage's folks moved back from Florida. Can't tell you what's keeping that boy, but I don't have the time to wait for him. Got an appointment in ten minutes to have that silly twit, Mavis, perm my hair again. Never had such a time keeping the curl in my hair before I started going to the girl. I have half a mind to do it myself from now on.''

During the monologue Ila had retrieved a huge bag from a closet, dug around in it for her keys, and continued walking through the kitchen to a back screen door. "You tell Cage I didn't make him any supper to warm up. He never ate what I fixed last night, and from the look of that sack in your hand, he's probably got other plans for tonight.'' The screen door slammed behind her, and her voice trailed over her shoulder. "Don't let me find no pet hair on the furniture.''

Then a car engine sounded, and Zoey dropped her gaze to Oxy. "That, I'm positive, was aimed at you.'' She set him down, and placed the bag of food on the counter. "Your entire future might just hinge on your behavior this evening, so keep that in mind.''

Zoey turned slowly about the kitchen, newly aware of the emptiness of the house. Not even to herself did she admit that her words could apply as much to her as to the puppy.

Eyes burning, Cage made his way through the cloaked shadows to the house. Ila must have turned some lamps on before she left, and their muted glow was welcoming in the silent, still darkness. The weather hadn't yet given in to the tumultuous rains that had been forecast, but heat lightning seared and scored the sky, and the air was almost too thick to breathe.

It was a measure of his weariness that he was almost to the front door before the sight of a car parked alongside the house registered. Slowly he backed up, squinted into the darkness. A long breath hissed between his teeth. It was too dark to discern the color, but he recognized the make. The hard band that had been forming in his chest all day loosened. The glow beckoning from the windows took on new warmth.

Oxy greeted him at the door, and he bent to rumple the dog's ears, but his attention was acutely fixed before him. Wasting no time, he straightened and went in search of Zoey.

He found her in the kitchen, a book in her hand and a soda on the table in front of her. She was seated on a ladder-backed chair with her feet curled beneath her, in one of those joint-defying positions that only women could seem to manage and men could only drool over.

Like a sneaky left jab, desire hit him square in the gut. She was wearing a white sleeveless top that made him think of the one she'd worn the first night he'd met her, but this one was softer somehow, with lace and ribbons tracing the edges. She was a breath of cool, sweet air after the mugginess of the day, a flash of blessed sunshine after the unbelievably savage crime reports he'd immersed himself in all afternoon.

Unfamiliar emotion surged through him—a simple sense of longing that was nearly staggering. For the first time, he realized how long it had been since this house had seemed like a home. Until he'd found her waiting in it for him.

Her eyes, when she looked up, were startled. She straightened self-consciously. "You may have to rethink Oxy's function as a watchdog. I had no idea you'd come home."

With effort, he matched her wary tone with a casual one of his own. "Now don't go blaming this little guy. He just hasn't learned to bark yet." The dog had followed Cage to the kitchen, and trailed after him as he went to the refrigerator to get a beer. Cage's gaze lingered on the thick, seasoned steaks lying on a plate inside, next to a bowl of fresh salad. He snagged a bottle with two fingers and straightened to face her again. Twisting off the top with a quick efficient movement, he raised the beer to his lips, grateful to have something to occupy his hands.

Zoey watched him searchingly. She'd never seen him look so fatigued, his shoulders slightly slumped as if from carrying a burden too great to bear. She had an overpowering urge to go and wrap her arms around him, let some of the tired cynicism he wore drain away.

Because the strength of the urge terrified her, she rose swiftly. "I didn't know dogs had to be taught to bark. It appears I've been neglecting Oxy's lessons." Cage was still leaning against the refrigerator, so she busied herself at the stove, fiddling with the broiler she'd found in the drawer beneath the oven.

Cage saw the nervous energy in her movements and wondered at it. "He'll discover that talent all on his own soon enough. Then you'll be wishing he could unlearn it." Thunder rolled ominously outside, followed by a crack of lightning. She started, her gaze darting to the screen door.

"I suppose we should close that."

He lifted a shoulder. "Every porch on this place—and I think it has six or seven—is covered. The rain's not going to hurt anything."

"I've been waiting for a while. I didn't realize you'd be late. I kept thinking you'd be home anytime...." She bit her lip when she realized she was babbling.

"I was involved in something." Not by the slightest inflection did he let on that he'd spent hours wading through reports of carnage and violence, and that the experience had left him weary and sick. And not for the world would he have her know the awful suspicion that drove the search, even as a part of him prayed to be proved wrong.

"I have steaks." Her voice steadier now, Zoey raised her eyes to his. "Maybe it's too late for you to eat. Or maybe you'd rather I'd go so you can be alone."

He pushed away from the refrigerator and went to her. Tipping her chin up with one crooked finger, he let his lips sink into hers, savoring her texture, her taste.

"No." His voice was soft when their mouths parted. "I don't want to be alone."

So while the thunder rumbled warnings outside, and lightning flashed to herald the long-awaited rain, Cage let himself enjoy the simple pleasure of just being near her. They broiled the steaks together, bickering amiably about the best way to cook them. When he refused a potato, they ate only the steaks and salad. The rain came, softly at first, then in a wild torrent that pounded against the windows and walls.

When he was pleasantly full, Cage sat back and drove Oxy into delirium by offering him small scraps of meat. "My mama had a custom for this kind of storm," he mused aloud, as he yanked his fingers out of the way of the puppy's sharp teeth. "The kind that built up for hours and hours and when it broke just poured for hours more. No matter what the season, or the time of day, she'd bully my daddy into building a fire in the fireplace in the den. Then the whole family would gather in there, stay to talk, read some, until it passed. When we were teenagers Nadine and I made like the whole thing was a big ordeal." One corner of his mouth lifted. "But we never have a rain like this that I don't think of those times."

An answering smile curled her lips. "Maybe that's what you need now. To build a fire in the den and curl up in front of it."

Abruptly his nostalgia vanished. He'd spent too many hours in that room last night, staring blankly into the darkness, fighting ghosts that refused to stay banished. "I don't think so." Because the words sounded harsher than he wished, he added, in masterful understatement, "I didn't get much sleep last night. After the long day I put in today, I wouldn't trust myself to start a fire, much less tend to it."

Was that a hint? she wondered. If so, it lacked his usual subtlety. All at once, she questioned her decision to wait for him. He had probably come home exhausted, and was just too well-mannered to tell her to go. "You must be tired." Zoey rose abruptly. "I'll just clean these dishes up and head home."

"You can leave them."

She looked at him askance. "No way. Did I mention I met your housekeeper?"

His lips curved. "Ila. I figured she must have let you in. And I'm just as afraid of her as you are. But tomorrow's Sunday so she won't be in. I'll do them in the morning."

She already had water running in the sink for the broiler, and had the dishwasher open.

"Or," he murmured, leaning back and propping his feet on the chair she'd vacated, "you could just clean those dishes right up." He sipped from his beer and watched her.

"It won't take me long at all," she assured him, turning from the counter to bend over the dishwasher rack, arranging the plates efficiently. With a subtle twitch and roll of her hips, she rose, turned for another handful of dishes and repeated the process. "I'll be out of here in no time."

He watched with great appreciation as she swayed and twisted, her shorts riding up with each movement as she leaned over the dishwasher, glimpses of muscles flashing in those fine legs as she straightened. "I'm in no hurry." He cocked his head consideringly and wondered if he had to choose the sexiest, most mouthwatering part of her, would it be those long, smooth legs or that sweet little butt? He tipped his head to get a different angle. Some decisions weren't to be made lightly.

One of the forks escaped her grip and fell to the bottom of the dishwasher. She gave a curse that she probably thought he couldn't hear, and bent to retrieve it.

"You can reach it." He offered the words as encouragement, paused for another drink. "Stretch on in there."

"I've got it." Turning triumphantly, she caught the wicked grin of pure enjoyment on his face and realized what he'd been up to. "You are a sick and depraved man, Gauthier."

He gave her a slow, lusty wink. "Funny you should say that. I'm feeling remarkably healthy."

She dropped the fork into the silverware holder, filled the soap container and slammed the door shut. Starting the appliance, she turned back to the sink, her cheeks hot. "I'm beginning to think that red meat is the last thing I should have fed you tonight."

"Did you have something else in mind as dessert?"

Her hands stilled in the act of scrubbing the broiler and she resisted the urge to press a wet hand to her fluttering stomach. She might be the writer, but she was more than willing to admit that when it came to double entendres, he was the master.

"The only thing I have in mind—" her shoulders jerked as a loud crack of thunder reverberated overhead "—is getting out of here so you can catch some sleep. I should have realized when it got so late that you'd be too tired for company."

One moment he was lounging in the chair, the picture of indolence, the next he was at her side. Her breath tangled in her throat as she looked up at him. He was so laid-back most of the time that it was easy to forget that he could move like a whip when he wanted to.

"I would have been too tired for company," he agreed, lifting a hand to smooth the hair away from her face. "But I can't think of a more welcome sight than finding *you* in my kitchen waiting for me." His hand lingered on her jawline, stroked lightly. "I don't think I can tell you how much I needed that tonight."

His words warmed her as surely as his touch. And when his lips lowered to hers, a candle of heat sparked to life, flickering along each and every nerve ending. Her heart began to thud.

The pressure was light, a mere whisper of movement. Then his lips firmed, rubbed against hers once, twice, and again. He savored her mouth with all the leisure and enjoyment of a man lingering over a prized wine. Or the decadent dessert he'd mentioned earlier. With a little sigh of pleasure, she leaned into the kiss.

For long moments thunder rolled overhead, rain pelted the windows, but she was oblivious to the elements. She sank against him, delighting in the feel of hard arms wrapped around her, of her breasts pressed against his muscled chest. If she'd been thinking, she might have been alarmed by how natural it seemed to be in his arms now; how *right*. But thought had danced capriciously away. Now there was only sensation.

Much too soon he lifted his head to rest his brow against hers, his voice slightly unsteady. "I believe I finally realize what Shelley meant. 'I arise from dreams of thee / In the first sweet sleep of night, / When the winds are breathing low, / And the stars are shining bright.'"

A shiver cascaded down her spine. "Shelley." Would he never cease to surprise her? "I'm impressed."

His lips brushed against her eyelids, her temple. "English lit, senior year. Mr. Gilhardy had a gallbladder attack and our sub was a twenty-something dewy-skinned college grad with high expectations and short skirts. For three weeks I was a star pupil."

She smiled, as he'd meant her to. But she was well aware that the bit of humor was meant to defuse the situation. She took a deep breath, and used every bit of willpower she could muster to step back.

"I was going." The slight distance seemed to help her head clear, so she took another step away. She looked around for the dog, which seemed to have disappeared. "Oxy?" she called. "Where did you get to? Here, boy."

The soft kissy noises she made to summon the mutt weren't particularly effective for Oxy, but Cage had to suppress his sudden savage urge to cover her mouth again, swallow the sounds. He jammed his hands in his pockets instead. One thing last night had taught him was the need for patience. Zoey had to come along at her own pace; she couldn't be hurried or rushed. Because right now, patience had never seemed more distant, he turned and went to look for the dog.

They found him curled up in a corner of the parlor, one long ear lying across his nose. A ghost of a smile passed across Cage's mouth. "Looks like he's made himself right at home. Why don't you leave him here? I can deliver him tomorrow."

She eyed the dog doubtfully. "I can't be sure he'll be this peaceful all night. He has a penchant for nocturnal wanderings, and I didn't bring any of his toys to chew on. I'd hate if he decided to chew on anything valuable. Ila would have my head."

Lightning flashed and it seemed as though the wind would drive the rain right through the windows. Cage cocked his head. "I'm beginning to think both of you would be better off right here for the night." A corner of his mouth pulled up when he saw her immediate reaction. "No need to worry. This house has about ten bedrooms, give or take. You can choose the one farthest away from mine, with the stoutest lock."

Silently she looked at him. He was telling her she had nothing to fear from him, but he needn't have wasted his breath. It wasn't Cage's restraint she was fearing, at any rate, but her own.

With an edge of desperation prodding her, she turned and went down the hall to pull open the front door. The rain came down in sheets, slanted by the heavy wind. Except for the frequent flashes of lightning, the darkness was solid. She couldn't even make out the shape of her car next to the house.

Without turning around, she knew he was behind her, could feel his breath in her hair. "There's no way I'm letting you go out alone in this." As if he sensed a protest coming, he added, "If you're set on going home tonight, I'll follow you in my car. Just to be sure you get there all right."

He'd managed to make her feel guilty. She knew he was exhausted. "That won't be necessary. It's only a couple of miles."

But he was already crossing the hall, pulling a rain poncho from the hallway closet and tossing it toward her. "Won't take me but a minute. And I wouldn't sleep tonight if I didn't get you home safely." His voice was muffled; he had his head deep in the closet.

She was being ridiculous. Already weary from little sleep and long hours on the job, Cage didn't need to be dragged out in the middle of a storm like this. And there would be no talking him out of this plan. He had an ingrained sense of responsibility that she'd only recently let herself become aware of. She took a deep breath.

"No, you're right." He straightened to look at her quizzically, a second poncho in his hand. "There's no reason for both of us to go out in this storm. I'll..." Inexplicably, her throat went dry. "I'll just...stay here for the night. That is, if your offer's still open."

There was a flicker of something indiscernible in his eye, then he turned away and replaced the poncho in the closet. "It's still open." She shut the front door and went to him, handed him the second poncho. When he'd hung it up he turned to her. "Why don't I show you the bedrooms? I think I'm going to take a page from Oxy and turn in for the night."

She nodded, then said, "Wait a second." She went to the kitchen and retrieved the book she'd begun reading. Reaching him again, she held it up. "I browsed through the books in the den while I was waiting for you. I hope that's all right."

He stared at the book for a moment, before giving her a smile that didn't reach his eyes. "That's fine." She followed him up a long, sweeping staircase that Scarlett O'Hara would have looked at home on, to a spacious hallway. The room he took her to was at the end of the hall. "You have an adjoining bathroom. If you'd like something to wear, I can get you a T-shirt or something.''

Her skin went hot. She couldn't imagine anything less practical than spending the night wrapped in something of Cage's. Something that still held his scent, his warmth. Something that would guarantee that if she got any sleep tonight, it would be filled with disturbing dreams of him.

Her gaze met his and her words were soft.

''I'd like that.''

Chapter 9

The wind continued to shake the graceful old Southern home and the rain continued to fall. But Cage couldn't blame his restlessness on the weather. It wasn't the occasional crack of thunder that kept him edgy. It wasn't the flashes of lightning that made it impossible for him to get the sleep his body so desperately craved. It was the woman down the hall from him. The one who'd probably been blissfully asleep for the past hour.

He stood shirtless on the porch that connected to his room by way of heavy French doors. The roof protected him from the worst of the rain, although the wind flung darting pinpricks of moisture against his skin. Outside he felt at one with the elements. The savage weather was a match for the frustrated emotions that churned within him.

Surely he was doing penance for some long-forgotten sin. Having Zoey only steps away and not being able to touch her was a temptation beyond description. He welcomed the occasional stinging needles of rain, the cold wind against his heated skin. But it didn't help. The only thing that would bring him relief from this fire burning him from the inside was the one thing he wasn't likely to get.

Something in the fierceness of the weather drew him. He walked to the railing, braced his fists against it. Closing his eyes, he raised his face to the rain.

That was how Zoey found him. The open French doors attracted her gaze, the man outside held it. She stopped midway into the room, the inner argument she'd been waging for the last hour forgotten. Mesmerized, she couldn't take her eyes off him.

The darkness and the lightning warred around him, first painting him in shadow, then strobing him with flashes of brilliant illumination that etched his body against the sky, before the night swallowed him up again.

She was unaware of taking the steps that brought her closer to him. Logic vanished, to be replaced by pure emotion. The trouble with unleashing her feelings, she was discovering, was that they took on a life of their own. Restraint disappeared, caution faded. What was left was as raw and wild as the storm raging outside.

He stiffened then, like an animal scenting her presence, and turned around. She was close enough to see the play of bone and sinew in his back and arms, then to note the lightly padded muscles of his torso, and the fascinating line of hair trailing into his unfastened pants. Desire chugged through her veins.

Cage blinked once, then again. But the apparition before him didn't disappear. The hand she held out touched his chest, trailed a wake of fire down to his stomach. When her fingertips paused at his waistband, he closed the distance between them with two quick steps and took her into his arms.

His lips were wet, but heated. His skin should have been chilled but it warmed her wherever they touched. When his mouth met hers, she fisted her hand in his damp hair and let the riptide of pleasure pull her under.

Yes, she thought dimly. *Yes, and yes and yes.* The inner

war she'd waged in her room was forgotten now, flooded by a sea of sensation. There was only the keen blade of desire, honed to an almost-painful edge, slicing away all semblance of control. He was as hungry as she, as fierce as the storm, when his mouth twisted over hers. Tongues battled, teeth scraped, while each strove to dive closer. She was vaguely aware that stray drops of rain still reached them; the only surprise was that they didn't sizzle upon impact with their skin.

He moved his hands up under the tank top she still wore. She was warm and smooth to the touch. He stroked her, fingers discovering the delicate vertebrae of her spine, the intriguing curve of her waist. Patience was elusive. He pulled the top over her head and dragged his mouth from hers, drank the rain from her skin.

A path of flame lingered on every inch he touched. Neither of them noticed that the grumble of thunder sounded slightly farther away; that the slashing rain was lessening to a steady drumming. They were immersed in a storm of their own making.

She arched her throat to him, forgetting the bargain she'd struck with herself to take what he offered and retain her distance. What had seemed entirely possible in the solitude of her room was swirling out of reach now. He could make her lose that carefully crafted control. He could make her *want*.

Her hand wedged between their bodies, fingertips trailing across the sculpted muscles of his chest. When her fingernail scraped his nipple she felt the hiss of his breath, the tightening of his arms around her. She made a pleased sound in her throat. She'd never before considered how much pleasure could be had in bringing pleasure to another. It was a discovery rife with promise.

Cage released the back catch on her bra, dragged the straps down her arms and dropped it at their feet. For the first time that evening, he damned the darkness. He wanted to see each curve and hollow, wanted to explore the contrast where light skin turned into rosy nipple. Since the shadows prevented that, he went on the sensual discovery by taste alone.

When he drew her nipple into his mouth, Zoey gasped, her fingers tightening in his hair. Colors fragmented behind her closed eyelids, a brilliant contrast to the surrounding night. Each flick of his tongue, each scrape of teeth, pulled her deeper into a vortex from which there was no return.

His mouth sealed hers again. She greeted it eagerly. Dimly aware of moving, it wasn't until she heard the quiet click of a door closing and the muting of the rain, that she realized they were in his room. He released her for a moment, then his arms were around her again, lowering her to the comforter he'd dragged from the bed. The down quilt cushioned them from the carpet beneath. Cage's hard body pressed her into the softness. Outside, the weather still raged. But the sensual storm had moved indoors.

Their hands lowered and battled, releasing zippers, tugging at clothing. Aided by determination and dexterity, they were soon free to touch. Damp skin glided against damp skin. Muscles jumped reflexively beneath heated fingers. Hearts thudded in unison.

They rose to their knees. Dreamily Zoey lifted her arm to his neck, only to have him catch it, press a kiss inside her elbow, before allowing it to complete its journey. If she opened her eyes she could see the doors behind him, the occasional flashes of lightning, throwing their bodies in sharp relief against the shadows. But she was too absorbed in Cage to notice. Everything else had ceased to exist.

His hands were everywhere, stroking and caressing, just a few degrees shy of desperate. He moved behind her, lifting her hair from her nape, dropping kisses there, trailing them across her shoulders. She leaned back against him, turned her head to meet his lips, reveling in the freedom the position gave him.

He buried his mouth against her neck, cupped her smooth breasts, trailed his fingers down her flat stomach and then lower. He couldn't see her response, but felt it in the way her muscles tautened as he traced the apex of her thighs. He waited for her to gradually soften against him before he cupped her damp center and slid a finger inside her.

Her breath came in whimpers, and she arched against him. Her skin was smooth and soft, and quivered helplessly beneath his touch. The evidence of her passion was brutally satisfying. He'd thought he'd known all there was to know about intimacy. A month ago he'd have sworn that pleasure was the same, regardless of the partner. A month ago he hadn't dreamed of the depths a man could fall to when he was steeped in one particular woman; the degree to which a man could want, his desire honed to a wickedly keen edge.

Zoey was no longer able to pinpoint the focus of her pleasure. Sensations were careening and crashing inside her. The unyielding muscles at her back thrilled, the faint tremors that spoke of dark and desperate needs enticed. His hands could be heartbreakingly gentle, mind-shatteringly knowing. This was the man beneath the layer of lazy affability. This was a measure of the ferocity that lurked beneath the easy charm.

She shivered, sensing danger even in the rising crest of passion. Need warred with doubt. Caution had served her well in the past. If she'd never before felt this level of emotion, neither had she worried about losing too much of herself in the process. As if he sensed her conflict, his touch slowed, became more languorous.

It was a measure of trust that had brought her to him tonight. Cage realized that, even as he felt her try to shut herself away from him. But it wasn't enough. He wanted more than she'd given to anyone else, more than she'd ever before allowed herself to give. This first time, with him, he'd settle for nothing less than all of her.

His teeth tested the rounded curve of her shoulder, and he was rewarded by a soft helpless sound she made in her throat. He explored her damp flesh with heated fingertips and felt the precise moment when she stiffened against him, surprise and pleasure drawing her up into a tight fist of need.

His whisper sounded in her ear, harsh and low. The words were lost in the roar of her blood. She twisted against him, reaching for something just beyond her grasp. And when the explosion rocked her, leaving her soft and pliant, drifting slowly into sweetness, she thought of nothing but him.

He lowered her to the blanket, caught her hands in his, laced their fingers. Then he pleasured them both by creating a moist path from her mouth to her throat, to her breasts where he lingered and savored, and then lower, his teeth nipping at her trembling stomach muscles, his tongue dancing in the indentation of her navel. Her breath caught; she twisted beneath him, sensing his intention, and perhaps even then, struggling against total submission. But when his tongue caressed her moist heat, her body once again betrayed her. It reveled in the hot intimacy, shuddered and strained beneath his teasing attentions.

He waited for her body to grow lax and weightless. He fought off the pounding in his veins, the hot clench of need in his gut. He wasn't ready to give in to the beast of his own carnality yet. There was more he wanted from Zoey. Much, much more. He released her hands, cupped her hips and devoured her.

Her breath strangled in her throat. He'd flung her effortlessly from contentment back into sensation. Her hands slid to his damp shoulders, clenched there. Her body softened, welcomed him. Wave after wave of pleasure battered her, one after another. Gone were the long fluid touches, the slow languid gentleness. In its place was a ruthlessness that was as arousing as it was unanticipated.

Greed took over—an urgent race born of hot sultry nights and need too long denied. Her fingers tangled in his hair, her hips lifted to his mouth—until it wasn't enough; until he wasn't close enough, deep enough, fast enough. She pulled at his shoulders frantically, and he raised his head from her and slid up her body, his muscles tense with tightly leashed passion, his skin damp with a sheen of perspiration.

He entered her with a long velvet stroke that had the breath shuddering out of her, and a mist fogging his brain. When he braced himself above her, he could feel his muscles quivering with restraint. He was desperate to see her face, to watch the flickers of unexpected pleasure chase across it before the culmination rocked her.

In the darkness he could see her eyes open, dazed and huge, to fix on his face. And in that moment he was desperately certain that what they shared here, right now, was a first. For both of them.

His hips lunged against hers and with each frantic movement the culmination shimmered just a bit closer. He felt her climax beneath him, swallowed her helpless cry. Her satin sheath was clenching and releasing around him, milking his own response. He fought the ending. It was too soon, too good, too much. But it wouldn't be put off any longer. With his gaze still locked on her face, the sensations slammed into him, and he surged violently against her one last time before following her in a dizzying freefall into pleasure.

When she found the strength to move, she raised her hand, stroked his damp hair. In response he pressed a moist kiss to the curve of her breast and shifted their positions. Now she was sprawled on top of him, her head pillowed in the hollow below his shoulder. He made a contented sound that rumbled in his chest, and swept his fingers up her spine and down again.

"The rain's letting up," she whispered. For the first time she realized why he'd chosen this spot to make love. The storm inside had reflected the one that raged without. The cocoon of intimacy that enveloped them had kept them safe from the ravages of the weather, engaged in their own tempest.

He didn't bother to glance outside. "A little. But it won't

be done until morning.'' He tipped up her chin and dropped a light kiss on her mouth. "If you're thinking of going somewhere, forget it.''

She shook her head, stretched her leg along his. "I don't think I could if I wanted to.''

He seized her words and interpreted them to suit himself. She didn't want to leave. A knot he hadn't known existed loosened within his chest. To lighten the feeling he said, "That's good. I'm known around these parts as a dangerous man to cross.''

She smiled against his skin. "I can see why. I saw the awards in the den when I was picking out a book.'' She felt him grow tense beneath her and wondered at the cause. "I didn't know you were a sharpshooter.''

He was silent for a moment, but when she didn't refer to any but the parish-fair awards, the tension eased from his limbs, one degree at a time. "You could say I followed in the Gauthier tradition. My daddy was a hunter, used to take me and Tanner out in the woods with him for whatever was in season. I never did get the taste for it. He and Tanner did some trapping and hunting. I preferred to practice on targets.''

It was a talent that had proved useful in his line of work. Unbidden, one of many scenes from *Hogan's Alley* flitted across his mind. The heavy ear guards to protect hearing, the outline of a man fifty feet away. Examining the target after he'd fired a round, satisfaction filling him as he realized he was still one of the steadiest hands in the NOPD. He never recalled wondering, back then, if the time would come when he'd doubt the ability he'd taken for granted for so long.

Her voice sounded in the darkness again. "I suppose the competition is pretty fierce at the annual parish fair.''

His smile came naturally, and he let his hand slide to cup her bottom. "It has its moments. If you talk real nice to me I'll let you tag along and bask in my reflected glory this

year. The fair is next month, to be held outside of Trumbel
Falls."

She was familiar with the name of the nearby town, but
had never been there. "You sound confident that you'll
win."

He lazily drew a finger down her arm, was pleased when
she shivered. "You might say I'm justifiably certain. The
chief of police won it for eight straight years until I entered.
I'm afraid that's one more thing he holds against me."

There was a suspect note of marvel in her voice. "Imagine someone not liking you."

"It is hard to believe," he agreed, investigating the hollows below her shoulder blades, "but there's no accounting
for taste." He leaned forward and nipped her mouth gently.
"As it happens, I've acquired a taste for you." His lips
stayed to linger, her flavor still on his tongue. It was startling
to feel this outrageous hunger for her when it had so recently
been satiated; frightening to experience this slow burn in his
belly that only she could extinguish. He reversed their positions again while their mouths mated, slid his hand up to
shape her breast.

"You're in my system, Zoey." His words were like silk,
sliding through the velvet of the night. "There's no getting
over it. I've passed the time when I'd want to."

How was it possible for such simple words to strike both
gladness and terror in her heart? She could feel her pulse
skitter, even as she formed her answer carefully. "I think…
Let's just concentrate on now. Can we?"

Because he recognized the layer of panic in her plea he
brushed his lips soothingly over her brow, her cheek, her
eyes. He dodged the blade of disappointment that stabbed
deep and instead focused on discovering all the secret places
that held her scent—behind her ear, the pulse below her jaw,
between her breasts.

Patience, he'd been told, was one of his virtues. As passion stirred between them again, he was very much aware

hat convincing this woman was going to take every ounce
of patience he could muster.

"Last one out of bed has to make breakfast."

With her usual morning-disposition gauge set at "surly,"
Zoey kept her eyes tightly closed and kicked in the direction
of that cheerful voice. For her efforts she received a yank
of the covers and a light swat on the rear. She rose in one
movement, ready to swing, and saw Cage, wearing nothing
but boxers and a smile, holding a cup of steaming coffee.

Only partially mollified, she took the cup he held out,
shoved her hair out of her face, and observed, "If you
haven't been told this before, it's only because people were
trying to spare your feelings. But it's a well-known fact that
everyone hates a morning person."

His smile only widened. "If it weren't for the morning
people, who'd make the coffee?"

She tucked the comforter around her breasts, closed her
eyes and sipped. Heaven. She was unaware of the sound of
contentment she made. It was several moments before she
reopened her eyes, feeling slightly more human.

"Did you mention breakfast?"

"Only that it was your turn to cook it."

"But I made supper last night."

"I helped."

Her lips moved suspiciously close to a pout. "But I'm
your guest."

"You are that," he agreed affably, leaning forward to
kiss the taste of coffee from her lips. "And if I may say so,
you're a lot better behaved than our guest downstairs."

It took a moment for his meaning to register, then her
eyes went wide. "Oxy! Omigosh, he needs to be let out
right away in the morning or else he—"

"He did."

She winced. "Tell me it wasn't on the rug."

"I can't tell a lie on the Sabbath."

"You're right." Guilt sank sharp fangs into her chest.

She pushed the coffee cup back into his hand. "I owe you breakfast." Arranging the comforter around her, she started to rise, only to find it impossible to move. She turned to see him with both feet firmly planted on one edge of the material, a cocky grin on his face.

"Where'd you say you were going?"

She looked pointedly at his feet, and then at him. "I was going to shower and then cook your meal—an offer I'm rapidly reconsidering."

"I can help."

"Good. Go get the pans ready."

"I meant with the shower." He picked up a fistful of quilt and slowly, inexorably, pulled more of the fabric toward him. Just as determinedly, she held on to her end.

"I believe I have enough proficiency in that area to handle things on my own."

He gave a mighty yank and pulled her closer. "But you don't know how to work the hot water."

Backing away from him wasn't the wisest course of action. She stumbled over the excess length of the comforter. "Something tells me I'm in hot water right now."

With one jerk he had her lying across his lap, and was laughing down at her. "Very hot water, indeed."

His lips were still curved when they met hers and her heart simply turned over. She'd never shared this with a man before, never engaged in this fun-loving sparring for fun's sake. If she wasn't careful, Cage would be much too easy to fall for. But she was, she reminded herself as she returned the increasing urgency of his kiss, a very cautious person.

He had her in his arms and was following her down onto his bed when the doorbell sounded. Sighing, he rested his brow against hers. The doorbell pealed again.

"Maybe if we ignore it they'll go away."

"Yeah, that's what they said about gangsta rap." He let out a breath and loosened her hands from around his neck, pressed a hard kiss to her mouth. He crossed to a dresser against the wall that looked to be more than a century old, took out a pair of jeans and drew them on.

"I'm coming," he mumbled as he headed down the stairs and the bell rang again. "But not the way I'd like to be." He pulled open the door to see one of his deputies standing there.

"DuPrey," he said flatly. "This had better be good."

The man's cheeks were flushed with excitement. "I sure am sorry about the interruption, Sheriff. I tried to call but there's a lot of phone lines out because of the storm last night. I've already checked with the phone company. They'll have trucks out shortly."

Cage propped one hand against the doorjamb and eyed the man with dwindling patience. "And you need to talk to me because…"

"Oh. Yeah." His Adam's apple bobbed nervously. "Chief Deputy Fisher said I should let you know. Doc Barnes had Stacy Rutherford transported by ambulance to St. John's in Baton Rouge last night. She's in pretty bad shape. Says Donny Ray tried to kill her."

The doctor came out of the patient's room and looked at the man leaning against the opposite wall. "You can talk to her, Sheriff, but she shouldn't get too agitated. And she's going to be difficult to understand." Cage nodded, stood, and forced himself to enter the room.

"Hey, Stacy."

She turned her head toward him and he swallowed hard. One of her eyes was swollen closed and her nose had obviously been broken. Her bottom lip was puffy and twice its normal size. "Sheriff."

He pulled up a chair and sat next to the bed, reaching out to gently clasp the hand that wasn't in a cast. "I know this is hard for you. I want you to take all the time you need. I'm not going to let him hurt you again, Stacy, but you're going to have to help me. You know it's past time."

"You want...a...statement." The words had to be pronounced carefully, but they were intelligible.

He consulted the form in the folder he was holding. "Doc Barnes said he found you collapsed in front of the clinic last night."

"I...ran." Her good eye closed for a moment. "I never seen Donny like that before...so full of mean and hate. I knew he was gonna kill me. He swore he would."

Cage's nerves tightened, but he kept his touch gentle. "Was he drinking again?"

She gave a slight nod of her head. "Some. He came in from the barn...had this queer look in his eye." She stopped and looked toward the table. Cage got up and poured her a glass of ice water, guided the straw to her bruised lips. When she finished she lay back again against the pillow, as if the single act had exhausted her. When she began speaking again her voice was eerily lifeless. "Donny Ray...asked if there wasn't something I should tell him. I said I didn't know what he meant. Then I saw the bag in his hand."

Cage felt a sinking sensation in the pit of his stomach. "What was in the bag?"

"The extra money you give me. And them little cards. I was thinking...I didn't want to have to go to one of them places where I don't know no one. I was gonna save up some, and if things got too bad I could run off. Somewhere Donny couldn't find me."

Tears squeezed from under the swollen eyelid and trailed down her face. Cage didn't think he'd ever seen a sight so heart-wrenching. "How did Donny Ray break your ribs?"

"Caught me by the woodpile. Staved them in with a big piece of kindling. I tried to fight back." She gestured to her cast. "He caught me in the arm."

"Stacy." Cage took her hand in both of his and waited for her to look at him. "Will you testify against him?" He could see the indecision on her face and bit back a curse. "He won't get near you again."

"Wouldn't have to be him," she whispered hoarsely.

You know how them brothers of his are. Any one of them ould do me in if I made trouble for Donny Ray.''

"I'll guarantee your safety," Cage promised grimly. "A ard will be posted outside your door for as long as you're re. When you're ready to be released we'll find a safe ace for you until the trial.''

"And then I could get far away?''

He nodded. He'd make sure the woman got clear across e country, even if he paid her way himself. "As far as ou want.''

A deep breath shuddered out of her. "Probably won't be trial, anyhow." Her hand trembled convulsively in his. f Donny Ray knows you're looking for him he'll hightail to the woods. Won't no one ever find him there.''

The full moon hung heavy in the sky. Zoey held Oxy on r lap, rocking slowly back and forth in the glider. When e car pulled silently into her driveway her heart gave a ttle leap. As Cage walked toward her, she could tell by the ay he carried himself just how long the day had been.

She put the puppy down and reached for the pitcher of monade she'd brought out with her, poured some in a glass d handed it to him as he dropped down beside her. He ank it in one long swallow. She poured him another and e curled his arm around her shoulders, urging her to his de. It didn't take much to keep her there. She'd worried out him all day. There had been grim purpose in his eyes hen he'd left the house that day. That and a sort of horrible nowing. She no longer questioned this need she had to ffer him comfort, and she refused to question the quiet tisfaction she felt at knowing he'd come to her for just at.

"Suppose you heard most of what went on last night.'' e sipped from the glass and let the tensions of the day ep out of him, a fraction at a time.

"I stopped by the Stew 'N Brew for lunch. Becky Jane led me in, and she had it 'on good account from Tommy

Lee.'" The last words were uttered in the inflection t
waitress had used.

Cage grunted, sipped from the glass. "Tommy Lee, hu
If that boy ever wants to make deputy he's gonna need
learn to keep his mouth shut."

"He didn't tell anything people weren't already buzzir
about. I ran into Fern Sykes later and she had even mo
details. That's the one thing this town never lacks."

He laid his head back against the swing and closed h
eyes. "I've never seen a woman more beat-up than Stac
was—face all bruised, broken arm and ribs. But she wa
still scared. I had to work at convincing her to swear out
statement. Even now, I'm not sure she won't back out aga
later."

He'd answered domestic-dispute calls in New Orleans,
course. Had dealt with the fear and the circle of violenc
before. When an abused woman returned to the batterer
household, he'd never failed to feel useless. Helpless.

Her hand skated down his arm, a warm source of comfo
"Sometimes we just have to figure that all we can do is o
best."

His eyes came open again, and he stared up at the porc
ceiling. "And if our best isn't good enough?" For an insta
he was no longer talking about Stacy Rutherford and oth
victims like her. It was Amy Lou Travers's image that flitte
into his mind and lingered.

Silence stretched between them. The night insects creake
and chirped in melancholy harmony. Her voice, when
came, was soft. "The day I won permanent custody of m
brother and sister was the most terrifying day of my lif
All of a sudden I was flooded with self-doubt. What if
was being just as arrogant as my aunt and uncle had a
cused? Was I only thinking of myself by keeping Carolir
and Patrick with me? The truth of it was, my relatives ha
the maturity and the means to provide for them more con
fortably."

He set his glass on the porch railing and picked up he

and, measured his palm against hers. Mildly he asked, "So it was selfishness and an overdeveloped maternal instinct that had you fighting for them?"

Her head snapped toward him. He couldn't see the flare in those beautiful green eyes, but he knew it was there. "My aunt and uncle would have stifled every wonderfully creative thought Caroline ever had. Patrick's high spirits would have been crushed for fear they'd lead him to delinquency."

He laced their fingers together. "So you made the best choice. Your brother and sister turned out okay, didn't they?"

She turned to face him fully, trying to make him understand. "Don't you see? I'm very proud of my brother and my sister, but there's no way for me to ever be sure that I did the right thing. Who knows? Maybe with the advantages my relatives could have given them, the kids would have been even better off. The fact is, there's no way of being certain. And I got to the place where I had to shut off all the questions, all the doubts, and just concentrate on doing my best. Because in the long run, that's all there is. Being able to look back and say we did as well as we could."

Her words rang in some distant place deep inside him; a place where he wasn't ready—not yet—to accept the simplicity of the message. "I wish it were that easy." He brushed his lips over her hair and drew in her scent. She smelled like springtime.

He drew a languid finger down her throat, lingered on the pulse that beat below her collarbone, and then dipped lower. "Where's your locket?" he murmured, leaning forward to press his lips to the spot where he'd often seen it nestled.

When she felt his tongue trace the upper curve of her breast, her pulse leaped, then settled into a skitter. "I don't know. I haven't been able to find it."

He raised his head, a smile curving his lips. "Maybe I could help you with that. Someone with my skills should prove invaluable in the search."

Her fingers twined in the hair at his nape. "You think

so?'' It was so easy when she was alone, when logic was uppermost and emotion suppressed, to believe that both of them could take what they needed from this relationship without regrets. So tempting to think he would be satisfied with the little of herself she was comfortable sharing. His fingertip traced the slope of her breast and with the gentlest of touches, brought her nipple to pebbled hardness.

And it was absolutely terrifying to discover the ease with which reason shifted aside, allowing dangerous emotions to surface.

"I know so," he affirmed. "And as a result of the experience I bring to investigative practices, I suggest we start the search—" he closed his teeth over her earlobe "—in your bed."

"That seems an unlikely place to look." She strove to ignore the shivers chasing over her skin and kept her voice steady. "I've never worn the locket to bed."

"In that case—" he swept her up in his arms and grinned wickedly down into her surprised face "—it's the floor again."

She laughed softly and hooked her arms around his neck. "Again?"

He brushed her mouth with his. "And again. And again."

He carried her into the house, and their laughter drifted into the night air, curling like smoke through the darkness. The sound reached the figure hidden in the distance. Night-vision binoculars were lowered. The familiar urges frothed and churned, but it wasn't time to let them run unchecked.

But soon. The figure smiled with hideous resolve—a balm to deep, twisted desires that wouldn't be denied.

Very soon.

Chapter 10

Cage looked up from the reams of printouts he'd downloaded from the computer and set down the highlighter he'd been using. He'd confined his search, for the present, to homicides that had occurred in the last ten years, and to victims who fit the physical description of Janice Reilly. And even as he started to read through the material that hadn't been eliminated, he wondered if he was wasting his time.

If so, it wouldn't be the first fruitless task he'd engaged in over the past few days. The search for Donny Ray Rutherford had yielded them nothing, despite the manpower he'd assigned it. Stacy's prediction had proved true. Donny Ray had taken to the woods, and so far had managed to elude the manhunt. The tracking dogs had been useless because the recent heavy rain had washed away any traces of scent he might have left. In any case, Donny Ray was wily enough to have used the river to end his trail.

Although Cage still had men combing the area, the search was going to be tedious and time-consuming. He was banking on the fact that Donny Ray wouldn't leave the area. In his warped mind, his violence toward his wife wouldn't seem serious enough for him to run very far.

Or maybe Cage wasn't giving the man enough credit. Maybe Donny Ray realized that the longer he stayed at large, the shakier Stacy would be about pressing charges.

If so, he'd be right. Each day that passed without her husband in custody, Stacy withdrew a bit more, got a little less certain about her actions. Cage had assured her over and over again that Donny Ray would be brought in, and he'd been sincere. But he harbored an equally sincere realization that timing in this instance was critical.

He turned his attention back to the printouts. Already, it looked as if the particular hunch he'd followed had led him straight up a blind alley. After narrowing the search, he'd combed the information for rape/murders with similar MOs, but no particular pattern was jumping out at him. In his experience, repeat offenders didn't change their style or their weapon of choice. Each had an individual preference— the impersonal power of a gun, the ruthlessness of a blade, the all-powerful feeling of strangulation. And once they'd established an MO, they might improve upon it, polish it, but they didn't alter it to a significant degree.

Which led him right back to nowhere.

He pressed the heels of his palms against his eyes. Black dots still danced behind his eyelids—a sure sign he'd been poring over these printouts for too long.

The door behind him opened, and Fisher's voice sounded. "I've got some good news, Sheriff."

Cage lifted his head and turned around. "I could use some, Delbert. What do you have?"

"Finally got a lead on the source of ether for the meth operation."

His attention sharpened, Cage asked, "You found where it came from?"

Fisher shook his head. "Not yet, but I've got a start. A

clerk at one of the last automotive stores we checked, positively ID'd one of the pictures we showed them.''

''And?''

''Said a man who looked like the photo I showed him of Donny Ray came in last winter and wanted to order a large quantity of ether. Gave the guy a song and dance about moving up north, and wanting to stock it up for the next winter so he could start his car. The clerk was wise enough to recognize the story for what it was and told him he had to report such orders to his manager. And then he said Donny Ray offered him a wad of cash to keep the transaction between the two of them.''

''Like I always said, Donny Ray's not the brightest bulb in the pack. Good work, Delbert. Guess we have a few more questions to put to ol' Donny Ray when we catch up with him. Keep Sutton and Baker on it, though. The Rutherfords ended up getting those chemicals from somewhere. Let one track the anhydrous leads and the other focus on the ether.''

''Yessir.''

Cage rubbed at a knotted muscle in his neck. ''Have you come up with anything more on Jeremy Klatt?''

A little of the jubilance went out of Fisher's expression. ''Not yet, sir, sorry. Checked with his employer, coworkers... Even his ex-girlfriends don't have anything too damaging to say about him. Unless being tight with money has become a crime.''

Blowing out a breath of frustration, Cage shook his head. ''If it was, we'd have our cells full pretty regular. Damn. Can't help thinking we're chasing our tails looking in his direction.''

''I don't know.'' Fisher reached up a hand, ran it through his thinning dark hair. ''Most times it turns out to be someone closest to the victim. I can't help thinking whoever did it is right under our noses.''

''Yeah, well, Klatt would make a helluva good suspect if we weren't coming up empty-handed on any evidence linking him to the crime. No, I think we need to re-examine our attentions in the case. I want you to reinterview the victim's co-workers, her friends, even her beautician. Ask them again about somebody new in her life.''

Fisher shifted uncomfortably. ''Sheriff, we went over those questions with them before—''

''So, do it again.'' There wasn't a snap in Cage's voice, not quite, but there was enough steel to have the other man subsiding. ''Janice Reilly dressed to go out that night to see someone. We haven't learned who it was yet. Concentrate on that.''

Fisher's face was as expressionless as his tone. ''Yessir.'' He'd turned to leave, when Cage's voice stopped him again.

''And Delbert?''

The man looked quizzically at him.

''Good job with the lead on the ether.''

A slight smile curled the other man's mouth, reminding Cage how long it had been since he'd seen one there. ''Thank you, sir.''

The door closed quietly behind the deputy and Cage shifted his gaze back to the printouts. His concentration slower to adjust. He'd gotten used to trusting his instincts when he was a detective with the NOPD. They'd saved his skin on more than one occasion. Was it possible to lose that intuition once the constant edge of danger was removed? He dropped his head to his hands, considered the question. Law enforcement in Charity had been, up until recently, a walk in the park. They'd handled the drunks, the reckless drivers, an occasional break and enter. There'd been that stolen-car ring in the southern part of the parish last year, but compared to his caseload as a detective, the work had been fairly routine. Until now.

He raised his head, stared blindly into space. He was going to have to hope like hell that a man couldn't lose instincts that had played such a large part in his life—because his sixth sense was still prodding him. His focus shifted to the sheaf of papers on the table.

And it was telling him that he'd find answers buried somewhere in that pile of information.

Zoey barely let up on the accelerator when she entered Charity's town limits. She'd been so lost in her work, the hours had gotten away from her. When she'd finally glanced at the clock, she'd only had ten minutes before she was supposed to meet Cage at the Stew 'N Brew for lunch.

There had been no time to change her clothes, as she'd planned. She'd had to be satisfied with grabbing her purse and running a quick brush through her hair as she'd backed the car out of the drive. Oxy had whined piteously when he'd realized she was leaving without him, and she knew she'd pay for the slight when she got home. The pooch was ingenious at getting himself into mischief when she wasn't around.

The diner was ahead, and she was mentally congratulating herself for arriving on time when a siren sounded behind her. For an instant she was certain it was Cage, making a spectacle for which she'd make him pay dearly. But a glance in the rearview mirror showed an official city car, not a parish one. Damn. Surely at some time in her life she had to have done at least one good deed for which an opportunity such as this would have been allowed to pass.

She pulled over to the side of the road and looked straight ahead rather than at the Potter sisters, who were peering out of Neesom's store window. There was no divine intervention in sight. Apparently God was having a busy Thursday.

She rolled down her window, ignoring the intense wave of heat. Arranging her face into a polite smile, she greeted the stern-looking policeman approaching her.

"Is something wrong, officer?" Experience had taught her that ignorance worked as well as any other ploy.

"I'll need to see your driver's license, ma'am. You were doing forty in a twenty-five-mile-an-hour zone."

Zoey handed him her driver's license and an apology.

"I'm sorry, I just wasn't thinking. I noticed I was late for an appointment and I..."

The man already had his ticket book out, and was writing carefully. "Discipline is the key, ma'am. Time is a gift. We all have to use it wisely."

The rest of her explanation slid down her throat. For the first time she noticed that despite the stifling heat, the man's crisply pressed uniform didn't show a hint of moisture. She rolled her eyes. It was just her luck to have to tangle with a superhuman law-enforcement robot.

From the corner of her eye she saw someone approaching and turned her head. Mentally she groaned. Cage had pulled his car up in front of the diner, and was sauntering across the street toward them, hands in his pockets. She'd always thought she had a sense of the ridiculous, but this was over-kill.

"Looks like you've caught yourself a dangerous criminal, Boyd." Cage bent to look in the driver's-side window, a broad grin on his face.

The ticket was ripped off the pad, and the officer handed Zoey a copy. "I've got the situation under control, Sheriff."

"I don't know." Cage straightened, and faced the man. "Maybe I'll just hang around in case she needs to be frisked. Did you run her plates? She may be wanted for something."

Zoey aimed a particularly lethal glance at him. His grin only widened.

"As I said, Sheriff," the officer went on imperturbably, replacing the pen in his shirt pocket, "just a routine traffic stop. Nothing for you to concern yourself with."

"Routine traffic stop?" Cage rubbed his chin and headed to the back of her car. "You probably caught the fact that the bulb is out in her taillight, then."

Zoey halted in the act of folding up the ticket, her jaw dropping. She poked her head out the window. "What do you think you're doing, Gauthier?"

"You know, you're right." The officer took out his book

again. Before her disbelieving gaze, the man wrote out another ticket and approached her with it. Cage, the low-down weasel, was bent over in a suspect fit of coughing.

"Now this one's just a warning, ma'am." Zoey fairly snatched the piece of paper out of his hand and jammed it into her purse. "You've got yourself a week to see about fixing that taillight. Safety should be a driver's utmost concern."

Only the fact that it was sure to result in another ticket kept her from backing over the man grinning at her through her rear window. Clenching her teeth, she slowly and carefully pulled away from the curb and parked in a free space in front of the diner.

Cage strolled across the street to meet her, and she got out of the car, her fingers curled. The police car pulled into the spot beside her. She whirled on the officer getting out of the car. "Now what?"

His eyebrows rose. "Ma'am?"

"I'm too close to the curb…too far away…my car hasn't been washed recently…what?"

"Uh…Zoey." Cage's voice sounded in her ear. She switched the focus of her glare to him.

"What?"

The policeman went by them, headed up the steps.

"I believe he's going in to eat lunch. That is—" his voice was full of laughter "—If he still has an appetite."

"Damn you, Gauthier." Her elbow jabbed his ribs with satisfying force. "Sometimes you're just too cute for words."

He rubbed at the spot where she'd caught him, his smile not dimming. Taking her elbow in his hand was as much an effort to protect himself as a gesture of politeness.

"Now, honey—" he fought to keep his tone sober as they walked up the steps to the diner "—Where's your sense of humor?"

"It'll be restored as soon as you fix my taillight."

It was, he figured as they entered the diner and found a booth, a lighter sentence than he deserved.

"I'll have the special today, Becky."

"Chicken-fried steak swimming in mashed potatoes and gravy?" Zoey sent him a reproving look. "I can almost hear your left ventricle slamming shut in protest."

"I've gotcha down, Sheriff. And how about you, Miss Prescott?" The waitress turned to Zoey, pen poised. "Gumbo again?"

Prepared to agree, Zoey looked from the expectant expression on Becky's face to Cage's knowing smile. A moment passed before resolve solidified. "Yes. Gumbo." The waitress wrote it down and turned away.

"Gumbo's always good," Cage said blandly.

Zoey narrowed her gaze at him. "I know what you're getting at, Gauthier. You're saying I'm predictable."

"Me?" His brows arched in exaggerated innocence. "I thought we were talking about Ethel's gumbo."

"There's nothing wrong with a little structure in life," she said primly. Not that there had been much structure in her life since Cage had entered it, but it was, in general, a philosophy she held dear. It wasn't inflexible to insist on control, she thought, lifting her chin. Surely it wasn't asking too much to keep things orderly, practical, with a slight protective distance between her and most of the world.

Her gaze dropped away from that laughing light in Cage's eyes. Distance, she'd found, spiraled away a little faster and more furiously each time she was with him. She smothered the chill the realization sent through her by changing the subject.

"Who was that drone to duty who stopped me, anyway?"

He chuckled at her words. "That was Charity's chief of police, Boyd Runnels."

She glanced up, interested, and turned her head to where the officer was sitting alone. "So that's your main opposition in the parish sharpshooting contest." She faced Cage again. "I'm not surprised you beat him. He's the kind of man to have technique down pat, but his kind lacks imagination.''

His brows climbed. ''You think imagination is important when shooting at targets?''

She sat back as Becky slid her soup and a steaming ''special'' plate on the table before them. ''I figure someone who knows how to think outside the lines might have an edge.''

Tucking her spoon into her bowl, she began to eat. He was slower to follow suit. She might like to keep herself held apart from the rest of the world, but as an observer she'd be perfectly suited for police work. She was a fair judge of character. He supposed that came in handy for a writer.

''Sheriff!''

He was no more than a third of the way through with his dinner when Ethel came to the booth to confront him, arms folded across her thin chest.

''I sure am enjoying your special plate today, Ethel.''

The flattery had no visible effect on her. ''You need to see to that Billy McIntire again. Folks are saying he's having one of his spells.''

Giving an inward sigh, he set down his silverware. ''Saw him just last week, Ethel. He seemed fine at the time.''

She glared at him, as if he'd just called her a liar. ''My grandsons were messing in the woods near his place, and he almost scared them to death! They come up on him and he was acting right strange, moaning and crying out at nothing. Someone needs to make sure he's all right.''

There was no doubt from her tone who she thought that someone should be. ''I'll do that, Ethel. But you tell those grandsons of yours to stay out of the woods until Donny Ray is apprehended. I don't know that he'd harm them, but it wouldn't be wise to test it.''

A startled expression came over her face. ''I'll be sure to mention that to their mother. That girl can't be thinking straight, letting them kids run wild.'' She turned half away, then back again, as if a thought had struck her. ''You might have a talk with the LaCostes, too. Their dog's been loose again, upsetting my chickens something fierce.''

To his credit, Cage's smile never faltered. ''I'll check into it, Ethel.''

''See that you do.'' She stomped back in the direction of the kitchen.

His attention shifted to Zoey. ''You've just witnessed one of the more glamorous aspects of law enforcement.''

She smiled with a sympathy she wouldn't put into words. ''Sounds like you're going to have your hands full. Who's this McIntire person Ethel was referring to?''

He went back to eating. ''Just a poor lonely fella who never got over Vietnam. You must have seen him. He mowed your lawn.''

Zoey's spoon froze halfway to her mouth. Aware that he was watching her curiously, she brought it to her lips, swallowed, then set the spoon back in the bowl. ''I can see how he might scare a couple of kids. I was a bit taken aback by him, myself.''

''He did something to frighten you?''

There was no need, she figured, to go into details that would just be embarrassing—to her. She shook her head. ''Not really. I didn't realize he was there, and I looked up, saw him standing before the kitchen window. I was startled for a moment.''

''Billy wouldn't hurt anyone, but folks around here get spooked by him sometimes. Ethel's right. I'll mosey out later and see how he's doing.'' A ghost of a smile lurked on his lips. ''I owe him one, anyhow, since he gave me Oxy.'' He reached across the table, picked up her hand. ''Now that lunch is out of the way, I have something important I've been meaning to ask you.''

Her mouth went dry, as much from the thumb he sent skimming over her knuckles as from the intent light in her eyes. ''What is it?''

''What are you doing for dinner?''

The breath that had been stopped up in her lungs slowly

released. "I'm letting you take me out. If you can fit me into your schedule after dealing with the LaCostes' dog, that is."

His smile was slow and wide and devastating. "The trick to being sheriff, sugar, is knowing when to delegate."

The McIntire place looked deserted. Cage walked up the new porch steps and peered in the screen door. He rapped against the doorjamb with his knuckle. "Billy?"

When there was no answer to his second knock, he opened the door and stepped inside. "Anybody home?" There wasn't a sound in the gloomy cabin. As he prepared to leave, his gaze landed on an object lying upon the table.

Curious, he picked it up, turned it over in his hands—a woman's barrette, delicately fashioned from wood and beads. Although it looked old, it had been cared for. Its surface was gleaming.

A footstep sounded outside and Cage looked up. Billy stared at him through the screen. "Whatcha need, Sheriff?"

Cage set the barrette down and joined the other man on the porch. "I was just looking for you, Billy." He nodded toward Lucy, the hunting dog, and the two remaining pups he'd kept. "Been in the woods?"

"Checked my traps." He whistled, and the dogs galloped over, nuzzled the hand he held out.

"Actually, I came out to see how you were doing." Cage squatted down and reached over to ruffle one pup's fur. "Heard you might be having a bad spell." His gaze lifted, fastened on Billy's face.

The other man hunched his shoulders, wouldn't meet his eyes. "Nothing new. Some trouble sleeping, is all."

Cage rose, nodded. "I know what you mean. Things can work on a man's mind in the middle of the night, can't they?" Silent for a moment, both men looked into the distance, considering specters that picked the midnight hours to haunt.

"Well, I'll be getting back to town." His tone sober, he

added, "I guess you know to get hold of me if you need anything."

The big man's hands clenched, then relaxed. "I guess I do."

Cage headed toward the steps, then paused. Turning back he said, "When I was looking for you, I couldn't help but notice that piece on the table in there. The barrette. Did you find it in the woods?"

Billy swung his head from side to side. "That was my mama's. She sure did set store by it. I try to keep it looking nice, like. The way it was when she was alive."

"You didn't happen to find a locket when you were mowing Miss Prescott's lawn, did you? A real pretty thing, all gold and fancy?" He waited for the man to shake his head, then continued down the steps. "Just thought I'd ask. You be sure and let me know if you need anything, you hear?"

Billy squinted into the sun as he watched the sheriff turn his car around in the narrow lane. He wished he'd had the courage to confess to the man; wished he could clear his conscience of at least one of the ghosts that lingered. A pup jumped up, begging for attention, and Billy reached down to lift it into his arms.

No one would believe him if he tried to explain—not even Gauthier. More likely than not, he'd be packed off to one of those hospitals again. His hands tightened around the pup convulsively. He was never going back to those small dark rooms, never going back to those doctors that poked and prodded at a man's mind until he couldn't tell the waking nightmares from the ones in his sleep.

He wasn't going to chance that again. Not ever.

Cage barricaded himself in his office and attempted to concentrate. It seemed as if there were always a million little details to catch up on anytime he stepped out of the office for a bit. And before he left the room again, he was determined to find whatever it was in that pile of computer printouts that still niggled at him with all the worry of a splinter under the skin.

Leaning back in his desk chair, he carefully began going through the information again. An hour later, his frustration was mounting.

Pushing away from the desk, he paced the room. He was spinning his wheels. He knew that, just as surely as he knew there was something—*some* thing—in those printouts that he wasn't catching. He rubbed his hands over his face. The small amount of sleep he'd been getting lately probably wasn't really conducive to conducting top-notch police work. All that had been happening recently—Stacy in the hospital and the hunt for Donny Ray—on top of their other ongoing investigations should be enough to exhaust him. But it wasn't exhaustion he thought of at the end of the day. It wasn't sleep he craved as twilight fell. No, that distinction belonged to Zoey Prescott.

She was just as much an addiction as his favored cigars that he limited so ruthlessly, just as much a need in the system, a fever in the blood. But unlike the tobacco, there didn't seem to be any way to restrict his craving for her. He no longer had the desire to try.

And she was going to be in his life for the long term. A rush of fierce satisfaction coursed through him at the certainty. He just needed to be patient, let her come to the realization in her own time, in her own way; helped along— subtly, of course—by him.

Just thinking of her brought a smile to his lips, one that quickly faded. Because he remembered something she'd said in the diner; something about thinking outside the lines. He looked at the sheaf of papers reflectively. Maybe that was his problem here. Maybe he'd get further if he stopped analyzing the crimes, and started focusing on the big picture.

Filled with a rush of renewed interest, he headed back to his chair to start all over again. He'd been concentrating on the MOs, and no particular pattern had emerged. It was time to readjust his thinking; to look for something, no matter how insignificant, that was reminiscent of Janice Reilly's murder.

He found it a half hour later—a detail slight enough to make him question its importance. Kathryn Barker, murdered six years earlier, had been shot, execution-style, in the back of the head. Her body had been found in her motel room with no other wounds except her lacerated knees and legs. The bits of glass embedded in her skin had matched the shards found on the floor of the bathroom, and were determined to have come from the bottles of the same wine she'd shared with her killer.

They hadn't found glass in Janice Reilly's knees and shins, he remembered grimly, but slivers from redwood chips. Quickly he skimmed through the rest of the reports, but could find no others that made a reference to similar injuries. He made a list of the investigating officers in each of the cases before him and reached for the phone.

As he began dialing it occurred to him, with a sense of irony, that one of the most puzzling details about Janice Reilly's murder just might lead to its solution.

The knock on the door rattled the glass in it, before the knob turned and it was pushed open. Cage looked up from the notes he was taking and continued listening to the Shreveport detective he had on the phone.

"Thanks a lot. I'm not sure where I'm going yet with this information, but I have a feeling it's gonna help. Yeah, I'll be sure to do that." He replaced the receiver and looked at his visitor quizzically. "Shouldn't you be off duty, DuPrey?"

"Yes, sir, but I thought you should be brought up-to-date first."

Releasing a breath, Cage twirled his chair around to face the younger man. It was already after six. The rest of the phone calls would have to wait until tomorrow. "You made the trip out to the LaCostes'?"

"Yessir." The younger man's face bore a sheen of perpiration, silent testimony to the fact that he'd been out in the heat, which had returned to brutal after the recent rain. "They promised to tie up their dog, but I can't see that it'll do much good, seein' as how he'll just chew through the rope again. I advised them to get themselves a stout length of chain, and they agreed to think about that."

"Well, I appreciate the update." Dismissively, Cage returned his attention to his files. Moments passed, and the deputy remained where he was.

With resignation in his voice, Cage inquired, "Was there anything else, Roland?"

"Fact is, sir, I think there might be."

Silence stretched. "Well?"

DuPrey's throat worked, and he wiped his palms along the sides of his uniform pants. He was the picture of a man screwing up his courage.

The chair squeaked as Cage settled back in it once again. Experience had taught him that this wouldn't be a quick process, and prompting would only slow the man further.

"Do you recall my suspicions about those strangers who appeared in town last summer?"

The memory wasn't a particularly pleasant one. "The ones you were convinced were here to case the bank? I seem to recollect it. Why?"

"It turned out they were only carnival workers, staying here while they worked the parish fair." The dull flush of color on the man's cheeks could have been caused by remembered embarrassment. It certainly should have been. It had only been quick thinking and fast talking that had saved them from a false arrest charge. That, and a case of Cage's finest Scotch.

Perhaps realizing that dwelling on the memory wasn't in his best interests, Roland hurried on. "Well, I learned my lesson that time, Sheriff. I surely did. That's why I came to tell you first, this time."

There was a dull throb starting in the center of his forehead. Rubbing at it, Cage asked, "Tell me what, exactly?"

"About the newcomers to town, sir. Two men, staying at the motel out on Route 20. Fairly tough-looking individuals, I've heard tell, and I got to thinking, the parish fair ain't for another month yet. You don't suppose they'd send workers this early to set up, do you?"

It was surely a phenomenon peculiar to small towns that every person passing through was subjected to the most avid interest, if not downright suspicion. Not for the first time, Cage reflected on just what Zoey had gone through when she'd first come to Charity.

Choosing his words carefully, he said, "Well, I surely do appreciate the way you stay so observant, Roland." Because the stress of the day seemed to call for it, Cage took out the lone cigar he'd tucked into his pocket that morning and thought about lighting it.

The man grinned, shifted his feet a little. "Thanks, Sheriff, but I heard about them from Josie over at the Gas and Go. You know Josie. If there's a new man within ten miles, she spots him, and to come up against two of them traveling together—she must have thought she'd died and gone to heaven."

Cage was harboring the distinct possibility that he'd suffered the same fate, only to have ended up at the exact opposite destination. "Josie's interest aside, we're just going to let these guys pass through the parish without a hassle, understand?" He pointed the cigar at the younger man for emphasis. "You just let them be."

Disappointment colored DuPrey's words. "If you say so, Sheriff. I just thought I'd tell you."

"And you have."

The deputy turned to go. "Guess I thought you'd be interested, what with all that's been going on in the parish recently. Especially seein' as how these fellas were asking after you."

He'd finally managed to snag more than Cage's irritation. "After me? Why?"

DuPrey turned back to him, shrugged. "All I know is,

Josie said they were just as interested in pumping her for information as they were in pumping gas. She got all moony eyed over how mysterious and dangerous looking they were. I got the feeling that she was put out some when she couldn't get them engaged in a subject other than you.'' Color suffused his face again and he shuffled his feet. ''No offense, Sheriff.''

''None taken. What kinds of questions were they asking?''

Roland scratched his jaw. ''First I guess they asked, did she know you, and of course, Josie said as how she did. Told them the whole story about her grandma and your granddaddy being cousins and all. She sure does seem to set store by that relationship.''

Cage had the sensation of sinking to the bottom of a very deep pond. There was no way to speed up the excruciating pace of the man's story. He'd just start over at the beginning.

''Then she said as how they asked what you did and where you lived, did you have family around here.'' He lifted a shoulder. ''Fact is, Sheriff, I didn't wait for her to tell me everything. Josie sure does take her sweet time in the telling.''

''I know the type.'' Cage tucked the cigar back in his pocket and headed toward the door. ''Maybe it wouldn't be such a bad idea to talk to these strangers and find out what's behind their curiosity.''

DuPrey followed him so closely he was in danger of entangling their feet. ''I think it'd be best if I came with you, Sheriff.''

Cage couldn't prevent a sigh. ''I was afraid you would.''

For once, DuPrey had gotten it right, Cage thought. The stranger who opened the motel-room door they'd knocked on was every bit as dangerous looking as he'd related. His dark blond hair was tied back in a short ponytail and there was an assessing look in his cool gray eyes. A faded white scar traced across his throat above the open neck of his shirt, attesting to the fact that he'd survived at least one perilous encounter.

"Evening," Cage greeted the silent man.

The man's gaze flicked to his badge. "Sheriff."

Cage aimed an affable smile meant to disarm. "Don't know how familiar you are with the workings of small towns, but I figure Charity's grapevine is as reliable as most. I heard you were asking about me. Thought I'd stop by and see what I can do for you."

A connecting door inside the room opened, and a second man entered, bare-chested, drying his dark hair with a towel. "Dammit, aren't you ready yet? I'm about to go back and try that steakhouse we passed without…" His words tapered off when he saw Cage at the door. He dropped the towel, and finger-combed his hair back carelessly.

"Sheriff heard we were asking questions about him." A long look passed between the two men.

The dark-haired man lifted a shoulder. "Better let him in, then."

Stepping back, the first man allowed Cage to enter. His gaze flicked to DuPrey, who was dogging Cage's footsteps. "Felt the need to bring along protection, did you?" There was no attempt made to mask the derision in his words.

Though his jaw tightened, Cage kept his tone placid. "Deputy DuPrey? Shoot, he just came along for the ride. Didn't you, Roland?"

The deputy looked at the two men before them, and then at Cage. "Uh, sure… I mean, I guess so."

"See?" Cage made an innocent gesture with his hands. "I bring him along for his brilliant conversational skills. He really keeps my wits sharpened." A casual smile tilted his lips. "Probably for much the same reason as you travel with him." He inclined his head toward the dark-haired man.

Curiously, the blond man's expression lightened a fraction. "Yeah, something like that."

Slipping something in his pocket, Cage said, "You fellas

seem to have me at a disadvantage. You know who I am but I don't believe I've had the pleasure of an introduction.''

"Sure talks fancy, doesn't he, Jed?''

The dark-haired man threw a warning look at his companion. "Jed Sullivan's my name. This is—'' his hesitation was infinitesimal "—my brother, Sully.''

Cage cocked his head. "Sully Sullivan? Guess your mama had a sense of humor.''

The man named Sully bared his teeth in what couldn't be mistaken for a smile. "You don't know the half of it.''

"You're right about one thing. We came to town looking for you.'' Jed looked meaningfully at DuPrey. "But what we have to say is private. I'm not sure you'd want to discuss this in front of your deputy.''

"I don't like the sound of this, Sheriff,'' DuPrey said in an undertone that was easily heard by all occupants of the room.

Scratching his chin, Cage said, "Private, huh? I'll admit to being a bit puzzled. Can't think what I'd have to discuss with two fellas I've never met before. Unless…'' His eyes widened, then he shook his head. "Nope. I don't figure you guys are part of that prize patrol that goes around awarding the sweepstakes money, are ya?''

DuPrey gave each of the strangers a thorough once-over, as if to make certain.

Sully looked at Jed. "I'm not so sure we ought to go through with this.''

"It's too late to back out now.'' Turning, Jed went toward the small desk tucked in the corner of the room and yanked open a drawer. It was absolutely the worst thing he could have done.

"Take cover, Sheriff!'' DuPrey yelled. He launched himself at Jed's back in a full-body tackle that brought them both to the floor.

"What the hell?'' Sully started toward the two of them, but was brought up short by Cage's arm against his chest. "I'll handle this.''

Sully sent him a black look and threw off his arm. "The hell you will."

They glared at each other for a split instant, before Cage's attention was diverted. "DuPrey, put that damn gun away." The deputy had drawn his weapon and was fumbling to release the catch on the set of handcuffs he carried on his belt.

"Good God," the man on the floor said, his voice muffled. "We've stumbled into *Mayberry R.F.D.*"

"I got a clear view of the firearm he was reaching for as soon as he opened the drawer, Sheriff." DuPrey had managed to unlatch the handcuffs, but due to Jed's lack of co-operation, was having a devil of a time using them. "I think I'm gonna need some help with this one."

"For Chrissake," Sully muttered. Exaggeratedly, he held his arms up in a gesture of surrender and headed for the drawer. "Just let me show you—"

"I guess I'll just look for myself." Cage stepped ahead of the man, aimed an easy smile. "If you don't mind, that is. Or if you do."

With obvious disgust, Sully turned away.

"Does somebody want to get this overeager cartoon character off of me?" There was no disguising the thread of danger in Jed's cool voice.

Cage stepped over the two on the floor and pulled the desk drawer the rest of the way out. Sure enough, there was a holstered gun lying on top of a large envelope. He picked up the gun and examined it. "Glock. Someone believes in firepower. Who's the shooter?"

"It's mine," said Sully flatly. "Along with the shield."

Curious, Cage probed under the envelope and found a flat black leather case. Flipping it open, he studied the official ID. Although it wasn't a particularly flattering picture, there was no mistaking the likeness of the man standing across the room. "No offense, son, but they didn't exactly capture your best side. What's DEA want in St. Augustine parish?"

"'DEA'?"

Taking advantage of the deputy's momentary lack of attention, Jed reared up and knocked him off-balance, then rolled and plowed a fist into his belly. DuPrey doubled over, the breath squeezing out of him. Picking himself up, Jed sent a dark look at Sully. "Thanks. A lot."

Although there was no smile on his face, it sounded in Sully's voice. "No problem."

Cage ambled over and guided DuPrey to the edge of the bed. "You'll get your breath back in a minute or so. You're not dying, Roland. It just feels like it." His gaze lifted to encompass the other two men. His voice steely, he said, "I'd like an explanation. Fast."

When it was apparent that Sully wasn't going to speak, Jed jerked his head in the direction of the desk. "You'll find your damn explanation in that envelope in there."

While the two brothers conversed in low tones in the corner of the room, and DuPrey slowly recovered, Cage opened the envelope and withdrew some documents, fanning through them quickly. Then he stopped and went through them with more care.

Propping his weight against the desk had less to do with comfort than support—because suddenly he needed it. His mouth went dry and an iron vice squeezed his chest. He felt as if he'd been on the receiving end of the sucker punch DuPrey was still bent over from. Air clogged in his lungs, and for a moment his mind went absolutely blank. Then in a dizzying rush it began to function again; questions crowded in, demanding, insistent.

"Well?"

Cage didn't know how much time had passed before that word, fraught with impatience, sounded. A minute…an hour…a week. Time had simply ceased to exist, as if they were suspended in the moment indefinitely.

Sully's voice was exaggeratedly patient. "Did you find your answers?"

"Sheriff?" DuPrey had recovered his powers of speech

and was looking at him quizzically. "Are these fellas both agents?"

"No," Jed stated evenly, his gaze trained on Cage's still expression. "We're his brothers."

Chapter 11

Zoey could tell the instant she opened the door to Cage that something was terribly wrong. Her gaze took in the freshly pressed chinos and T-shirt, the bottle of wine in one hand and the cluster of brightly colored flowers in the other. His jaw was freshly shaven, the familiar smile curled those well-formed lips but his eyes were the color of gunmetal, signaling a storm brewing.

She held the screen door open for him and reached for the flowers he held out. "What's wrong?"

"This isn't a criticism, you understand, but I hope you're not one of those women who think every time a man comes bearing gifts that he's been up to no good."

Cage strolled past her and went to the kitchen, placing the wine on the counter. She followed him and rooted through the cupboards for something that would serve as a vase.

"The thought hadn't occurred to me, but it does bear consideration." She found an old vase, dusty from disuse, at the back of the shelf and stuck it in the sink. While she turned the water on, she watched him from beneath her lashes. She remembered the first time he'd come to her, tension tying him in knots, and his unwillingness to talk about it. "Is it the case again?"

The case. He drew in a deep breath, turned to the refrigerator. Somehow wine didn't appeal to him tonight. He took out a bottle of beer and twisted off the top. "There's plenty about the case that's bothering me." The phone calls he'd completed to the investigative detectives on the unsolved cases just might result in links to the Janice Reilly murder. He didn't know whether to be elated or horrified. He put the bottle to his lips, took a long swallow.

"Charity's been a pretty eventful place today. Reckon you'll hear about it sooner rather than later." He nodded toward the vase. "I think you've got plenty of water in that thing."

With her attention diverted for the moment, he sipped from the beer again. It was hard to know how to explain the events of the last couple of hours. Harder still to examine the welter of emotions still churning crazily inside him.

Having finished arranging the flowers in the vase, she turned back to him, then dipped her head to smell them. "I didn't thank you for the flowers. They're beautiful."

He wisely refrained from mentioning that he'd thought so, too, when he'd passed them in Widow Parson's garden. He hadn't thought the widow would mind him picking some when she had so many, but he wasn't sure Zoey would be as appreciative of the sentiment.

She set the flowers in the middle of the kitchen table, and pulled out a chair, settled on it. "I'm listening."

But his focus was no longer on the events of the day. "You look gorgeous tonight. Do you realize I've never seen you wear a dress before?" It was a casual denim outfit with thin straps and a front that snapped all the way down. He figured he could have her out of it in about three seconds. Five, tops.

"I've never seen you in a dress before, either, so we're

even. And quit trying to change the subject. I'm not letting you sidestep this time, nor am I going to wait to hear it on the street. Tell me what happened.''

"What happened,'' he said, pausing for another drink, "was that my past caught up with me." He gave her a humorless smile. "Damn near steamrollered me, as a matter of fact." His words were a peculiarly fitting description of how he'd felt after reading the contents of that envelope. Court documents, original birth certificates, for each of his half brothers as well as him, and old pictures. A death certificate for a mother he didn't remember, from a long-ago life he couldn't deny. The weight of the evidence, attesting to relationships he hadn't been entirely convinced he wanted to explore, had nearly flattened him.

In the interest of time, he gave her the abridged version. Even in the telling, the scene in the motel room took on a surreal quality, mixed with a dash of the unbelievable.

"You're certain...of the relationship?''

"If I wasn't in the motel room, I was when I got home.'' The look he directed her way was steady. "The information I had in that unopened envelope at home was sketchier, but there was enough there to match what Jed and Sully showed me." Not that he'd needed the corroboration. He'd felt an awful certainty as he'd read through the documents they'd brought, an inexplicable knowing that had been proof in itself.

"Well." She breathed out the word in one long stream of air. "Not an auspicious beginning, to be sure." She watched him carefully. He drained the beer and set it on the counter, turning to the refrigerator for another. "That's what this is, you know, whether you were ready for it or not. A beginning.''

He twisted the top off the beer with a single savage movement. "A beginning? Not hardly. An ending, maybe. An answer, at last, for the questions that have plagued me from time to time.''

She waited for him to go on, and when he fell silent, she asked incredulously, "That's it? That's all this is to you?"

He lifted a shoulder, his gaze fixed on the bottle's label. "Good thing Nadine isn't around to hear me say it, but she was right. What use is it to go poking in the past? What does it do but confuse the memories—fond memories—I have of my childhood?"

What good, he wondered, came from more guilt, sneaking up layer by insidious layer as Jed and Sully had given him scraps of information about their childhoods? What good came from concluding that he'd escaped the awful slums and a drugged-out mother, while Sully had struggled to grow up with the same? That he'd been adopted by loving decent parents, while Jed's adoptive parents, from the little he'd said, must have been lacking in both respects? He'd wondered about his past, had made an attempt to explore it but the reality was fraught with complicated emotions he hadn't completely considered.

His attention shifted to Zoey. She'd risen and approached had placed her hand on his arm. "I can't imagine what it must have been like today. But I know it's got to be swirling around inside you, chewing you up. Give it time to settle in. No matter what your sister said, establishing a relationship with these two men doesn't detract from what you had with your adoptive family. It's just…more."

He stared at her reflectively, then reached out a finger smoothed a strand of hair away from her face. "It's not quite that simple."

"Nothing worthwhile is." Even as she spoke the words they hammered home a truth she was too honest to dodge. How could she suggest that he consider a relationship that might leave him open to pain, to disappointment? How dared she be convinced it was the right move for him when she herself embraced distance like an insulating force field?

Because the thought made her feel like a hypocrite, she stepped back. "How about if we take a break from every thing for a few hours? I have a proposition that you may find interesting.''

Recognizing the distraction for what it was, he leaned more of his weight against the counter and let himself enjoy it. And her. ''I'm a sucker for propositions.''

''I'm not surprised. Here's mine. I'm going to let you take me to dinner. You can wine me, dine me.... Then, if you're very, very good, I'm going to let you bring me home—'' she leaned close enough to nip at his bottom lip ''—and you can help me look for my locket again.''

His brows arched and he captured her nape in his hand when she would have moved away. ''Still haven't found that pesky thing, hmm?'' he murmured against her mouth. The kiss he pressed there melted her muscles to warm wax. ''I know some places we haven't looked yet. I'm thinking we should start—'' he nibbled his way down the side of her throat ''—in the bathtub.''

''Ah...'' Her mind turned to mush. ''Another interesting idea.'' It took a great deal more strength than it should have to draw away from him. She resisted the urge to press her palm against her fluttering stomach and instead pushed her hair over her shoulder. She was relieved to note that her hand was almost steady.

Because he was looking entirely too pleased with himself, she said, ''Oh, and Gauthier...while we're eating this evening, maybe you'll entertain a few more ideas if I tell you what I'm wearing under this dress.''

She swayed forward, whispered in his ear.

He swallowed hard and his gaze raked her form. ''Not a stitch?''

''Nothing but a few dabs of perfume and excellent muscle tone.'' Content with his reaction, she pulled away, started from the kitchen. ''Put your tongue back in your mouth, *sugar*. You're drooling.'' She'd never realized that playing these little sexual games could be so satisfying, so... arousing. But then, she'd never had the urge to play them before she'd met Cage.

Awash in hormones, he trailed after her. "You've got a streak of cruel, honey."

He was pretty sure that shouldn't be such a turn-on. But he was damn sure that he liked her idea of distraction.

The music in Jonesy's was loud, the tables were crowded and the beer was cold. "I haven't been here since my first night in Charity." Once they'd placed their orders with Lilah, Zoey amused herself by twisting around in her seat taking in the decor. "I believe I failed to fully appreciate the ambience."

Her actions were causing her dress to ride higher on her thighs, lower across her chest. He caught a few patrons at the bar gawking at her and gave them a glare. He had to fight an urge to reach over and tug up that suddenly scanty material. He was wryly aware that he'd never experienced such a compulsion with any other woman. Quite the opposite, in fact.

"I suppose you know everybody in here."

Cage slouched a little in his chair and stretched his legs out in front of him. "I'd be surprised if I didn't. I recognize most everyone in the parish, at least to nod to."

His phrasing had her lips twitching. She'd lived in Chicago her entire life and it was doubtful she knew a fraction of the number of people he did, nodding acquaintances included. His easy manner and lazy charm would attract people, women and men alike. He didn't have an ounce of that wall of reserve that was so much a part of her.

That *had* been such a part of her, she corrected herself uneasily. She wondered how difficult it would be to rebuild that wall once it had been scaled.

Uncomfortable with the thought, she scanned the occupants of the room. "Who's that gentleman in the corner? The one giving Lilah a hard time?"

Cage craned his neck to see whom she was talking about. "Oh, that's Vince Segrem. Lost his wife last year and he's been making time with anything female ever since."

She looked at the man again with new sympathy. "What did his wife die of?"

"I didn't say she died, honey, I said he *lost* her. Claims he went to New Orleans shopping and misplaced her in a mall there. She hasn't found her way home yet, so maybe that's the way she likes it."

Aware that she'd just walked into the trap he'd baited so neatly, she resisted the urge to stick out her tongue. She was very mature that way. "And that lady at the bar with the red hair? What's her story?"

He didn't have to turn around to know she was talking about Cindy Ann Putney. "There was bad blood between our families years ago, but Cindy Ann and I never paid it no mind."

"How noble of you both."

Grinning at the thinly veiled sarcasm in her voice, he continued, "There was a story around our house that only got told after my daddy had had a few and he got to teasing Mama. Seems Cindy Ann's mother was sort of lonely after her divorce and my mama thought her eyes were roving a little too often in my daddy's direction."

Zoey was fascinated despite herself. "What'd she do?"

"Well, being the refined, Southern gentlewoman my mama was, there was nothing to be *done*. Ladies with breeding certainly wouldn't resort to violence or threats. Still…" He drew the tale out by pausing for a drink. Lord, he loved the way she looked when she was listening to a story, all bright-eyed and impatient, as if she were writing it in her mind as it was spinning out.

"There was the time," he continued, "that my mama and Mrs. Putney were working together at a church picnic. They were setting the pies out on the table. No one was ever able to say exactly how it happened, but my mama had an unusually graceless moment and Cindy Ann's mother ended up with a faceful of cream pie." He paused for a moment to contemplate the mental image. "It was all a terrible accident, you understand. But I gather that was the last time

Mrs. Putney cornered my daddy for some 'business advice.'"

Zoey gave a delighted laugh. "This may sound strange Gauthier, but I like your mother."

Absurdly touched, he reached over to cover her hand with his. "She'd like you, too." The words were sincere. Althea Genevieve Gauthier had been a kind, gentle spirit, but she'd admired those with strength as much as her son did. Thinking of her summoned memories of the Sullivan brothers and he swallowed around a inexplicable sense of betrayal.

"Don't look now, but the gentlemen who just walked in are staring at you." Contrary to her advice, she studied the duo with interest. "I hope they aren't another couple you've tangled with. They don't look like the type to walk away from trouble."

He turned to look in the direction of her gaze and was unsurprised to see Sully and Jed lounging against the bar, waiting to be seated. He raised a hand, which the two acknowledged by inclining their heads.

Zoey looked at Cage sharply. "Don't tell me they're old friends of—" Her words stopped and she swung her gaze back to the men, and then to Cage again. "My, my, my," she breathed.

"The Sullivan brothers." He couldn't say *his* brothers. His mind shied away from the thought. It was an idea that was going to have to sneak up on him, settle slowly. If it settled at all.

"Lilah." Cage caught the waitress as she bustled by. "I'd consider it a personal favor if you'd seat those two fellas standing at the bar as quickly as you can."

"What in blazes are you thinking, boy?" She waved a hand toward the crowded room. "Look at this place. We've got 'em stacked three deep as it is."

"I'd consider it a favor."

Her gaze sharpened when he repeated the words softly, and she threw another glance at the two. "I'll see what I can do."

Zoey touched his hand as the woman hurried away. "That was a nice gesture."

He shrugged. "No use leaving them to stand there attracting everyone's attention. Truth is, I'm downright fearful for them if Cindy Ann gets them in her sights. Like her mama, she can be a bit single-minded."

She watched Lilah lead the men to a table that had suddenly been vacated. If Vince Segrem was annoyed by his sudden change of seating, it didn't show. He sidled up to Cindy Ann while he enjoyed a beer on the house.

"I'd like to meet them."

He looked dismayed. "I'm not so sure that's a good idea. Things between us are a bit…tense."

She eyed him, not without sympathy. "You're half brothers, Cage. The relationship isn't going to go away, even if they do." When he didn't respond, only reached for his beer, she rose. "I can introduce myself."

He practically tripped over his chair in his haste to follow her. The downside to strong women, he mused silently as he wove through the full tables in her path, was their stubbornness. There was something to be said for a woman who would smile sweetly and listen to reason.

It occurred to him then that such women had never held his interest for long. Being cursed with a gift for looking at the positive, he shoved his hands into his pockets and focused on the sway of her hips, which, his excellent memory reminded him, were bare beneath the dress. He might be slightly put out with her, but he wasn't blind.

"Gentlemen." Since she had her hand stuck out, Jed had no choice but to take it. Both he and Sully stood, looked at her quizzically. "I'm Zoey Prescott, a…friend of Cage's."

"Ma'am."

Sully took her hand in turn, then looked over her shoulder. "Looks like he's caught up with you, ma'am."

"It's a pleasure to meet his brothers." It was, to her surprise, the truth. She studied both men carefully. There were few similarities among the three. Jed was darker and taller

than the others. Sully might be an inch or so shorter than
Cage, and blond. There the resemblance stopped.

Or so she thought until she looked at their eyes. A breath
trapped in her throat. Both men had gray eyes, the shade
almost identical to Cage's. That single similarity was staggering.

An awkward silence fell when Cage joined them. Finally,
Sully cleared his throat. "Didn't see many places to eat.
What's good here?"

Rocking back on his heels a little, Cage took his time
answering. "Steaks are all good. Rib-eye is the specialty."
Another silence stretched.

It was clear to Zoey that the men could use a little help.
They reminded her of three wolves, circling warily, readying
to pounce. In an unusually social act that had Cage widening
his eyes comically, she pulled out a free chair. "Do you
mind if we sit down for a while? We could get better ac-
quainted."

Jed and Sully exchanged a glance that was as cautious as
Cage's tone when he spoke.

"Sweetheart, I think Lilah is serving our salads."

Her gaze was as direct as her words. "It can wait." Each
of the three men seated themselves. And then Zoey, with,
if not sweetness, enough charm to placate even Cage, began
what could only be termed a "friendly inquisition."

At the end of fifteen minutes there had been more information elicited, and returned, than in the entire two hours
or so the three had spent together earlier that day. Of course,
Cage justified silently, they'd gotten off to a rocky start this
afternoon, and only a woman would be able to coax Jed,
and the more taciturn Sully, to speak freely about their
wives, even getting them to pull out their wallets to show
her pictures. He shook his head in amazement when Zoey
finally gave him a smug smile and said, "Please excuse me,
gentlemen. I'll be right back." Chairs scraped as the men
scrambled up, all eyes fixed on her as she gracefully wended
her way through the crowd to the ladies' room.

"Nice lady," Sully said laconically, when they were seated again. "Wonder what she sees in you."

"You mean other than charm, intelligence and outrageous good looks?" Cage shrugged. "You got me."

With a snort, the other man reached for his beer. "Well, you are a pretty boy, there's no doubt about that." There was no mistaking the gibe in the words. "Isn't he a pretty boy, Jed? Got a face like a choirboy."

Cage studied him over the top of his bottle. "You know, I'm beginning to think it's a shame that we weren't all raised together. You could have used a pounding or two along the way to cure that attitude."

"Yeah, it's too bad you landed instead in that cushy plantation house and a big pile of money," Sully retorted. "Did Daddy's cash buy your job, too?"

Watching Cage's gaze heat and narrow had Jed intervening. "Knock it off." The man—*his brother,* he corrected himself with a lingering sense of astonishment—had a much longer fuse than either he or Sully. But something in his eyes said the explosion at its end was something to be wary of. They weren't here to exchange insults, regardless. "We didn't exactly plan to spring the information on you like we did." What they had planned was to check him out carefully before contacting him at all, but they'd failed to take into account small-town gossip.

After a glance at his brother, Sully added grudgingly, "Yeah. It's a lot to get used to." Both he and Jed at least had had some forewarning before they'd met the first time. Sully wasn't willing to give Cage Gauthier much credit— not yet—but he'd answer to his wife, Ellie, if he didn't at least give the man a chance.

"How long will you be in town?" Cage asked.

"We'll drive the car back to the airport and take planes out on Sunday."

Cage nodded and stood. "I'll be in touch before then."

Zoey rejoined Cage at their table, placed her napkin on her lap with a flourish, and began stabbing at her now dry salad. "What'd you do, cut and run the minute I turned my back?"

"It was more like five minutes. And you did the Potter sisters proud, honey. At least, I assume that's where you learned those interrogation techniques."

She refused to take offense. "What good is being taught by masters if you don't take the time to practice?"

He reached over and smoothed a finger across her hand. "I know what you tried to do, but something like this can't be rushed." He fell silent when Lilah put their steaming steaks in front of them. When she'd left he continued, "If—" he gently emphasized the word "—I decide to pursue any kind of relationship with...the Sullivans, it's going to take some time. Some careful consideration."

Her voice softened. She knew what it was to take things slowly and cautiously. "Just so you give it consideration."

The front door of Jonesy's suddenly burst open and several men entered, their voices raucous. Elbowing each other and guffawing loudly, they made places for themselves at the bar and called for service.

Cage didn't have to turn around to recognize their voices. "Perfect," he muttered. Deliberately, he sawed at his steak, brought a piece to his mouth. "This isn't exactly the evening I had planned for us."

She was frowning over his shoulder. "Does it always get this rowdy in here?"

"It does when the Rutherfords come to town."

Her fork paused halfway to her mouth. "The ones who shot at your house?"

Imperturbably, he continued eating. "I expect so. They're like rats—like to travel in packs." He glanced up, recognized the look in her eye and uttered a warning. "Don't even think about it."

With effort, she returned her attention to her meal. "What?"

"Save the innocent act. If you're planning on going up there...saying anything..." Just the thought sent a cold chill down his spine. He didn't want Zoey anywhere near that clan, and especially not when they'd been drinking. Even sitting across the room was too damn close. "I could get Lilah to wrap up our steaks. We could finish them at home."

"And pass up the chance to dance with you later?" She nodded at the couples who were moving about the tiny dance floor in front of the jukebox. "No way."

"All my best moves are better suited for privacy."

Wanting to smile, she brought her wineglass to her lips. "I'll be the judge of that. I like to be very...thorough...in my research."

He had, she discovered later, more moves than she'd expected. He guided her around the postage-stamp-size dance floor with a fluidity that spoke of practice. The crowded space forced them to dance close. The heat of his gaze urged her even closer. She rested her head against his chest, let her eyelids droop. She could hear his heart thudding in her ear, feel the subtle play of muscles beneath his skin. He had one hand at the base of her spine, lightly caressing. The fingers of his other hand were wrapped around her palm, occasionally brushing against her bare shoulder. Molten warmth suffused her veins and every pulse point jumped in time to the song's backbeat. She was aware that they were doing little more than swaying together. She was also aware of an intense desire to be alone with him.

She opened her eyes, tipped her head back, and saw her desire reflected on his face. Her heart stuttered in her chest. Without a word, they turned and began making their way toward the door.

They were no more than halfway when a voice rang out, "Well, lookee, here, boys, it's the high-and-mighty sheriff of St. Augustine parish."

Zoey glanced at Cage, concerned when his face hardened. "Let it go. They're all as drunk as skunks."

He might have been able to do as she advised. He'd never know—because the next thing that came out of Lonny Rutherford's mouth had his fingers clenching. "Don't blame him for leaving early. I wouldn't mind going home and plowing into that one myself." Shoulders set, Cage turned.

"Go on outside and wait in the car, Zoey."

She didn't know whether to be outraged or amazed at the order. "Not unless you come with me."

He seemed not to have heard her. Sauntering closer to the bar, he faced four of the Rutherfords, all cackling at their brother's witticism. "I believe I must have misunderstood you, Lonny. Even low-down scum like you know better than to talk like that about a lady. But seein' as how you're probably under a lot of stress and all, lately, I'm going to allow you the chance to apologize."

Lonny snorted and spat on the floor. "Stress? What stress?"

"Well, there's your younger brother still in jail. Your worthless other brother on the run. Takes a miserable excuse for a man to pound on a woman, doesn't it?" The gaze he flicked over the group was derisive. "Of course, that's about what I'd expect from your family."

His words effectively wiped the grin from Lonny's face. It was replaced by a mask of pure mean. "Both of them was your fault, Gauthier. First you framed Carver, then you poked your nose into Donny Ray's business, too. What goes on between a man and his wife ain't no one else's never mind."

"It is when that man is a cowardly drunk who uses his wife for a punching bag." With the smell of trouble in the air, the patrons at the bar sidled away, most choosing a place across the room with a good vantage point.

Zoey watched money exchange hands and realized with amazement that some of the men were betting on the outcome of the altercation. Determinedly, she moved forward. "Cage, please take me home now."

Without turning his head, he said mildly, "Zoey, if you take one step closer, I'm going to be mighty put out with you."

Strong hands captured both of her elbows, guiding her

away from the bar. Looking up, she was relieved to see Jed and Sully. "Thank God you're still here. Let go of me and get Cage out of this place before somebody gets hurt."

They deposited her in a safe corner and turned back to the dispute. "Doesn't look like that's going to be possible, ma'am."

She looked at Jed impatiently. "Of course it's possible—"

"You've been asking for this for a long time, Gauthier." Lonny's words had her attention snapping back to Cage. The four men had pushed away from the bar and were slowly encircling him. "It's about time you found out what happens to people who mess with us."

Cage ducked the fist that Lonny sent his way and punched the man twice in the gut.

"Nice move," Jed said in an aside.

"Not bad," Sully agreed.

Astonished, Zoey yanked at their sleeves. "What on earth is wrong with you both? Get out there and put a stop to this!"

As Lonny doubled over, another Rutherford spun Cage around and sent a right jab into his face.

Sully winced. "That's gonna leave a mark."

"You imbeciles!" Zoey seethed. She pushed at them both, but they were as immovable as brick walls. "Do something!"

Jed glanced at Sully. "Care to make a little wager?"

Sully dug into his pocket for a bill. "Twenty says they wipe the floor with him."

Jed watched consideringly as a third Rutherford jumped on Cage's back with his forearm pressed across Cage's throat. "Okay, but you have to give me two-to-one odds. There are four of them."

"Men! You're all morons!" Zoey pushed between them and started toward the fray. Four hands grabbed for her, pulled her back.

"Now, ma'am, that's certainly no place for a woman."

As they watched, Lonny recovered his breath and motioned to his brothers. Two of them wrestled Cage's arms behind his back and endeavored to hold him still while Lonny wound up. Cage let the two men take his weight and kicked out, catching the eldest Rutherford square in the chin before he could land the punch. He dropped like a giant redwood.

Jed rubbed his jaw. "You know, I think Cage probably *could* have rearranged your face for you if we'd grown up together."

Sully was offended. "If he was that good, this would be over already."

"When this is over, I'll rearrange both your faces."

The two men knew when to be selectively deaf. They pretended not to hear Zoey's gritted comment.

He put up a damn good fight, Sully thought, as one man was sent flying over Cage's back. But it was easy to see he was tiring, and with three opponents still in the brawl, there were always fresh reserves to rush him. Apparently, the same thought had occurred to them—they fanned out and approached him from all sides, pouncing at the same time, sending Cage crashing across a table. They were on him at once, fists flying.

"Well, shoot," Jed said finally. "Now they're just piling on."

"Nothing sporting about that."

The two brothers looked at each other. Zoey gave a strangled cry and their attention returned to the fray. One of the Rutherfords had picked up a chair.

One second Sully was in front of her, and the next he was tackling the man, knocking the chair to the floor and sending a fist into his face. When a second body landed hard on top of Sully, he was rolled over. His short jab snapped the other man's head back. Jed waded into the fight, evening out the numbers. He focused on the Rutherford doing his best to strangle Cage, and left Sully to ward off the one rushing toward them with a broken bottle.

By the time the sirens in the distance had become uniforms rushing through the door, the floor was littered with crushed glass and crumpled bodies. Cage, Jed and Sully picked themselves up and leaned against the bar.

"Looks like a bloodbath happened in here." Deputy Baker flipped over one unconscious Rutherford and handcuffed him. "Want to file the report tonight, Sheriff, or wait?"

Cage put his fingers to his throbbing jaw. "I think I'll wait until tomorrow. You and Morris take some statements, get these guys locked up. They're going to be guests of the parish again."

He grinned at Sully, but carefully. "I do want you to know, son, I appreciated not having to deal with that chair coming at me."

Sully touched his right eye, which was rapidly swelling shut. "Well, it was looking kinda unfair by that point." A tinge of admiration entered his voice. "But that one you sent flying over your back? Pure poetry."

Cage clapped them both on the shoulders. "Did you see Jed here trip Garrett and send him toppling into Marvin? Looked like human bowling."

One corner of Jed's mouth curled up. The other side was split and bloody. "You really owe me for the guy with the chokehold on you. I think he had to be knocked unconscious to set you loose."

A quiet voice laced with latent danger interrupted their laughter. "Well, isn't this a touching picture of male bonding."

All three of them straightened when Zoey approached them, and shuffled their feet self-consciously.

Her arms were folded across her chest to keep herself from reaching out and knocking their heads together. "If I'd known all it would take was some gratuitous violence to get you three relaxed, I would have beaten you silly earlier this evening."

She looked ferocious enough to do it, too. Unfortunately,

her stance and words reminded Jed so much of his wife, Julianne, that he smiled again. It was a mistake.

"You!" She approached him. "You're still practically a newlywed! What will your wife have to say when you come home all bruised?"

He cleared his throat and strove for a straight face. "Pretty much what you said, ma'am."

"You're the oldest of the three Sullivan idiots, aren't you?" Her glare dared him to disagree. He wasn't foolish enough to do so. "It's not too late for you to set an example."

"And as for you!" When she whirled on Sully, he had to force himself not to take a step back. He wasn't used to wild-eyed outrage and tongue-lashing women. Ellie wouldn't have scolded. Not much, anyway. But her silent disapproval would have had him groveling within minutes. "You're a federal agent! Your superiors might have something to say about you brawling in a roadhouse with a bunch of redneck hillbillies."

"Well, I think they'd understand once I explained...." The words dried up in his mouth when she pinned him with a look. "I guess you're right, ma'am."

If the meek tone was meant to pacify, it failed miserably. Her focus on Cage now, she stepped forward, shoved her face close to his. "And *you* are the *sheriff*." The words were measured. Her temper wasn't. "You are supposed to symbolize law and order in this parish. What are people going to think when they hear about you resorting to violence?"

He'd never seen her look more beautiful. "Isn't she the sweetest thing?" His tone had his brothers exchanging a look. Cage recognized the instant the heat in her eyes turned to flame and he held up his hands placatingly. "Now, honey, remember, violence isn't the ans—" The breath whooshed out of him when her fist rammed into his belly. "Good one," he said weakly, his breathing strangled. "I think we could have used you in the fight, after all."

She straightened, slightly more calm. ''You three have ten minutes to get to my house so I can clean you up.''

''But I drove,'' protested Cage.

She reached into his pocket, withdrew the keys. ''I'm riding alone. If you were in the car with me, I'd be tempted to run it into a tree.''

He rubbed at the lingering ache in his stomach as she swung away from them and marched toward the door. His voice was marveling. ''She sure is something, isn't she?''

By the time she'd sent Sully and Jed back to the motel, bandaged and holding ice packs to their wounds, she'd cooled off a little—enough that she fussed a bit over Cage, made him remove his shirt so she could check his ribs. She wasn't sure what broken ribs looked like, but he didn't flinch under her gentle examination. As a matter of fact, as she watched his face for signs of pain while she trailed her fingers up and down his sides, all she saw was…ill-concealed pleasure.

She scrambled upright and stifled the urge to smack him. He tapped his lips. ''It does hurt here.''

''Not as much as it could,'' she threatened meaningfully.

Turning away, she gathered up the boxes of bandages, towels and the container of ice. He was silent as she cleaned up the kitchen, content to watch her for a time. She'd been glorious in her ire, but he'd recently learned the folly of saying so out loud. When there was no longer anything left to put away or scrub he took a risk and spoke. ''How mad are you?''

She threw him a look that softened slightly when she saw him holding ice to his jaw. ''Very.''

''You can hit me again if it would make you feel better.''

The words, delivered in that teasing tone, summoned a surge of embarrassment. She had never, in her life, hit anybody before, had never contemplated the volcanic emotion it would take to do so. Even when she'd learned the depth of Alan's betrayal, she'd done no more than plot revenge, made sure he was punished to the maximum extent for his crimes.

Opening the floodgates to emotion, she was finding, could be downright dangerous.

She lifted a shoulder. "I think there's been more than enough violence for one evening, don't you?"

"My position, exactly. I was wondering if you would mind me staying here tonight." He strove for an innocent expression. "Could be I'm concussed."

"I'm sure your head is much too hard for that." But she did wonder about the possibility. "Maybe it wouldn't hurt for Doc Barnes..." The panicked look he gave her had her weakening. "Well, it probably would be better if you had someone to check up on you during the night."

Better, he agreed in smug silence, for both of them. He got to his feet, swayed a little. Immediately she was at his side.

"Where are you going?"

He set the ice on the table. "I'd like to take a shower. Wash the stench of Rutherfords off me."

She could understand the sentiment so she helped him up the stairs, her arm placed carefully around his waist. "Careful," she instructed. "If you feel dizzy, just lean on me a little."

He did so, for the sheer pleasure of turning his face into her hair and inhaling the gut-wrenching fragrance that always lingered there. She guided him into the bathroom and turned on the shower. Then she busied herself bringing out towels and a washcloth.

"Okay." She set the items down, scanned the room. "Is there anything else you need?"

"Just you."

Her gaze flew to his and she stood still while he closed the distance between them. Framing her face in both of his hands he pressed a gentle kiss to her lips. "You're all I need, Zoey. All I want. I guess that should scare me half to death. I know it does you."

She moistened her lips, unable to look away from his smoky eyes, the intensity of his expression. "This is still new to me."

He ruthlessly suppressed a surge of disappointment, and nibbled his way along her jawline. "I'm just asking you to give it a chance."

Somewhere in the recesses of her mind where thought was already dimming, reason fading, she knew what he was asking for, and a familiar panic circled. But she didn't want to combat the fear and paralyzing doubt right now. With his lips cruising her face, his arms tight and strong around her, she wanted to wrap herself in that cocoon of intimacy that wove so quickly between them; to give herself up once more to swamping sensation.

She gave a little gasp as he released the snaps on her dress in one sneaky movement and pushed the straps of the garment down her arms.

"Two seconds." There was fierce satisfaction in Cage's voice. "I've been wanting to do that all night."

Staggered and aroused, she pressed her bare breasts to his chest, eyelids closing at the sudden rush of pleasure. Her hands wedged in between their bodies, fighting to release his pants. They broke apart for a second to dispense with their remaining clothing and then he caught her in his arms, guided her backward into the shower.

The stinging needles of spray were hot, sending shivers over her skin before it adjusted to the temperature. Cage's mouth was heated, too, and avid as it roamed her throat, her shoulders, following the tiny rivulets that cascaded down her. He closed his teeth over her nipple then, and drew deeply from her.

Her knees weakening, she leaned more fully into him. The sinews of his neck and shoulders were taut and straining beneath her fingers. She slicked her hands down his wet back to his hips, and kneaded the tightly bunched muscles there. His big body jerked helplessly against hers when she trailed her fingers lower, cupping his masculinity.

He raised his head, one hand shoving the wet hair back from his face. His expression was pagan; possessive. The raw emotion she saw there should have frightened her. Instead, she reveled in the fierceness of his need, a response that was equal to her own.

Lifting her with his hands beneath her bottom, he pressed her against the wall of the shower, wrapping her legs around his waist. She stiffened. The unfamiliar position left her open, exposed, and totally vulnerable. She clasped her arms more tightly around his neck, and their gazes fixed on each other.

He entered her with a slow, sure stroke that had them both moaning. He paused, buried deep inside her, and rested his brow against hers. "This is more, Zoey." The words she'd used earlier that evening came back to her, took on new meaning. "You and me."

Withdrawing from her a little, he surged again, his hips slapping against hers. Her vision hazed. She clutched him tighter. There was no room for thought, nothing between them but the pleasure crowding in, the sound of their mating, the feel of wet skin against wet skin. The sensations spiraled wildly, careening and cascading inside her with every thrust.

He worked his hand between their bodies, touched her where she was exposed and throbbing, and her hips twisted, pistoned against his frantically. They crested together, their labored breaths mingling, fingers clutching.

The water cooled long before their passion did.

Chapter 12

Flickers of candlelight waved and danced in the dark room, illuminating the couple in the tub. Zoey sat propped against Cage's chest, her head resting on his shoulder, sipping from a glass of wine. She had no idea what time of night it was; it didn't matter. Time had ceased to exist.

Cage's hand brushed her breasts in an absent caress. "I think I've died and gone to heaven."

The purely male satisfaction tinging his voice made her lips curve. "Somehow I doubt you'd arrive there without first doing some serious penance."

He bent forward and nibbled the cord at the side of her neck. "Honey, you're not still harboring a grudge over that little wager we made, are you?"

She pinched his leg, just hard enough to draw a wince. "Next time I'll know better than to be hoaxed into playing a shell game with an accomplished con man. Where'd you learn to bait and switch like that?"

One of his hands slid down her thigh and up again. "Tanner and I never missed the carnival in Trumbel Falls. The old guy who ran the game was an expert. I paid attention.''

It had been a combination of curiosity and competitiveness that had drawn her to accept his bet. Since the thought of losing never occurred to her, she hadn't been discouraged by the prize he'd named. In fact, the idea of one of them being a 'slave' to the other for the rest of the night had been too tantalizing to pass up.

Her neck arched, allowing him better access to the spot behind her ear that had never been sensitive until he'd found it. He'd been an obnoxious winner, of course, insisting first on popcorn and sodas, then, after they'd both been stuffed, suggesting a full-body massage. That had turned out to be an exercise in mutual gratification, since having free rein to concentrate on his body had been as arousing for her as it had for him. And there had been no doubt he'd been aroused. Being a fair-minded man, he'd reciprocated, and their desire had re-ignited.

By the time he'd requested they share a bath, the hot water had recovered, but their bodies hadn't. She felt completely boneless as she relaxed against him, a sensation that had little to do with the wine, and everything to do with Cage.

He took the wineglass from her, sipped, and handed it back. ''I'm thinking we can just stay in here indefinitely. As long as the hot water holds out, I don't see a blessed reason why we ever have to move out of this tub.''

She allowed herself a moment to consider the tempting possibilities. ''It would take a while for anyone to come looking for me. But how long do you think you can be absent before a search party is sent for you?''

His mouth skimmed her shoulder, his tongue dancing over the curves and hollows. It was a moment before he responded, regret lacing his words. ''I'm usually at the office by seven. I'd give them until seven-thirty before they track me down. And of course, the second place they'd look for me is here.''

His words gave her pause. "You think so, do you?"

"I know it. We were seen dining together at Jonesy's, after which we were dancing close while you gazed adoringly into my eyes." Though she made a rude sound, he went on. "We left together so you could lovingly bandage my wounds…"

"You've got a gift for revising history. The way I remember it, we left separately."

"But obviously with the same destination in mind."

"How about the punch in the gut I gave you?" she asked sweetly. "Does that factor into the conclusion at all?"

His voice was dismissive. "Window dressing. Come to think of it, maybe no one will look for me until noon. We were obviously a couple intent on make-up sex. Everyone knows that can take all night and half the next day besides."

She choked on her wine. "Is there some small-town handbook I should be reading? Something that will clue me in on these mutations of common sense that pass for customs here?"

"Actually, there is." When she offered him the wineglass, he declined. He enjoyed having his hands free. His fingers slid down her sides, curled around her hips. "I've added a chapter or two myself along the way."

"I can imagine which ones." His caressing hands leeched strength from her muscles, and fired a frisson of pleasure along her spine. She no longer marveled at how easily his touch restoked her passion. Her automatic response would have terrified, if she wasn't becoming certain she wielded a similar power over him. For a woman who'd never given much consideration to her own femininity, the knowledge was heady.

"Maybe I'll add an entry to that handbook myself." He made an interested sound, while nibbling his way down her sensitive throat. "One that dictates a day off for a sheriff who performs heroics in his off-duty hours."

That had him lifting his head, a smirk sounding in his voice. "Heroics? Well that's a real sweet way to refer to my love-making, sugar…'' The pinch she gave him then had him hissing in his breath. She was dangerously close to a highly sensitive area. ''Ah…I guess you meant me taking on the Rutherfords, didn't you? As I recall, you referred to those actions a bit differently earlier tonight.''

She guided his mouth back to the spot he'd abandoned. ''Well, it's not my opinion, obviously, but the public might be thankful to have the parish scourged of the Rutherford clan, even for a few days. As a matter of fact,'' her voice held a teasing lilt, ''when you bring in Donny Ray you'll probably earn another medal to hang on your wall, Gauthier.''

The silence that followed her words was physically palpable. She could feel tension pierce his limbs. It permeated the air, turning it thick with unspoken regrets, none of which she understood. He lifted his head, and the air chilled the area his lips had warmed. An involuntary shiver raced over her skin. ''Cage?''

She tried to turn to look in his face, but he looped his arms around her waist, keeping her stationary. It would be easier, he expected, to tell her if he didn't have to look at her while doing so. Easier, because he didn't know if he could bear to watch pity turn to disappointment when she found out just how far from a hero he really was.

''Heroics is a funny word. There were some in New Orleans who applied it to me a couple of years ago. It's never sat right with me.''

She reached for his hands, linked her fingers with his, then pulled their arms more tightly around her. She couldn't have expressed her feelings more eloquently.

He rested his chin on her damp hair. ''There was a case I was working for a few months. Young women were turning up missing within a twenty-mile radius within New Orleans. Never found any bodies, but it was plain the disappearances were linked. The kidnapper wasn't particularly clever, just lucky for a time. His luck ran out. We got a description, discovered his identity, and began closing in on him. Five women had been snatched from their families; it was a high-profile case in the city." High profile didn't begin to describe the relentlessness with which Cage and his partner had hunted for the man. Concern in the department had risen in accordance with the number of victims. A task force had been assigned and Cage had made it a personal promise that the perpetrator would be caught before he claimed another victim.

He rubbed his thumbs lightly along the soft skin of her palms. The sensation helped center him somehow, pulled him back from the abyss his memory was approaching. "My partner and I tracked him to an abandoned warehouse. We called for backup, but we couldn't wait for the other units to arrive." They hadn't dared wait when the screaming had started, the bone-chilling, terror-filled shrieks. They'd entered the building and confronted a hellish scene that still revisited in Technicolor reruns in his dreams.

His voice, when he continued, was hoarse. "Colby Neesom was a serial rapist who fancied himself something of a collector. Got the idea of setting up his own personal harem. The women…he kept them naked, bound and gagged when he wasn't savaging them. When we broke in he was attacking Amy Lou Travers at knifepoint." He stopped for a moment as the crashing waves of memories engulfed him—the wide-eyed shock in the eyes of the women when they'd seen them, the terror and hope warring in the eyes of Amy Lou as the scene unfolded.

As if sensing the horrible brutality that was replaying in his mind, Zoey brought his hands to her lips, pressed a kiss to his knuckles. The sweetness of her action was so at odds with the scene he was immersed in, he felt a moment of vertigo, lost between two worlds. "Neesom pulled Amy Lou in front of him and put the knife to her throat. Kept telling us she'd die before we could get a shot off. But he was a bit taller than she was; part of his forehead was visible behind her. Only a couple of guys in the department could have made that shot. I was one of them."

She knew, without his saying it, that what had happened that night still haunted Cage. She could hear the regret throbbing in his voice, recognized the unspoken pain that still lingered. "It was a horrible position for you to be placed in."

He recognized the solace she was trying to offer, but wouldn't, *couldn't* accept it. "More horrible for those women, I expect. Most horrible for Amy Lou. Because I hesitated, only for an instant, although it seemed longer. Tried to weigh whether taking the shot was worth the risk to the victim; to decide if there wasn't some way to bring an end to it without bloodshed. When I saw Neesom's fingers tighten on the knife, I pulled the trigger. He'd plunged the knife into her throat a fraction of a second before the bullet hit him."

The breath clogged in his lungs as he watched the scene unfurl in a mental movie fixed in slow motion; watched as the impact from the bullet blew away part of Neesom's brain; saw Amy Lou's body crumple; watched himself catch her, hoping that most of the blood on her belonged to her attacker.

And saw, once again, Amy Lou Travers die in his arms; read the condemnation for his hesitation in her lifeless eyes.

Zoey pulled at his arms to free herself, and twisted around in the tub until she was astride him. Both hands slid up to cup his jaw, and her lips brushed his with exquisite gentleness. In contrast, however, her voice was fierce. "Don't you dare blame yourself for her death, Cage. What kind of man would you be if you hadn't weighed her safety when considering that shot? Lay the blame for Amy Lou Travers's death squarely where it belongs—with her killer."

He rested his forehead against hers, his arms going around her to hold her tightly. "Blame's a funny thing, honey. It doesn't shift around where you'd like to put it. It sticks where the doubt's the strongest."

"Then that's where you start." Her lips went to his eyelids, his cheeks, that straight arrogant nose. "You said it yourself. Few could have made that shot. Yet you did, saving four women. Let it be enough." The words were whispered against his mouth, her lips a fraction away. "Let go of the doubt, Cage."

When her mouth settled over his he slid a hand up to her nape, cupped her head in his palm. He returned her kiss with all the emotion that still churned and frothed inside him. Minutes later, his attention focused on the woman taking him slow and deep inside her, he felt a glimmer of peace that had long eluded him.

And if it wasn't accompanied by a marginal lessening of guilt, it was, at least, a celebration of life. He'd accept that much for now.

Having decided his shirt was a lost cause, Cage walked downstairs wearing only his chinos. He needed to go home and change before work, anyway. So it was a good thing that he'd awakened in Zoey's bed alone, right? And that he'd soaked away the aches that were naggingly making themselves known this morning, also alone.

But no amount of convincing could make him resent his solitude any less. It hadn't taken him long to get used to the feeling of having Zoey sprawled out beside him. Or over him. Or beneath him. He tucked the erotic thoughts away. For the first time he was uncomfortably aware that there must have been a woman or two in his past who'd felt just as cheated when they'd awakened after he'd left during the night.

His daddy had always said, "What goes around comes around." His relationship with Zoey proved the phrase true. The first time he'd been the one to want more from a woman, he'd chosen one who was wary about taking it; terrified about giving it. But the connection between them was too real to deny. Last night had only intensified it. It was past time Zoey accepted it, as well.

He heard her voice then in the kitchen, and padded softly in the direction of the sound. At first he thought she was talking to Oxy, but as he neared, it became apparent she was on the phone.

Planning to swipe a kiss on the way to the refrigerator, he was halted in his tracks by the one-sided conversation floating toward him.

"That's great, Mark. I'm glad you liked it." There was silence again, then she laughed delightedly. "From your lips to the publisher's ears." There was another pause. "Just how long a book tour are you planning, anyway? That's a lengthy time to live out of a suitcase. Well, we can iron that out when I get back to Chicago."

She continued to speak, but Cage stopped listening. Sheets of ice settled over his skin, a layer at a time. She was planning to go back to Chicago. There was no doubt about it. Maybe not for a month or two, but it was definitely on her mind. Leaving Charity.

Leaving him.

The frigid lance of pain that pierced him had the bitter sting of betrayal. He found it wasn't to his liking. It was easier, far easier, to feel anger.

She looked up then, saw him standing in the doorway. "I'll talk to you later, Mark. Let me know how negotiations go." She hung up the phone and strolled over to Cage, slipping her arms around his waist and kissing his unshaven chin.

"You were sleeping so soundly I thought it best to leave you be while I made coffee."

"And a phone call." Unhooking her hands, he set her away from him, went to the cupboard for a glass. "Who's Mark?"

Puzzled by his attitude, she watched as he poured himself some orange juice. "My agent. He left a message for me on my machine last night. He had the greatest news." Wonder entered her voice. "He's got offers from three publishing houses for the book I'm writing. We haven't settled on one yet, but they're all talking book tours, astronomical advances— What's wrong?"

He leaned against the counter and drank the juice. It wasn't a good choice for a throat that already felt tight and raw. "Sounds big. How soon do you leave?"

Comprehension coursed through her, and she chose her words carefully. "The book isn't even done yet, Cage. I haven't really thought that far ahead."

The smile he aimed was devoid of humor. "That's kind of the problem, isn't it? You're not thinking about much of anything. Not concerning us, anyway."

"That's not true." Her hands slipped into the pockets of her robe, hugged her body defensively. "I was awake most of the night, thinking."

"You were awake most of the night, sugar, but not thinking. Unless you do your best planning while you're naked and moaning."

Her lips thinned. "Don't be crude."

He gave a polite nod that was at odds with the heat in his eyes. "All right, I'm listening. Why don't you tell me what you came up with?" At her silence, he coaxed, "Well, come on, sweetheart, let's have it. Just tell me about the parts that involve us."

She turned away, reached out a finger and traced a shape on the table. "I haven't had a lot of luck planning futures with men. My ex-fiancé is serving time for robbing me blind while I was making the wedding arrangements." She steeled herself against his reaction to the disappointment she knew she was dealing. Again. Defensiveness edged her words. "I'm not like you. Trust doesn't come easily for me. I don't have an endless supply of it."

Her words tore through him with jagged, gnashing teeth. After the incredible gift of her support last night, her failure to offer her trust to him as easily couldn't possibly wound more deeply.

"That's bull." He made no attempt to disguise his anger. "I'm willing to bet you never let your ex get close to you, either. Your brother and sister, sure, but no one else. It doesn't matter to me, because I don't want what he had, anyway. I want it all. Everything you have to give. I won't be satisfied with less.''

Her heart jammed like a fist in her throat. He couldn't have said anything more guaranteed to terrify. She sorted through the false denials, the explanations; then, in a desolate tone, she uttered a slice of the truth: ''You want too much.''

The simple words struck hammer blows at his heart. ''So how long am I going to have to pay for what that creep did to you?'' He took care to make sure none of the desperate emotion churning inside him made it to his voice. ''Another week? A month? A year?'' He slammed the glass down on the counter and went across the room to her, taking her arms in his hands. ''Give me a clue, Zoey.''

''I don't know!'' she shouted at him. She pulled away from his touch, her body suddenly trembling. ''It isn't about him, anyway, it's about you!'' She paused when she saw the hurt wash over his face, and her heart wept. Hurting Cage was the last thing she wanted to do.

She dropped her gaze to the floor. ''I was ready to marry Alan. His betrayal shook my structured little world. But it didn't shatter it.''

Her last sentence arrested his attention. ''And what if it was me, Zoey? What if I betrayed you?''

It was as if he'd reached deep inside her and ripped out the last desperate question that had been torturing her relentlessly. ''I couldn't get over that,'' she whispered achingly. ''I don't even want to think about having to try.''

He opened and closed his hands helplessly, feeling as if he had one chance left, but it was dancing just out of his reach. ''I don't suppose I can promise that I'll never hurt you.'' He watched her flinch at his words. ''But I can promise to try my best not to.'' He waited, but she made no response.

Not by so much as a flicker of an eyelash did he reveal how deeply her silence stabbed him. ''I reckon we both know what the other wants. It'll be all or nothing for me, Zoey. Guess you know where to find me when you decide.''

Burying himself in his work was as good an escape as any. Cage called the remaining detectives on the list, each conversation adding to the feeling of foreboding inside him. When he'd finished with the phone calls he returned his attention to the stack of printouts in front of him. He removed only the ones in which the detective had relayed details about superficial wounds to the victim's knees and shins. When he was finished, he had a stack of seven unsolved cases that involved rape/homicides.

Each of the women had knelt or crawled in something that lacerated the skin. Gravel, glass, wood chips—the material had varied. Two victims had died of gunshot wounds, one had been poisoned, three stabbed, and two strangled. No wonder he hadn't caught a pattern before. Looking at MOs had been a futile task. The shooting victims had been killed with different makes and models of guns. The stab wounds indicated different murder weapons, as well. And one woman had been strangled with a pair of panty hose; while regular clothesline had been used on Janice Reilly.

Eight women in ten years, if Janice Reilly was included. All victims were in their early to mid-twenties, all attractive. All had been brutally murdered, some of them tortured first. He felt bile rising in his throat. He didn't like the suspicions that were growing more certain by the hour; didn't enjoy envisioning a killer at work in the state, with eight homicides behind him, possibly more. A serial killer, who, to Cage's knowledge, wasn't being hunted as such.

He got up, went to a drawer and took out a map of the state. Unfolding it, he tacked it up on the bulletin board. Then he went through each of the files again, wrote dates on slips of paper and carefully pinned them up on the map, designating the locations of the bodies and the sequence of the deaths. The resulting pattern made the hair rise on the back of his neck.

The first had happened a little less than a decade ago, the second three years later. Two murders had taken place in the next four years, spaced an equal distance apart. Then it had been only eighteen months until the next. The cycle had accelerated with the last two victims—Cage checked again—killed within a space of five months.

He was no expert in the area but he knew what that escalating cycle could mean. He scrubbed his hands over his face once, hard, then reached for the phone.

It was time to call in the Louisiana attorney general's office.

Many states finance a government agency that law-enforcement officers can turn to for help in complex crimes. In Louisiana, the investigative offices of the attorney general were at the disposal of law-enforcement officials.

After driving the fifty miles to Baton Rouge, then cooling his heels in a waiting room for over an hour, Cage was ushered in to an assistant attorney general by the name of Tom Lane. He'd feared he'd be handed off to one of the several political types rushing to and from through the waiting room. But the man seated behind the desk before him had to have experienced at least fifty years, most of them hard ones. His dark hair was liberally streaked with gray, and his craggy features could have been hewn from stone.

"Sheriff Gauthier." The man rose, shook Cage's hand firmly. "What brings you all the way to Baton Rouge on such a miserable day? Way I hear it, another storm is brewing."

Reseating himself, Cage crossed one leg over his knee. "Hope that doesn't prove to be the case, sir. We still haven't completely dried out from the last one." Pleasantries over, he eased into business. "You might have heard about the murder victim discovered in St. Augustine parish a while back."

The man nodded. "Do you have any leads?"

"Not many, until yesterday. Now...well, now I'm not

sure exactly what I have." Quickly he updated the man on the research he'd been doing.

By the time he'd finished, Lane was already shaking his head. "That's impossible, Sheriff. No serial is operating in the state, thank God. So far, we've managed to avoid that plague."

"I sincerely hope that's true." Cage handed the man a sheet on which he'd typed the pertinent information and sat back while the man scanned it.

"These injuries to the victims' legs—that checks out for all of them?"

"I called the investigating officers on each of those crimes in the last twenty-four hours. I asked about it particularly, and eliminated the victims who didn't fit. I know the MOs are all over the place. Can't figure a guy changing the way he operates from one crime to the next. That part doesn't figure."

"Maybe, maybe not," the other man muttered, glancing up. "It wouldn't be unusual for a serial to change the way he commits the crime. It's the signature that would remain static."

"You think these injuries to the victims' knees and shins indicate what the killer does to fulfill himself?"

"Could be." Lane's voice was reluctant. "Let's say, purely for the sake of speculation, that there was some nut out there who feels compelled to punish women. What does he do before he kills her? Does he make her beg, plead for her life?"

"Or pray." All would require the victim to take a position of supplication on some sort of painful surface. That might elicit the rush of power that was so important to a demented mind.

"Do you have anything else?" It was clear from the man's tone that he was hoping Cage would respond in the negative. Silently Cage handed him the file he'd brought along. Lane took his time reading through the cases. He

stared for a long time at the map Cage had drawn indicating
the sites of the bodies and the dates of the deaths.

When Lane finally looked up, concern had etched a few
more lines in his face. He considered Cage for a long moment. "I told you when you came in here, Sheriff, that we
have no knowledge of a serial killer working in Louisiana.
I still believe that." His gaze dropped to the open file folder
before him. "However…you've presented some compelling
information, which I feel requires further examination."

"What exactly will you be looking at?"

Lane raked his hand through his hair. "I'll be interested
in seeing if there's a similarity in how each of the bodies
was disposed of. What were the crime scenes like in the
homicides where the crime scene was discovered? Some of
these freaks like to take trophies from the kills. Was anything missing from each of the victims?" He shot Cage a
grim smile. "The more I think about it, the more questions
I've got."

"Yeah. Me, too." Cage was silent for a moment. "We're
still speculating, right?" He didn't wait for the other man's
nod before going on. "What kind of guy would do this?"

"Hell, I'm not a profiler…"

"Me either." His soft words effectively stemmed the rest
of Lane's protest. "But you've had some training; so have
I. What are we looking for here? I figure white male; the
victims are all Caucasian, and these kind of crimes rarely
cross racial boundaries."

"We don't know what kind of crimes these are, yet,"
interjected Lane, but his words were perfunctory. "*If* these
crimes are related, this guy is the toughest kind to catch.
He's smart and highly organized. He's careful with details,
hence the lack of evidence at each crime. And if your theory
is correct, he's had plenty of time to perfect his technique."

Cage stared at the other man, but he wasn't seeing the
assistant attorney general. His mind was racing. "This has
to be someone who wouldn't attract attention. No witnesses
were ever found in any of the cases who noticed anyone

unusual nearby. The killer didn't have to use force to kidnap any of these women; there was no evidence of blitz-style attacks or blunt trauma to the head. So the women trusted him, at least initially.''

"Maybe this guy is as smooth as Bundy." Lane was getting into the brainstorming now, leaning back in his chair and fiercely contemplating the ceiling. "Or maybe he dresses like an authority figure who would normally command respect.''

"Or else he seems so damn harmless no one would ever suspect him.''

The two men fell silent, exchanging a long, grim glance. Finally Lane got to his feet. "I'll see that this information gets passed on, Sheriff, and keep you updated. I've got to tell you, I'm hoping like hell that you're way off base about this.''

Cage rose, feeling as if he'd aged a dozen years. "So do I, sir. So do I.''

It was almost ten o'clock before Cage left his office for home. The promised storm hadn't broken out of the suffocating cocoon of humidity, and he was glad to find that Ila had left the air conditioning on. He slipped off his shoes and wandered to the kitchen, intent on finding whatever the housekeeper might have left for him to warm up. The tuna casserole didn't look particularly appealing, but he figured if he didn't eat it, Ila would quit cooking for him altogether. After heating it in the microwave, he grabbed a beer from the refrigerator to wash it down.

He stabbed at the unappetizing stuff on his plate, and shoveled in the food, more intent on fuel than taste. Lucky thing, too. He grimaced, reaching for the beer. He'd never much cared for tuna, and he had a sneaky suspicion Ila knew it, too. She made a point to remember things like that. No doubt she was paying him back for not eating the last few meals she'd fixed for him. As a tactic, it was pretty effective. He made a mental note to pick up some of that toilet water

at Neesom's Ila was so crazy about. He wasn't above a bi
of bribery to do a little fence-mending with the woman. I
shouldn't have been necessary, but it was hard to maintain
a proper employer-employee relationship with a woman
who'd diapered his bottom, and tanned it more than a few
times over the years, as well. Besides, Cage had always
found it more efficient to get around obstacles with a wink
and a smile, than with out-and-out confrontation.

At least he had until he'd met Zoey. The swift stab he
name brought him was becoming too familiar. He pushed
his half-eaten meal away and propped his feet up on the
chair across from him. Taking the cigar from his shirt
pocket, he gave more attention to lighting it than the ac
required.

He was a man known for his steady persistence, but he'
shown none of his usual patience this morning. The though
of her leaving, of her lack of faith in their relationship, had
had logic clouding and emotion taking over. He'd pushed
hard, when he should have known better. He could have
bided his time, used the next month or two to bind her to
him so closely that she couldn't fathom leaving him. Bu
instinct had reared up, born of fear of losing her.

Thunder rumbled sullenly in the distance. Although the
promised rain showed no signs of beginning, he was stil
reminded of the first time he'd made love to Zoey. His body
tightened at the memory. The helpless feeling he'd left he
house with was as foreign as it was frustrating. She seemed
to hold their future in her palm, and there wasn't a blessed
thing he could do about it.

To divert himself, he concentrated on blowing a trio o
perfect smoke rings. Ila would have his hide for smoking in
the house, and she had a nose like a bloodhound. He
couldn't bring himself to care.

It took more effort than it should have to force his mind
back to the meeting he'd had with Lane. He'd half hoped
the man would scoff at his suspicions, point out flagran
inconsistencies in his tenuous theory. But instead, he'

iven it credence—the kind of credence that Cage had been
alf hoping it lacked.

Instincts that had nothing to do with logic told him that
urther investigation would eliminate doubt about the hom-
cides being linked. And those links might point to a com-
non thread between the victims, one that could lead them
o a killer.

Narrowing his eyes, he considered the haze of smoke be-
ore him as if it held some much-needed answers. The lo-
ations of the murders were scattered all over the state. At
his point, trying to predict where the killer would strike
ext seemed futile.

That was the biggest question in his mind: where. It didn't
ccur to him to wonder when. It had been five months be-
ween the last two victims the killer had claimed.

There was no doubt in Cage's mind that if something
lidn't break soon, another would be claimed before the
ummer was over.

Zoey's progression through the small house was signaled
y the lights that winked on, one after another. They shone
ike tiny beacons in the darkness. She moved out of the
itchen, onto the attached screened-in porch. Backdropped
gainst the light spilling from the kitchen door, she appeared
or a moment to be haloed by the glow.

Senses heightened, the figure watched silently in the
ight, each beat of a pulse throbbing like a wound. Dagger-
dged expectancy sliced deeply among varying emotions,
nd an urgent need rose to an almost unbearable pitch.

It could happen now. Eyes slid shut; the scene unfolded
n the depths of a twisted mind. The lock on the door would
e no problem, and the shock on her face would be sweet.
'he moment when that shock switched to terror would turn
he keen blade of anticipation into a painful rush of power
hat was dizzying in its intensity.

It was more difficult than usual to turn back the swell of
emptation. But everything had to be perfect. Details took

careful planning. Surely Zoey would understand the importance of planning.

It wouldn't be much longer before Zoey would understand…everything.

Chapter 13

The gunmetal sky was pierced with occasional jags of lightning, and the rain fell in sheets. Cage glanced out the office window. Although lacking the winds of the previous storm, the weather threatened to persist for hours. It matched his mood after a singularly sleepless night. As a matter of fact, it seemed to match the mood of just about everybody he encountered today.

He rubbed the stiffness from the back of his neck. He'd been a cop long enough to know how intangibles like weather, barometric pressure and a good old-fashioned full moon could affect human behavior. And, true to form, they'd been dealing with phone calls from disgruntled parish citizens all day. Ethel was certain she'd spotted Donny Ray peeking in her windows bold as could be this morning, and Fern had called to describe a car she'd spotted parked near the woods where "it shouldn't oughta be."

Even his own employees weren't exempt. Surely the dreary day was to blame for Luanne and Patsy sniping at each other about who made the best coffee. Hell, while he was at it, he could blame it for Fisher's short temper with DuPrey's incessant questions, as well. Not to mention Tommy Lee's foul humor after returning from lunch at the Stew 'N Brew. Although to be fair, that could just as easily be the result of yet another rejection from a certain blond waitress.

Hearing the shouting emanating from the area of the cells, he heaved a long breath. It'd just go to figure that the Rutherfords would be as susceptible to the rotten weather as anyone else. After all, they were human, too, all evidence to the contrary.

Rising, he strode to his door, but it opened before he could reach it. He spoke, stemming the words that threatened to tumble from Luanne's mouth. "I know, I heard. Our guests object to the quality of the food here. I'm on my way to remind them it comes straight from the diner. If they want to complain about Ethel's cooking, I'm going to make them say it to her face. That should put the fear of God into the lot of them."

But Luanne's plump face remained creased with urgency. "Baker and Sutton just radioed in. You'd better head on out to the woods behind the old Carney place. They found Donny Ray hanging from a tree out there. Looks like a suicide, Sheriff."

The steady rain didn't prevent a crowd from gathering, hampering the efforts of the deputies. DuPrey had been given the duty of crowd control, and he looked to have his hands full. When Runnels and one of his officers arrived, DuPrey waved them through.

Tarps and spotlights were being utilized to preserve the scene, efforts that would no doubt be wasted. Doc Barnes was still bent over the body where it had been lowered to the ground. Cage stood next to him, knowing the man well enough to avoid rushing him. Scanning the area, his attention was arrested. Well beyond the crowd, amidst the dense foliage, was Billy McIntire. Their gazes meshed for a moment, before Billy turned and melted into the woods. Cage made a mental note to search the man out to get a statement. If he'd been wandering in the woods at the same time Donny Ray had, he might be able to shed some light on his death.

His attention drifted back to the body. "What do you think, Doc?

"I think he's dead," was the testy reply. "Hasn't been long, though. No more than an hour, maybe two. He knew how to do it right. Picked a tree with a hell of a drop. Broke his fool neck." With effort, the older man got to his feet. "Any sign of a note?"

Cage motioned to Fisher, who pulled on latex gloves and took out an evidence bag. He squatted down and began to go through the corpse's pockets. Runnels knelt beside him.

"Think we've got something, Sheriff." Runnels took the evidence bag from Fisher and held it so the deputy could ease his finding inside. Cage bent to see the sodden piece of paper Fisher smoothed out once it was in the bag.

I done my best to rid the world of evil.

"Well, there's your suicide note." Fisher rocked back on his heels. "Not exactly what I'd expect from Donny Ray. Of course, hadn't figured him the type for suicide, either."

"He may have been despondent over his wife leaving him," Boyd observed. "Or life on the run became too much for him."

"I'd hardly considered surviving in the woods he's known all his life as being on the lam, Boyd." Cage's voice was dry. He tended to agree with Fisher's assessment. Men of Donny Ray's ilk sometimes committed murder-suicides, victimizing their wives or girlfriends, but he wouldn't have predicted the man would take his own life.

Cage bent over the body again. "Let's see what else we can find."

"Sheriff."

He looked up to see Deputy Sutton addressing him.

"What about the next of kin?"

"Shoot." He rose, thinking quickly. He hated the thought of having Stacy hear this news over the phone, but they wouldn't be free for hours yet. "You'd better call Stacy at the shelter. Make sure you talk to the director first, so she has somebody there for her afterwards."

Sutton nodded.

"And Donny Ray's brothers will have to be told." His eyes met Sutton's. "It probably wouldn't hurt for you to stick close to the office until I get back." The deputy nodded and turned away.

"There. Right there."

Runnels's voice was pitched with more excitement than Cage had ever heard in it. He returned his attention to the two men squatting beside him.

"It's sticking to the back of that match book cover you just dropped into the bag. What's that?" Runnels held the evidence bag in front of one of the spotlights, and Cage and Fisher peered at the object he was pointing to.

Everything taken from Donny Ray's pockets was clumped together, saturated by the rain. The flash of color pressed against the dark match book was an incongruous sight. Cage was no expert, but the long false nail looked a likely match for the color Pearly Pink. The polish Janice Reilly had had applied the day before she was murdered.

Zoey stared blindly out the window into the gloom. The steady rain showed no signs of lessening. The dismal weather was a perfect match for her mood.

Oxy sat at her feet, his head cocked, as if to gauge whether she was ready to burst into tears or start throwing things. She'd done both that day. Neither had helped. Nothing would relieve the feeling that she'd had something precious within her grasp, only to throw it away.

The rain ran in tiny rivers down the windowpane to cluster, shimmering, before dropping to the ground below. It wasn't as if Cage hadn't known what he'd been asking. He'd read her fears as if they'd been written on her face, and he'd made his demand in spite of them. Or, perhaps, because of them.

Turning away from the window, she began to pace. He couldn't possibly know what it was to have only yourself to depend on, while others were counting on you. Once control was learned, it was difficult to give up. It was easy to preach about letting others near, but closeness established vulnerability. Where one was vulnerable, one could be hurt.

As Cage could hurt her.

She walked through the house, not noticing the toy Oxy had left in her path until she stepped on it and it emitted a squeak. Alan hadn't had the power to wound as deeply as Cage could, because of the emotional distance she'd maintained. Hadn't that saved her from the worst of the pain from his betrayal? It shouldn't make her a coward to want to spare herself that.

She'd tried to keep a similar distance with Cage, but the man had simply made it impossible. Sinking to the floor, she let Oxy climb onto her lap, and then hugged the animal close. She should have paid closer attention to those alarm bells that sounded whenever she was in Cage's arms. Somehow, he'd slipped past her defenses. And somehow, he'd made her glad of it.

The dog gave a yip, and she loosened her hold. Oxy immediately made his escape. How long, she wondered, had she been kidding herself imagining that the choice was still hers to make? The risk of losing Cage couldn't be any less painful than the possibility of being hurt by him at some time. If distance was what she wanted, she'd long since passed the time where it would have been effective. Long past the time when she'd fallen in love with the man.

It wasn't an abrupt realization; more like smoke curling beneath a door that she'd kept stubbornly closed. She'd been deceiving herself thinking she still had time to step away from Cage. What he wanted from her still had the power to make her palms sweat and her throat go dry. She hated to think of disappointing him; hated to believe that maybe she wasn't capable of giving him what he was looking for.

But she'd despise herself as a coward if she didn't try.

Rising, she headed to the phone and called his number. Though it was early evening, the phone rang endlessly. Next she called his office, only to be told by the impersonal voice on the phone that he couldn't be disturbed.

The message she left took a ridiculous amount of courage. "Will you tell him Zoey called and asked him to come by her house when he's finished? Tell him…I have the answer he's been waiting for."

"I guess I'm not following you, Sheriff." Fisher surveyed him placidly. "Why would you even raise the question of whether Donny Ray died by his own hand? Suicide note looked to be his handwriting, didn't it?"

Cage blew a smoke ring, and considered his deputy's questions. The answers were both affirmative. The inverted-V bruise on the back of Donny's neck had indicated hanging rather than strangling. What was holding him back from washing his hands of the whole mess? He had a chance to wrap up a couple of cases with a nice big bow. Runnels's final words that evening were probably correct. The taxpayers would be spared the expense of two trials. And despite what the chief thought, Cage's reluctance to be convinced wasn't due to Runnels being the first to spot the evidence labeling Donny Ray as Janice Reilly's killer.

He reached out, tapped the ash from his cigar into the ashtray. Trouble was, he was having difficulty putting all the details together in a way that made sense to him.

"I guess you could say it's the false nail that's bothering me," Cage mused aloud. "I just can't see a reason Donny Ray would have for killing that girl. Assuming, of course, that it does prove to belong to Janice Reilly."

"We know he's capable of violence toward women. And Morris found an empty envelope from a Baton Rouge bank. He could have seen the victim on the street sometime he was there and planned the whole thing out."

"Planned the whole thing," Cage echoed. Maybe that was what was bothering him so much. "Donny Ray might have had it in him to murder someone in the heat of the moment, especially if he was liquored up. But he doesn't strike me as being able to carry out a murder and leave no clues. And it's a sure thing that a woman like Janice Reilly wouldn't go with him without force. Her body didn't show signs of drugs or head trauma. What would cause her to go near a man like him?"

Fisher frowned, considering. "With both of them dead now, I guess we'll never know all the details of her murder."

Cage looked up, caught the weariness in the other man's face. "Well, it's been a long day. There's nothing more that needs to be done tonight. Why don't you go on home, Delbert. Who's on the night shift tonight?"

"Baker, for one."

"Ask him to swing by Billy McIntire's place. If he can find him, I'd like to talk to him."

The door closed behind Fisher. Narrowing his eyes, Cage exhaled a stream of smoke. Maybe he was just being bullheaded. He should be overjoyed to find that the speculation he'd engaged in with Tom Lane was just that—that their concerns about a serial killer operating in Louisiana were based on exaggerated coincidence.

Problem was, as a detective he'd learned never to trust coincidences. Especially if there were lives at stake. He strove to set aside bias and focus on fact. Whoever had murdered Janice Reilly was someone she felt safe with. Someone with good communication skills, credibility or a harmless appearance. None of those descriptions fit Donny Ray Rutherford.

But they would describe the kind of killer who had murdered eight women without leaving a shred of evidence.

Patsy ducked in and handed Cage a piece of paper. "Didn't want to interrupt you before, Sheriff. You had a phone call."

His stomach did a slow pitch and roll as he read the message Zoey had left. He folded the note and creased it carefully with his thumbnail. There was no way of knowing just what Zoey's answer was; no way to be sure if it was the one he was so desperate to hear.

He stubbed his cigar out in the ashtray. He was just cowardly enough to consider putting off seeing her until tomorrow. Then, at least, if it wasn't the answer he wanted, his mind would be clear to muster a convincing argument.

"You gonna answer that message, Sheriff?" Patsy asked in an arch voice.

Cage slowly shook his head. "I don't think so. Is there any more coffee out there? I think I'm going be here awhile."

The rain had slowed to a steady patter. Zoey decided to prepare stir-fry, which would be quick and easy to fix when Cage came. *If* he came.

To distract herself from the nerves that were flashing and jittering inside her, she drew a knife from the butcher block and concentrated on slicing up chicken breasts. She was going to think positively. Cage *would* come. And she would tell him what was in her heart, no matter how daunting the act was—because the thought of him not being in her life was even more terrifying.

A knock sounded at the front door, and she pressed a hand to her heart. It was rocketing in her chest. Taking a deep breath, she headed down the hallway, Oxy trailing her, and opened the door.

Her heart plummeted to someplace in the vicinity of her shoes. "If you're looking for Cage, he isn't here."

"Are you expecting him?"

She hesitated. *She was,* she assured herself firmly. "Yes, soon I hope."

"Mind if I wait for him?"

She held the door open in invitation.

The desire to go to Zoey warred with a healthy dose of sheer apprehension. Her note was in his pocket. Its message was less easy to tuck away. Deliberately, he forced his mind back to the events of the day.

Folding his hands behind his head, he leaned back in his chair. Instead of trying to still the niggling doubts about the case's solution, he opened his mind, let them spill out, to be sorted through one at a time. Something was still nagging him strongly about the case, and it wasn't going to leave him be until he considered it from all angles.

If he didn't like Donny Ray as the suspect in Janice Reilly's murder, it meant her killer was still at large. But that wouldn't mean he wasn't any closer to identifying the killer than he had been yesterday. Not at all.

Because someone would have had to plant that false nail on Donny Ray. Someone with a reason to direct their attention elsewhere.

It went to figure that the someone was probably the killer himself.

Frigid fingers of ice traced up Cage's neck. The killer lived in the parish; had to. He'd known the woods well. Janice Reilly's body had been left in the wooded area near the river; Donny's body had been discovered in the woods. A stranger in Charity aroused talk. This would be someone accepted. Maybe even looked up to.

Someone who seemed above suspicion.

Despite the chill creeping over his skin, sweat popped out on Cage's forehead. He wished he knew more about the disposal of the other murder victims. Because suddenly the arrangement of Janice Reilly's body took on a horrifying significance. Her hand had been nailed to the tree in a macabre greeting. Was it intended for the unfortunate soul who would discover the body? Or the man most likely to investigate the murder?

His mind was racing now, thought fragments forming too rapidly to complete them. He stared fiercely into space, ideas formulating, shifting; details clicking into place. He shook his head hard once, as if to rid it of the awful suspicion that had lodged there. It didn't help.

The idea was too horrible to contemplate. But his next thought seized the heart in his chest in a vise grip. Because if there was the remotest possibility he was right, he already knew who the next victim would be.

Panic layered with dread circled in his gut. He sprang from his chair and charged through the office. Patsy looked up at him in amazement.

"Call all the men to duty. Now. Tell them it's red alert. And send a backup unit to Zoey Prescott's place."

"What's keeping Cage?"

Zoey shrugged. "The office, I suppose."

"Someone's going to have to teach that boy what all work and no play does to a body." Tanner shrugged out of his raincoat. "Where should I put this so it doesn't drip on your floor?"

She resumed cutting up the chicken. "Out on the back porch." She was about to point the way, when he walked by her in the right direction.

"Now." He re-entered the kitchen and stood looking around. "Put me to work."

"Do you have any experience in the kitchen, Beauchamp?"

He grinned. "Actually...no. But I do work well under supervision."

"Okay." She turned around and gestured to the vegetables she had set on the counter. "Get yourself another knife and chop those up. Careful with your fingers."

"Sweet Zoey, 'careful' is my middle name."

Busying herself making a sauce to marinate the chicken

in, she listened to Tanner with half an ear. His stories about the mischief he and Cage had gotten into over the years made her smile. The tales of their exploits in high school had her shaking her head. But his constant patter soothed nerves that had been jumping and quaking all day. Until the talk turned to the day's excitement.

"Guess you heard about Donny Ray hanging himself today."

"No." Shock clutched her throat. "I hadn't heard."

He gave an easy shrug. "No big loss, if you ask me. But the biggest surprise was they think they can link him to Janice Reilly's murder."

She leaned against the counter for support. "You're kidding! Is that what Cage believes?"

"Hard to tell what Cage is thinking right now. But he's a smart guy. Maybe not as smart as me—" his teeth flashed immodestly "—but smart, all the same. He'll put things together soon enough."

She was still reeling at the news. "I had no idea. How did they connect Donny Ray to the murder?"

"Seems he had something on him he'd taken from the victim. It's said killers like to take souvenirs of their kills." His voice slowed, went a little dreamy. "I hear tell they take out their trophies and relive the thrill. Do you like souvenirs, Zoey?"

Something about the man's manner disturbed her. She glanced at the clock, wondered how much longer Cage would be. "I'm not much for tokens, no."

"Really? Then this doesn't mean anything to you at all?" He turned to face her, and from his fingers dangled her locket.

She stared at it, nonplussed. "Where did you get that?" She would have liked to snatch it away from him, but an inexplicable thread of caution warned her to stay where she was.

He closed his fingers around it again and slipped it into his pocket. "You're a very sound sleeper, you know." He grinned. "So is that puppy of yours. The lock on your back door wasn't much of a challenge." When he took a couple of steps toward her, she backed away, her eyes fixed on his face.

"I almost took even more that night." He threw his head back, let himself relish the memory. "It would have been so easy as I stood over your bed, watching you sleep. But anticipation makes the prize all the sweeter. No matter how many times I was tempted, I held back until the time was right. The time *is* right, Zoey. You know that, don't you?"

Casually he picked up the butcher knife he'd been using, and moved toward her.

She put the table between them, her hands shaking, ice crawling through her veins. *Cage had been wrong.* Her temples throbbed with disbelief. Janice Reilly's murderer *was* in their midst. He was standing in her kitchen. It was as if the novel still taking shape in her mind had sprung to sudden, vivid life. "Don't be a fool, Tanner. Cage will be here at any moment." Perhaps if she wished hard enough, her words would come true.

His smile was curiously detached. "I'm counting on it." And he stalked her with slow, deliberate steps.

It took all her strength to summon logic from the nasty, panicked pool of emotions. What was important to a sick twisted individual like this? Power? Control? She desperately needed a way to divert his attention so that she could make her escape.

"I'm not afraid of you, Tanner."

"Really? How curious." He licked the edge of the blade and blood welled on his tongue. He grinned at her—a macabre grimace that lacked human emotion. "I guess that's your first mistake."

She gave a mighty shove of the table, turning it over in front of him, and made a dash for the door. The blade was at her throat before she got out of the kitchen. "You're going to be the best of them all," he whispered in her ear. "*They* didn't want to be pure, but you do, don't you? I'm going to purify you, Zoey. And this time it's going to be...perfect.'' He pulled her to the counter, forcing her to lean back against him.

"I learned about purifying the sinning spirit from my dear old daddy, did I tell you that?'' The knife point under her chin pressed menacingly.

"No.'' The word was barely audible.

"My bitch of a mother left the sick old bastard. Guess she didn't want to be purified, but she left a little something behind. Namely me. So I was pretty damn *pure* by the time he'd kicked off. He made sure of that.'' For the first time emotion crept into his voice. Frightening emotion. Rage.

"Drop the knife, Tanner.''

Zoey's knees almost buckled with relief when she heard Cage's voice, saw him enter the room in a crouch, gun pointed.

One quick glance assured Cage that Zoey was all right. For the time being. "I can make sure you get help, Tanner. But it has to end now.''

"As usual, ol' friend, I have to agree with you.'' He grinned at Cage over Zoey's head, as casual as if they were sharing a beer in Jonesy's; as if he wasn't holding a knife to Zoey's throat. "I'm good, but sooner or later someone was going to catch up with me. I decided there is nobody I'd rather match wits with than you. I planned the whole thing carefully. I think you'll agree, it's really quite brilliant.''

Cage felt encased in a nightmare he couldn't wake up from. This was Tanner. The man who was like a brother to him. The one who knew him better than anyone else. The one he was just beginning to understand he'd never known at all.

Tanner took the blade and pressed the flat end against Zoey's skin, running it over her cheek. "'Course, I gave you more than a running start. Thought I was going to have to draw a diagram for you, but you finally put all the pieces together, didn't you, son? I'm a little disappointed it took you so long, but I suppose even a supercop's instincts would be a bit dulled after being out of the city for so long.''

His instincts had been dulled, Cage thought sickly, by his failure to consider his friends and acquaintances as suspects. Even now the reality was hard to comprehend.

''I'm not going to let you hurt her, Tanner.''

Zoey watched Cage circle slowly to keep them in his sight, countering every move of Tanner's with one of his own, and felt a lick of despair. There was no way he could get a clear shot. Not with Tanner holding her so close. Not with the emotion that must be tearing at Cage's heart.

She moved her head, and felt the prick of the knife. She thought of the other knife she'd used to cut up the chicken only a few feet away.

Tanner tightened his arm around Zoey's neck. ''Does this remind you of anything, Cage, m'boy?'' The blade nicked her skin and she jerked helplessly. Cage's hand tightened on the gun, his eyes never leaving Tanner.

''No? What about Amy Lou Travers? Does her pretty face still haunt you at night? I'm betting it does. You always had a nagging conscience. I always figured it was a helluva lot more comfortable not have one at all.'' He dragged Zoey backwards until the wall was at his back. ''How was he holding Amy Lou at the end? Like this, wasn't it?''

It took effort for Cage to keep his hand steady. Tanner's voice was an evil, insidious echo of the guilt and regret he kept tucked away. ''Remember, Cage? Amy Lou thought you'd save her, too, but she was wrong, wasn't she?''

Her eyes had been wide, hope and despair battling wildly there. Neesom had shielded his body with hers, holding the knife pressed to her throat.

Cage saw the direction of Zoey's gaze, gave a sharp shake of his head. She didn't have a chance of getting to the other knife before Tanner cut her.

''You still a sharpshooter, son?'' Tanner grinned at him over Zoey's shoulder. ''Let's see how good you are. You were a second too late for Amy Lou, weren't you? You wouldn't make the same mistake twice. Or could you?''

Zoey's eyes met Cage's. He knew she was recalling the memory he'd recounted for her. Knew the doubt and fear that must be battling inside her. He shifted a bit, steadied his gun hand, and swallowed, wishing the memories could be banished.

One instant. Just a second's hesitation to figure whether he could make the shot... Whether he should take the risk.

His throat felt dry and rough. He needed to clear his head. He couldn't afford to take his eyes from Tanner. This wasn't New Orleans. It wasn't going to happen again. It couldn't.

He saw Zoey look at the other knife again, then at him. *The gun and the knife had been used almost simultaneously. The woman's blue eyes had widened in shock, before going lifeless, falling beneath the weight of the man's body.*

No, not blue. With effort he shook the vision from his mind. Zoey's eyes were green. She was looking at him now, trying to determine whether her best chance lay with him or in a desperate lunge for the knife. She twisted in her captor's grasp.

It was Tanner's body partially visible behind Zoey, as he easily overpowered her struggles. Not Neesom's. It was Tanner's voice echoing the words that screamed across his mind. *"Amy Lou..."*

The sound of the gunshot in the small room was deafening. The cold blade bit against Zoey's skin, before Tanner's grip loosened, released her.

Cage kept his gun pointed at the man on the floor even as his free arm reached for Zoey, pulled her to him tightly.

Tanner pressed his hand over the hole in his chest, looking dazed at the amount of blood seeping through his fingers. Then his gaze reached Cage's, as void of feeling as the smile on his lips. "Did I ever tell you what really happened to Tooner?" His wild, eerie laugh was still sounding as sirens filled the air.

Chapter 14

Zoey appreciated the comforting presence of Jed and Sully, but had refused to let them persuade her to go home once she'd given her statement. She was determined to wait for Cage, for as long as that took. Finally the two had shrugged, given up their efforts, and propped themselves against the wall.

When Cage entered the office, he looked fatigued and heartsick. But his arms were welcoming when Zoey walked into them, and held her close.

Her grip was just as strong. He'd lost so much today, in the space of a few minutes, it was a wonder to her that he was still standing at all.

Jed cleared his throat from across the room. "Guess you've got the guy taken care of?"

Cage released Zoey reluctantly, but kept her at his side with one arm looped around her waist. "He'll be under heavy guard at the nearest hospital until he can be moved. After that—" she felt, rather than saw, his slight flinch "—

it'll be up to the courts. I figure they'll want to order tests to see if he's fit for trial.''

"We heard some of the deputies talking," Sully said. "Have you figured out his connection with that homicide victim found here a while back?''

With subtle nudging, Zoey managed to move Cage across the room and into a chair. He gave a slight tug, and pulled her into his lap.

"Actually, we've tentatively connected Tanner to eight murders, and from some of the things he said, I'm wondering if we shouldn't investigate as far back as his college years.''

"What in hell turns a man as twisted as that?" muttered Jed.

"He was horribly abused by his father," Zoey said, meeting Cage's gaze.

"More than I ever suspected," Cage affirmed. "I mean, we were always getting into trouble when we were kids. My second home was the woodshed. But with Tanner's daddy…'' His jaw tightened. "Old Jean-Paul drove off his pretty young wife when Tanner was just a baby, probably with his treatment of her. With her gone, there was no buffer between him and Tanner.''

"Tanner blamed his mother for that," Zoey added. "It was clear in what he said to me. But…why punish innocent victims for something his parents did to him?''

Cage brushed his lips over her hair. "That's one for those fellas in the Behavioral Science Unit, honey. I suspect he killed his first victim by accident, in a fit of rage. And after discovering how much he liked it…'' He took a deep, shuddering breath. Better not to think of the animal they were discussing as Tanner. Better not to remember the years they'd spent together—the secret Tanner had carried.

Cage's voice was hoarse when he continued. "I imagine he improved on his style a little more each time. I do believe that with each murder, he was punishing his mother for leaving him to be abused by Jean-Paul.'' He reached out to pull Zoey closer. "Once he decided to include me in his plans, you were in danger because of your relationship to me."

Sully looked at him. "You think he intended to get at you all along?"

"He was a planner." Cage tried for a weary smile, didn't quite pull it off. "And every time, he'd try for a bigger thrill, take more risks. What could up the stakes higher than going head-to-head with the man who knows him better than anyone else?"

Jed was clearly trying to put the pieces together. "So what does this have to do with the hanging?"

"Tanner threw us Donny Ray as a solution to the murder, all wrapped up nice and neat. He had a violent past, he was involved with drugs...I suspect Tanner forced him at gunpoint to write the note, planted one of the victim's fingernails on him and made him hang himself. One of my deputies brought in Billy McIntire, a fella who wanders the woods around here. I thought he might have seen something today, but turns out what he witnessed was Tanner disposing of Janice Reilly's body. He was afraid no one would believe him if he came forward."

Zoey was shaking her head against his chest. She felt good in his arms, pressed up against him like this. It reminded him of his vow to keep her near. He dipped his head. "What is it, sugar?"

"I still don't understand how you knew I was in danger. I thought—I hoped you would come, but I wasn't sure."

He squeezed his eyes shut, remembering the stray thought he'd had about postponing their meeting. "I was putting it all together, probably just the way Tanner meant me to. Earlier today Fern Sykes had described a car like Tanner's hidden near the woods." He hadn't wanted to believe what that might mean. He still didn't.

Sully looked at Jed. "Can't say things don't stay interesting around him."

Cage tipped Zoey's chin, considered her mouth. Touching

her seemed to be his only line to sanity right now. He smoothed a finger over her jaw and let himself concentrate on her lovely face. "Stick around. They're about to get more interesting."

Jed cleared his throat and the two men drifted to the opposite side of the room.

Zoey looked into Cage's eyes and a breath shuddered out of her. "I've never been so scared."

His hand stroked her hair soothingly. "I know, sweetheart. But you did…great. I was so afraid you were going to go for that knife. You didn't stand a chance."

"I considered it. But in the end, I guess I had to trust you, after all. I thought if I could just get him to change position a bit, you'd have a better shot."

Her reward for the words was a bruising kiss, which turned softer and lingered. When their lips parted, he whispered huskily, "I believe you had something to tell me."

"You know, kids," Sully informed them politely, "that's what back seats are for."

"Stuff it." Cage's eyes were gleaming. "Every guy is entitled to a little romance at his big moment."

"Is that what you're after, Gauthier?" asked Zoey, her head tilted back to look up at him.

He recognized that glint in her eye. His smile was a slow lazy promise. "I fall for it every time."

The wedding was going to go off without a hitch. It was, Cage assured himself. But that didn't explain the clutch of nerves in his stomach, or the sweat on his brow.

Julianne Sullivan smiled at him, not without pity. "Stop fidgeting, honey. Everything's fine."

He sent a quick grin at the blond woman, recognizing the teasing light in her eyes. "I'm not nervous."

"Of course you aren't." Laughter danced in her wide brown eyes and she crossed the small room in back of the church with lazy grace. "Because there's absolutely no reason to be." She curled a hand around his nape and pulled his face down for a light kiss. "That's for luck, which you don't need. And a belated welcome to the Sullivan family."

Cage rested his hands on her shoulders, bared by the long gown she was wearing. He gave her a light squeeze. "Thanks, sweetheart. I gotta tell you, so far the Sullivan women are the best part of this family."

Jed raised a brow. "Is that why you have your hands on my wife?" Cage was astute enough to hear the warning in the even words so he gave Julianne another quick kiss, and grinned at his older brother's reaction.

"My turn." The mound of Ellie's stomach was only a slight obstacle between them, as Cage dropped a gentle kiss on her lips. "I'm so glad they found you, Cage." She turned and smiled at her husband. "Glad for all of us."

"Why is it that you're handling our women?" Sully grumbled. "Get your own wife."

Cage checked his watch again and straightened his tie for the hundredth time. "I plan to. The sooner the better." He ducked out of the room and headed toward the front of the church.

Nadine was seated at the organ, and as she began the music, the wedding party clustered into order. Behind Patrick and Caroline, Sully led his wife up the aisle, handling her as carefully as if she were made of spun glass. Although he'd scoff at anyone who said so, the thought of becoming a father in three months intrigued and terrified him by turns.

"Who would have thought you'd have to put on a tux so quickly after Jed and Julianne's wedding?" Ellie teased.

Matching his steps to hers, Sully countered, "I'd do anything to get pretty boy tied up with another woman. He's entirely too free with other men's wives."

"He is handsome, isn't he?" At Sully's quick scowl, Ellie patted his arm. "I tend to go for the deep and dangerous type, myself." She exchanged a smile with her husband.

Jed suspected that Julianne was in her element as they walked smoothly down the aisle. Having all eyes in the church zeroed in on his wife wouldn't make her the least bit uncomfortable. Quite the opposite.

"There's something you should know, Sullivan." She smiled brightly at the guests crowded into the small church. "Ellie will beat me to the maternity ward, but I'll be darned if Zoey does. You've got some work ahead of you."

Jed dipped his head. "I'm willing to practice for as long as it takes."

She stole a quick kiss. "See that you do."

It was anxiety, rather than the heat, that had perspiration beading on Cage's brow. But when the music changed and the vision in white made her way down the aisle, nerves faded away. He knew he was grinning like an idiot, but he didn't care.

His voice was pitched low when Zoey reached his side. "What are you wearing underneath that dress, sugar?"

Her lips curved. "I'm afraid you're going to have to wait until tonight to find out."

He faced the minister, content. He'd wait, all right. For a while. They had the rest of their lives, after all. And he was nothing if not a very patient man.

*   *   *   *   *

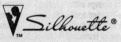

Of all the unforgettable families created by
#1 *New York Times* bestselling author

NORA ROBERTS

the Donovans are the most extraordinary. For, along with
their irresistible appeal, they've inherited some rather
remarkable gifts from their Celtic ancestors.

Coming in November 1999

THE DONOVAN LEGACY

3 full-length novels in one special volume:

CAPTIVATED: Hardheaded skeptic Nash Kirkland has *always*
kept his feelings in check, until he falls under the bewitching
spell of mysterious Morgana Donovan.

ENTRANCED: Desperate to find a missing child, detective
Mary Ellen Sutherland dubiously enlists beguiling
Sebastian Donovan's aid and discovers his uncommon abilities
include a talent for seduction.

CHARMED: Enigmatic healer Anastasia Donovan would do
anything to save the life of handsome Boone Sawyer's
daughter, even if it means revealing her secret to the man
who'd stolen her heart.

Also in November 1999 from Silhouette Intimate Moments

ENCHANTED

Lovely, guileless Rowan Murray is drawn to darkly enigmatic
Liam Donovan with a power she's never imagined possible. But
before Liam can give Rowan his love, he must first reveal to
her his incredible secret.

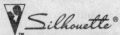

Available at your favorite retail outlet.

Look us up on-line at: http://www.romance.net   PSNRDLR